JUST DESERTS

Elizabeth Bailey

SAPERE
BOOKS

JUST DESERTS

Published by Sapere Books.

24 Trafalgar Road, Ilkley, LS29 8HH,
United Kingdom

saperebooks.com

ISBN: 978-1-80055-951-6

CHAPTER ONE

London 1786

An eerie silence pervaded the mist-shrouded park. This early on a raw February day only the hardiest spirits would venture forth. But Lord Christopher Chiddingly, inured by long custom to the discomforts of the English weather, sat his mount at his ease while the elegant grey mare blew steam clouds and tossed an impatient head.

He held her in, listening intently. The sound came again. A muffled thrumming of hoofs, distanced by the enveloping whiteness of the world about him.

Chiddingly frowned. Who else could be out at this hour on such a day? Only a fanatical horseman like himself, surely. Yet this was no ordinary airing. Whoever it was that was charging towards him was riding as hard as he could to the devil.

Nearer the rhythmic crescendo came. Louder, thundering out of the blanketing mist. Peering into the gloom, Chiddingly saw at last the vague outline of a horse and rider. A moment later, at full gallop, a monstrous brute of a chestnut burst into view. Catching sight of the obstacle in its path, it came to a plunging, snorting halt. Dark eyes rolled, nostrils flared wide, and with a whinnying cry it reared up, almost unseating its rider, whose wide-brimmed hat went flying.

A mass of gold locks was revealed, loosely tied at the nape of the neck and flowing over the shoulders of a man's double-caped greatcoat.

A furious imprecation in some foreign tongue rent the air.

Chiddingly's amazed glance caught the flashing eyes in an obviously feminine face, before the frightened horse veered away, hurtling over the greensward and vanishing into the mist.

Through his mind flicked the realisation that if there was a groom in attendance to prevent mishap, he had been left far behind. But Chiddingly was already on the move, urging his fleet Persian Arab to her swiftest pace. What woman was this, who rode a fierce-looking devil of a stallion and held it together through what should by rights have been a rattling fall? That she was not now lying with a broken neck was no fault of her own. But if it was not bolting now, he was no judge of the matter. Ahead of him he could see the chestnut's uneven pace, with the rider bent low over the withers, her voluminous petticoats flapping behind the saddle.

It seemed to Chiddingly an age as the grey crept closer, gaining steadily on the more powerful chestnut. But in fact it was a matter of seconds before they were neck and neck, the mare closing in obedience to the pressure of his knee, as he transferred the reins to one hand and reached out with the other to seize the chestnut's bridle just above the bit.

Once more there was a snorting, stamping muddle of hoofs and horseflesh until both mounts were still under an iron hand.

The lady, however, appeared far from grateful. There came a low, vibrant command: "Let go my rein!"

Then she raised her whip and the lash descended with a sharp crack on Chiddingly's gloved fingers. With an oath, he wrenched his hand back, clutching it against the numbing pain.

"How dare you?" The lady's voice was husky with passion. "Do you imagine me incapable of controlling my own mount, you — you blackguard?"

Chiddingly gazed at her in mingled astonishment and wrath. The confining ribbon had come loose, freeing the glorious mane of golden curls to riot about her flushed cheeks. She was undeniably handsome in the classic mode. Oval face, straight nose, and finely sculptured lips, even with their present scowling pout and the flashing anger of deep grey eyes.

But Chiddingly was in no mood to appreciate these attractions. He found his tongue. "I *beg* your pardon?"

"You may well. How dared you interfere? I allow no one — but no one — to touch my bridle as I ride. Do you understand?"

Fury engulfed him. "You may think yourself fortunate I do not drag you from that saddle!"

Her flush deepened. "Who the devil do you think you are to address me so?"

"The same whom you, madam, dared to strike at."

"It is no more than your deserts. Standing like a stock in the middle of the green! The wonder is I did not run you down. And then to chase after me!" She growled in her throat like a cat. "You had no right to stop me."

"If you have no more conduct, madam, than to ride without an attendant groom, that is your own affair. It is nothing to me how you disgrace yourself. But stand by and see a horse — any horse — misused, I will not."

"Misused?" She showed her teeth in a most unladylike snarl. "Let me tell you, I have never ridden a horse — *any* horse — above its capabilities."

"I find that hard to believe."

"I don't give a damn what you believe," stormed the lady, using quite unbecoming language, "but you are a fool if you cannot see that this unmannered hellion has taken no sort of hurt."

"No thanks to you."

A heavy thudding of hoofs interrupted them. Out of the now thinning mist a rider came. Triumph entered the lady's voice. "My groom!"

"Belated, but nevertheless welcome."

She gave a mirthless laugh. "If your English servants cannot hold their own on horseback, that is to their disgrace, not mine."

With which parting shot, the lady wheeled her mount and cantered away. The groom, who had only just come within reach of his quarry, gave an audible groan and turned his horse.

Chiddingly called after him. "You there!"

The man checked his mount and looked back. "Me, sir?"

"Who in the fiend's name else do you see about you?" Chiddingly brought his own mount level. "What in Hades were you about, to let your mistress ride unattended?"

"She ain't my mistress! For which I thank my stars."

"I don't doubt it. Have the goodness to answer my question."

"It weren't my blame, me lord."

"You know me?"

The man nodded with enthusiasm. "O' course, me lord. Every groom in London knows Baron Chiddingly."

The groom had recognised him at once, for Chiddingly's figure was distinctive. He was a rather loose-limbed man, with a large frame made powerful by constant exercise. He was also somewhat careless of dress — his top-boots and dark frock-coat were serviceable rather than fashionable — and he chose the military style of pigtail wig, blackened in preference to powder, with a bicorne atop.

"Miss up and took that there tedious brute out of his lordship's stable without so much as a by your leave, she did," continued the groom. "Most mettlesome beast we got. Danged if she doesn't fig him out herself, saddle, harness an' all. By the time I came into the stable yard, Miss was already riding out of the mews. I followed as fast as I could, me lord, but —"

"Hold your tongue! Be damned to you for a prating fool! Who is your master?"

The groom looked scared at this, but volunteered the information that he worked for the Earl of Rossendale.

"Rossendale?"

"Aye, me lord. Grosvenor Square."

"I know very well where his lordship lives, I thank you. Were I he, I'd have a deal to say to you, my lad. You had better make haste now and catch up with your mistress before she leaves the park. For her to be riding about the London streets unattended would be the outside of enough."

He put spurs to his horse on the words, but the groom shouted after him.

"She ain't my mistress, I telled you!"

Ruefully, Lord Chiddingly flexed the muscles of his injured hand. It was aching dully. Slowing his mount, he stripped off his glove. An angry weal showed red across his knuckles. It was a trifle swollen, the skin broken in spots.

He drew in a hissing breath. Damn the little cat to hell! Pray heaven he never again met with such a harridan.

Horse-mad Baron Chiddingly might be, but he was also a member of the *bon ton*, which carried with it certain obligations. While he might, with impunity, wear riding dress all day when at his home near Faversham in Kent, in town it was unacceptable. Fashionable matrons took justifiable exception to the aroma inseparable from horses and would have been grossly insulted had he brought it into their parlours.

So when Mrs Cordelia Harraton came looking for her brother at his lodgings, she knew that, although he was bound to have been out riding, by nine o'clock she might expect to find him changed and probably breakfasting.

This did not prevent her, upon her entrance into the parlour, from taking him to task in a sarcastic fashion. "I declare, I am fortunate indeed. I made sure I should find you newly come in from your beloved stables."

"Oh dear Lord," Chiddingly groaned, looking up from the dish of ham and eggs to which he was addressing himself with a healthy appetite. "What now, Cordelia?"

They were by no means a fond pair of siblings. Chiddingly was wont to refer to her as *my sister Harridan* with reference to her nagging and sometimes spiteful ways, while Cordelia was inclined to despise him for what she called his *addiction to the turf,* and considered his attempts to breed racing champions an extravagant waste of a fortune long since found to be inadequate for the purpose. It was characteristic of her that before she got down to the business that had brought her, Cordelia should revert to a favourite theme.

"I know you claim to be purse-pinched, Christopher, but why you must wallow in squalor is a matter passing my comprehension."

"I am not squandering my precious blunt on a town house, Cordelia," Chiddingly said, his manner weary, "so don't waste your breath."

"You will have to do so when you get married."

"Are you at that again?"

The death in the war in America of young Captain Phineas Chiddingly ten years previously had left the baron the last of his name. Cordelia had been trying ever since to get him to the altar, introducing him to a succession of debutantes year after year, upon whom he turned an unresponsive back.

"When I can like a woman better than any of my horses, my dear sister," he said now, "I shall be happy to oblige you."

His sister gave him a sour smile. "I'll warrant you'll oblige me sooner than that."

Mrs Harraton was a strapping matron, a year or two older than her brother and very like him in looks, though she did not share his taste for riding. She looked well in a cherry-red greatcoat dress with triple capes, worn as an open robe over a softer shaded petticoat in muslin with a flounced hem, topped by a huge hat with a soft crown and ribbons falling in bows over the wide brim. But the iron-grey wig, frizzed and curled in the prevailing mode, did not agree with her sallow complexion. When she smiled, as now, the contrast with her excellent white teeth had an unfortunate effect.

"You look like a Cheshire cat, Cordelia," her brother remarked, effectively slaying the smile.

"I declare," she said on a huffy note, "I have a good mind to leave you without disclosing my news."

"I wish you would."

"Well, I will not." Mrs Harraton pulled out a chair and sat down. "You may give me a cup of chocolate."

Chiddingly sighed, but he reached for the chocolate pot and poured some of the thick dark liquid into his own unused cup and gave it to her. Cordelia sipped at her chocolate and put the cup down with an air of determination.

"Well, Christopher, I shall come to the point."

"Not before time."

She chose to ignore this. "I shall not again remind you that you are the last of your name, for I have done so times out of mind and it has been quite without effect."

"You have taken notice of that, then? I am glad."

"You know as well as I that it is your duty to marry. However, since that does not weigh with you, I am pleased to be able to offer you a reason which is more likely to do the trick."

"Don't prose, Cordelia. You are about to dangle an heiress under my nose, I dare say, but if you can find one with fortune enough to tempt me —"

"I have done so," she interrupted, smug satisfaction in her features. "No, you do not know her. The girl is newly arrived in England."

"A foreigner?" asked Chiddingly, betraying some slight interest.

"No, indeed, though I gather she had as well be. Her father is a nabob. They are but just returned from Bombay, it seems."

His suddenly intent gaze was riveted on his sister's face. "Where had you this?"

"From Alice Chumleigh. You know she is my particular friend."

"Lady Alice? Is she not Rossendale's sister?"

"Of course she is. It appears that this Mrs Winsford is his aunt. She is a younger sister of Lady Rossendale. The whole family is staying in Grosvenor Square at this very moment."

Lord Chiddingly looked thoughtfully at the wound across his knuckles. The swelling had subsided, but a bluish tinge was creeping into the red slash.

"And this Miss Winsford," he said, an edge to his voice, "is the sole heiress?"

"I believe there is another sister," Cordelia said, shrugging. "But the nabob is so enormously wealthy that I am sure it cannot signify in the least."

Chiddingly frowned. "How can you know that? Often enough these East India merchants returning with vaunted fortunes turn out to be much less full of juice than anyone bargained for."

"Very true, but in this case you may be easy. Alice tells me that her mama nearly swooned with shock when her sister told her the sum of the daughter's expectations."

"Well, what are they?"

Delighted to have at last succeeded in confounding her abominable brother, Mrs Harraton produced her smug Cheshire cat grin. "Setting aside the fortune to be inherited on the father's death, you are looking at a cool one hundred thousand."

If Baron Chiddingly was displeased to see his sister, his emotions were as nothing to those exhibited by Viscount Digby Norton-Fitzwarren when he visited him later that morning.

"No, hang you, Chid," protested his friend, waving a well-manicured hand in dismissal as he saw the baron's reflection appear in the mirror before which he was engaged at his morning toilette. "Go away! I won't be fidgeted by your starts at this disgustingly early hour."

"Early hour? It is almost eleven of the clock," Chiddingly told him, coming up behind him and grinning into the mirror.

"Not yet eleven?" He wheeled round on his stool and faced his friend. "Have you taken leave of your senses?" He turned to his valet who was standing by, ready with the powdering jacket. "Who let him in, Weeke? Can't that fool of a butler recognise an undesirable?"

"Have done with these affectations, Fitz. They are quite wasted on me."

Chiddingly was rewarded with a faint smile and a quizzing twinkle. "Shall we let this disreputable fellow stay, Weeke?"

The valet permitted himself a tiny smirk. "I venture to think that his lordship may prove impossible to remove, my lord."

"How right you are," sighed the viscount. "If he's here, he's here, I suppose, eh?"

"As your lordship says."

Chiddingly cast up his eyes. "Enough. And get a move on, Fitz. I need your help. Why, I can dress in a tithe of the time it takes you with your finicking ways."

"And it shows, dear boy," muttered his friend plaintively, running a pained glance over Chiddingly's attire. "Believe me, it shows."

"Fop," retorted Chiddingly, grinning.

Fitzwarren raised a teasing eyebrow, but he said nothing more, merely turning back to the mirror and removing his nightcap.

"My toupée, Weeke."

His valet took a wig from the stand on a side table and placed it carefully over his master's head. Unlike the baron, Fitzwarren was highly fashion-conscious. The wig, which the valet was adjusting to the correct angle, was in the very latest mode, with a frizzed foretop and width at the sides. Once it was in place, Fitzwarren donned the powdering jacket and held a mask to his face while the valet puffed white powder over the already snowy toupée.

During this operation, Chiddingly retired to the far end of the dressing-room. "If you must be a dandy, why can you not install a powder closet?"

"Because I have no wish to choke to death in one," Fitz said, emerging from the mask and examining the results of his valet's ministrations in the mirror.

"No, you had rather your friends did so."

Fitz was unsympathetic. "Well, you would come."

Next he was assisted into a double-breasted waistcoat, horizontally striped in green and white, and then — not without difficulty — a tightly fitting dark green frock-coat with a high-standing collar was tugged on. Once dressed to his satisfaction, he dismissed his valet, saying he could manage the rest, and gave his attention to his friend.

They were on the surface an ill-assorted pair, the one brusque, careless of his appearance and wholly given over to racing pursuits, the other urbane, *point-device* and an acknowledged arbiter of beauty — both of objects and people. When taxed with his odd friendship with Chiddingly, Fitz would smile in a dreamy fashion.

"Oh, but there is great beauty in Chid, after all, don't you find? A beauty of passion."

In fact the odd friendship had been founded at Eton and had weathered every difference of taste or opinion.

"What is so vital, Chid," enquired Fitz, "that you must needs come seeking me out at the crack of dawn?"

"My sister Harraton has been with me this morning."

"Another eligible?"

Chiddingly nodded. "But for once I believe it may answer."

Fitzwarren's brows flew up, and he paused in the act of affixing a fob to the chain at his waist. "You don't say so. What particular virtue has this damsel to fire you up? Or need I ask?"

"Yes, she is an heiress. Or so my sister says."

This was no surprise to Fitzwarren. He was almost as familiar with the state of his friend's finances as he was with his own, knowing that the cost of importing bloodstock, together with the heart-breaking failures of hopeful and costly matings, resulted always in a distressing lack of resources.

While he had produced a few good winners, Chiddingly had not yet achieved his burning ambition, which was to breed a super-champion and found a money-spinning equine dynasty. The search kept him forever on the edge of financial ruin. A wife with sufficient capital to repair his flagging fortunes would be a worthwhile investment.

"How much?" demanded Fitz, coming straight to the point.

"One hundred thousand."

Fitz gave a low whistle.

"And heaven knows how much besides on the old man's death."

"Small wonder you are straining at the leash. But how comes it about I know nothing of this supremely endowed female?"

"As I understand it, she is but just returned from India."

"A nabob, then. But that does not explain how your sister Harraton has got her teeth into this tidbit while I — usually beforehand with the news — am ignorant," Fitz complained.

"Oh, that is easily done. She is thick as thieves with Rossendale's sister, and this girl is some sort of a cousin."

"Rossendale? Then you have not a moment to lose. You may be sure the dowager will not allow him to let this little goldmine slip through his fingers."

Chiddingly nodded in gloom. "What is worse, she is actually staying in his house."

Fitz flung up his hands. "Good grief, then you have not a cat's chance in hell!"

"Oh, be damned to you, Fitz!"

Impatient, Chiddingly flung across the room and back, thrusting his hands in his pockets so violently that the sudden agony of his forgotten wound made him jerk them out again. He cradled the injured knuckles, his breath hissing between his teeth.

"What's this?" Fitz came across and took hold of his reluctant hand, examining his hurts in silence. He let go the hand and looked his friend in the eyes. "I thought there was more here than your manner warranted. Out with it, man. What ails you?"

Chiddingly met his look squarely. "The fiendish truth is, Fitz, that I think I have met her."

"The heiress?"

"And if I am right, I can tell you this. Had she *two* hundred thousand to call her own, I would sell every nag in my stables before I took one step up the aisle to meet her."

Since Chiddingly would never keep his horses standing in weather such as this while he paid a lengthy social call, and flatly refused to permit his friend to order his own carriage for the purpose, Viscount Fitzwarren was obliged to accompany him on foot for the short distance from South Street in preference to calling up a hackney, a suggestion he rejected with loathing.

"Entrust my person to one of those malodorous rattletraps? You must be mad. Nor, before you open your mouth, will I take a chair. The last time I did so the wretched fellows nearly overturned me."

But as his affectations were largely assumed for the purpose of teasing his friend, Chiddingly paid no heed to him. They reached Grosvenor Square without any undue mishap occurring, such as the ruin of Viscount Fitzwarren's stockings by a splattering of mud, or a sudden downpour soaking him to the skin, both of which horrors he had loudly prophesied would overtake him. In fact, the lifting mist had given way to one of those clear blue skies that occasionally warmed late February with the promise of spring, though a sharp chill in the air made the crackling fire in Lady Rossendale's yellow saloon a welcome sight.

They were by no means the only callers to descend upon her ladyship that morning.

"News travels fast," Fitz murmured in his friend's ear. "I see at least two fortune-hunters here already."

"But where is Rossendale?" Chiddingly wondered, failing to spot his lordship's stocky figure as he glanced around.

"My dear Chid, the fellow has no need to make one of a herd. He may pursue her at his leisure in private."

At this point, Fitz was obliged to break off to greet his hostess, who had come up with hands held out.

"Fitz, how delightful. Though to be sure you find me in the wretchedest case. I vow, I am at sixes and sevens," declared Lady Rossendale, showing by her flowery speech and high-strung manner her tendency to the melodramatic.

The viscount bowed over her hand with rare grace. He was always in demand among the fashionable hostesses, particularly when they had a *protégée* to launch who might win the accolade of his approval that would ensure her instant success.

"I must introduce you to my sister. She has but just returned among us. Twenty-five years, can you believe it? I was thrown into strong hysterics and do not yet know if I am on my head or my heels." Then she took in his companion and a rather brittle laugh escaped her lips. "Chiddingly, too. I'm sure I wish you good fortune. No doubt Cordelia is here on the self-same errand." She gestured with her fan and then, tucking her hand in Fitz's arm, she bore him off.

Chiddingly looked around and saw that his sister Harraton was indeed present, over in the far corner of the room, and deep in conversation with a lady wearing a wisp of lace for a cap, who had her back to him.

18

Trust Cordelia to come and see for herself. To pursue his suit for him, too, if she had the chance.

He took in then that the other lady's cap imperfectly concealed a quantity of golden hair, cascading in ordered ringlets down the back of a gown of blue dimity, tied with a wide sash.

Chiddingly stiffened, suffering a resurgence of the emotions he had experienced this morning. Mentally willing her to turn and show her face, he watched her cross the room to talk to a bluff-looking man of some fifty summers, his deeply tanned features leaving Chiddingly in no doubt of his identity. This was confirmed in a short while by the voice of his friend in his ear.

"The nabob himself. One Archibald Winsford, packed off in disgrace in the fifties for some unmentionable misdemeanour, so his lady wife informs me," Fitz told him, amusement in his voice. "Which leads one to wonder just how he acquired his fortune."

"Who cares a straw as long as he cuts up warm?"

Fitz regarded him with a lurking twinkle. "Do I take it that this is not then the girl of this morning's ride?"

"I don't know yet, fiend seize it. The wretched female won't turn about."

But at that very moment, the lady in the lacy cap did turn, affording their lordships a perfect view of a classic face, whose features, framed by curling gold locks, were unmistakable.

"By heaven, it is she!"

"But she is quite enchantingly pretty, Chid. You said nothing of this, you dog."

"You would not have thought so had you seen her this morning, scowling and raving like the veriest shrew. I grant you she looks well now, when — for a wonder — she is at least smiling."

The sculptured lips were indeed parted in a warmth that embraced the whole company, and the grey eyes sparkled as she threaded through the room, exchanging a word here, a smile there.

Wrath surged up in Chiddingly's breast. That she should look so unconcerned after her atrocious conduct, actually daring to raise her whip against him! He stepped forward a few paces to intercept her, a challenge in his curt voice.

"Miss Winsford, I believe?"

She looked up at him in innocent enquiry. "Yes?"

There was no trace of recognition in the grey eyes as they scanned his face in a questioning look.

"You do not remember me?"

She smiled. "Should I? Have we been introduced?"

"You know very well we have not," Chiddingly snapped.

The grey eyes blinked. "Oh dear. But if we have not met —"

"Allow me to remedy the fault," said Fitzwarren, stepping in.

Miss Winsford turned to look at him and her eyes registered unexpected enthusiasm. "Oh, I know who you are. Mama was just pointing you out. I am so very glad to meet you, Lord Fitzwarren, for I have heard all about you and you are the very man I need."

"Then I am naturally at your service," Fitz said promptly, bowing, though his eye gleamed and his lips twitched.

Noting these signs of amusement, Miss Winsford burst into a delighted peal of silvery laughter. "Oh dear, my *unusual manners*. My poor aunt is quite distracted. I am so glad you are not shocked." She put out an impulsive hand and Fitz took it automatically in his. "You must not mind me," she said, her tone contrite. "I am afraid I will be considered dreadfully forward and pert, you know, for we have not been used to mind our tongues in the least back home — oh, drat! I mean in Bombay. I am not yet accustomed to remember that we *are* at home in England."

"I beg you will not think of minding your tongue on my account," Fitz said, kissing her hand. "I find your manners greatly refreshing."

She laughed and retrieved her hand, saying ruefully, "I dare say you will find yourself alone in that."

"Very likely," Chiddingly put in, his tone acid, and the grey eyes turned back to him in mute question.

He had been standing by all this while, growing steadily more incensed. He thought he had never seen anything more disingenuous. She must know quite well who he was. Yet she prated gaily on in that sweet, musical voice — quite unlike the raucous tones she had used this morning — that would charm the birds off the trees, and himself as well, had he not been privileged to see her in quite another guise.

He lowered his voice. "It will not do, ma'am. Do you dare to stand there and assert that you don't recall our encounter in the park?"

She was evidently startled. "So that is who you are! That explains it."

"Explains what?"

"Why you have been glowering at me so ferociously." Then, to his utter astonishment, not say fury, her eyes began to dance and her lips trembled on the beginnings of a laugh. "Oh dear, I do beg your pardon. But it is — it is so droll."

"Droll?" Chiddingly's blue eyes smouldered dangerously. He lifted his hand and thrust a closed fist before her face. "I trust, then, ma'am, you will find this equally droll."

Miss Winsford looked at his hand and caught her breath, the mischief vanishing from her eyes. "Did — did I do that?"

"I am very much afraid that you did, Miss Winsford," interposed Fitz, stirred to compassion by the shock in her face. He smiled at her. "Come, don't refine too much upon it. Make your excuses and there's an end."

"Oh, but it is quite dreadful," she burst out, forestalling Chiddingly, who had turned a kindling eye on his perfidious friend. "I had no idea that — I mean, it was not — I did not *know*. Indeed, sir, you have cause to be angry with —" she broke off and bit her lip, then continued more smoothly — "to be angry with me. Pray forgive me."

"There, Chid, you are amply recompensed," Fitz said with cheerful unconcern. "Now, Miss Winsford, let us move aside. We have drawn all eyes with this little comedy."

She glanced about and saw that the altercation had attracted some attention from those nearest to them. As Fitz guided her to one side, he saw the mischief was back in her face.

"I am glad to see you are merely amused at having caused a stir."

"It is not that," she confessed, eyes dancing again.

His brows flew up. "You are not still laughing at poor Chid?"

She bubbled over. "No indeed. I can't tell you — it was very bad, of course, but it is excessively amusing nevertheless."

Her laughter was infectious and Fitzwarren found himself obliged to join in.

"Miss Winsford," he observed, as he drew her to a sofa by the wall, "I perceive you are an incorrigible tease."

"Yes, I am," she admitted, sitting down. "It is too bad."

"On the contrary, it is delightful. But you have not yet told me in what way I can serve you."

"Oh, that." Miss Winsford smiled up at him engagingly and patted the seat beside her. He took his place on the sofa and she leaned towards him with a confiding air. "Well, I hoped you would consent to instruct me, you see."

"Good grief, at what, pray?"

"Why, at fashion, to be sure." She read puzzlement in his eyes and laughed. "Oh, I don't mean female dress, how should I? My aunt Rossendale is very well able to attend to that. It is in how to cut a dash that you are to advise me."

"Now, how should I be able to do that?"

"Well, of course you are able to. You have carved a very significant niche for yourself, have you not? You must be able to devise something for me."

For a moment he was taken aback. Then he burst into laughter. "Upon my soul! You have as few illusions about me as has Chid, it seems. I beg you will follow his lead, however, and pretend to believe I really am an arbiter of beauty, in public at least. I shall otherwise be quite undone."

She twinkled at him. "I will not give you away if only you will help me."

"But why are you so anxious to — er — cut a dash?"

"Oh, if you had lived in Bombay, you would not ask. Only conceive of parties with the same few dreary persons year after year. A stranger in our midst was cause for avid rejoicing, I can tell you. As for an eligible *parti*, I might have taken my choice of at least three. The new curate, if only he had not been given to strong liquors. My father's one bachelor writer for the company, though to be sure he is only a matter of thirty years my senior. Or of the military there was —"

"Enough! I am riven with compassion. Say no more. I comprehend perfectly. When is your debut?"

"In a week or two. Not before time. Do you realise that we are —?" She broke off and bit her lip. "Oh, drat. I mean, I am quite on the shelf. Very nearly one and twenty, you know. Is it not shocking?"

"Shocking indeed." But his eyes belied him.

She twinkled. "I knew you would say so. I hope you mean to come to our — my debut. You will certainly receive a card."

"Then I will certainly attend."

"Then will you show me a way to make a stir in the world?"

"I will bend my mind to the problem."

"Lord Fitzwarren, we have a bargain."

He smiled. "I wish you will call me Fitz. Everyone does so."

"Oh, certainly, I abhor ceremony. You may have observed it."

His eye gleamed. "Not at all. The personification of maidenly reserve."

Her laugh rippled again. "Would it be quite outrageous for you to address me as Pen?"

"Pen?"

"Penelope, you know. It is my name. Such a mouthful. But not as bad as Per —" She broke off again in some confusion.

"I beg your pardon?" Fitz said, puzzled by these frequent hesitations in her speech.

"Oh, nothing. Well, will you?"

"Call you Pen? I would be honoured. But as it is quite incorrect that I should do so, you will have to bear with Miss Winsford. In company, that is — Pen."

He said it so softly that her eyes danced and she glanced about to see if anyone was within earshot. But their attitude of close conversation had ensured a certain privacy, skilfully fostered by Lady Rossendale, who was only too pleased to have the arbiter approve her niece.

Miss Winsford saw no sign of Chiddingly. "Your friend has gone. Who was he, Fitz?"

Fitzwarren gazed at her in genuine horror. "Good grief, Miss Winsford, if we are to talk of manners —! I beg your pardon. In all the bustle I forgot to introduce him. He is Baron Chiddingly. Christopher Chiddingly, you know. One of the racing men."

"Oh, he likes horses?" Her eyes lit with sudden interest.

"Likes is too tame a word. Do you?"

"Me? Well, yes, but — but not as much as — I mean —" She broke off again and laughed. "Oh dear, I must seem wretchedly tongue-tied."

"There is no need for embarrassment. I should perhaps tell you that I know all about your escapade this morning."

To his amusement, her eyes began that merry dance and she giggled. "Yes, I — I do ride."

"Ride? I am led to believe you are a nonpareil. I am tempted to rise hours before my time only to witness your prowess. Should I meet you if I did so?"

The mischief in her face deepened. "It is possible. But whether it would be worth the effort I cannot say. You might not find my — my unusual manners quite so agreeable as you thought."

CHAPTER TWO

"I tell you, she has a temper like the fiend."

Fitzwarren shook his head. "I cannot believe it."

He sat at his ease in one of the comfortable chairs provided by Mr Padiham in the cosy parlour set aside for those of his patrons who came for the company and not to play at dice or cards. It was a favourite haunt of the racing men, for Paddy, as the proprietor was affectionately styled, had been a knowing tout who had often put the gamesters on to a good thing. When he retired, having grown fat on the proceeds, he opened a discreet gaming establishment which rapidly became the rage.

Fitz came for the play and the company, since Chid was not the only one of his friends to all but desert the older and stuffier White's or Brooks's.

It was a day or two since that memorable morning when the outrageous Miss Winsford had burst into their lives, but Chiddingly was still nursing his grievance.

"She behaved as though the entire episode had been wiped from her mind. If there is one thing I cannot abide, it is duplicity."

"Perhaps she had genuinely forgotten."

Chiddingly gave a short laugh. "If she had, then she is either a madwoman or a fool."

"Well, she is certainly not a fool." A reminiscent smile hovered on Fitz's lips. "And though she might be considered eccentric, I cannot think her insane."

"It is as I told you," Chiddingly said with impatience, turning to the fire where he stood with one hand resting on the mantelpiece, and kicking the logs in the grate with an impatient foot, "she may be as charming as you please in a drawing-room, but the woman has the temper of the devil when she is roused."

"Well, for the love of heaven, man, so too have you! Do you mean to turn your back on a fortune merely for a fault you have yourself?"

His friend looked at him. "For that, no. But for a liar and a cheat, yes."

There was a brief pause. Fitzwarren broke it, his tone strangely despondent. "That is what puzzles me."

"There is nothing to puzzle over. She had a use for you, so she must needs employ arts to attract. As for myself, no doubt she saw how her conduct must seem in the eyes of society had I chosen to put the tale about, so she pretended to forget. When that failed, she enacted a pretty little scene of contrition."

"If that is so, then my judgement of character is sadly at fault."

Chiddingly tossed off his wine and set the glass down on the mantelpiece with a snap. "Perhaps you think I invented the tale?"

Fitz's quizzing twinkle dawned. "Well, in one of your hot-headed moods, you are inclined to exaggeration, dear boy."

Chiddingly regarded the blue and yellow bruise which still decorated his knuckles. "Exaggeration, eh? Very well, Arbiter. Accompany me to the park tomorrow morning. Then we shall see."

"Good grief, must I?"

"If you wish to settle the question, yes."

But when, in spite of a good deal of complaint and protest, Chiddingly inexorably led him to the park at the outrageously early hour of half-past seven the next morning, it seemed they were doomed to disappointment.

Though they rode for half an hour, there was no sign of Miss Winsford or anyone else.

"For the love of heaven, let us go home! I am chilled to the marrow, and besides having had little sleep, I am like to contract an inflammation of the lung in this hideous damp."

"Nonsense. It has doubtless done your constitution a power of good."

But Chiddingly turned towards the gate that would lead them out of Hyde Park and back into Piccadilly. They had not ridden more than a few yards when the sound of several sets of hoofs was heard, together with the rattle of wheels.

A vehicle swept into view around the bend ahead. It was travelling at breakneck speed, and the two horses were hurriedly wheeled apart to seek the safety of the turf at either side of the wide road that ran through the park.

They both watched the rapid approach of a stylish phaeton pulled by a team of good-looking bays which Chiddingly instantly recognised. They had been his own, sold at auction by Richard Tattersall last year and ending up in Rossendale's stables.

His incredulous gaze took in the driver. Clad once again in an overlarge gentleman's frieze greatcoat, golden hair escaping from under the big cocked hat and flying behind, was Miss Winsford. Perched quite alone, whip at an excellent angle in one hand and reins threaded between her competent fingers, she drove her team at the gallop with an apparent unconcern for life or limb.

The phaeton flashed by and Chiddingly turned his stunned eyes to his friend on the opposite side of the road. Fitz was gazing after the phaeton with his mouth agape.

"What did I tell you?"

Then he wheeled his mount and set off in pursuit. He was aware in a moment of Fitz's long-tailed black thundering beside him, and their two horses had no difficulty in overtaking the phaeton which had slowed for the next bend.

"Miss Winsford! Miss Winsford, I say!"

She turned her head and saw the riders, automatically checking her team as she did so. Her eyes passed over Fitzwarren without a change and came to rest on Chiddingly. They narrowed.

"You again!" The voice was once more husky and low. "What do you want of me?"

"Are you completely out of your mind? This neck-or-nothing style will not do for London, let me tell you, whatever may have been acceptable in Bombay."

Her eyes blazed. "Do you dare again to censure my conduct?"

"I care nothing for your conduct. It is those horses that concern me. If they have not strained a tendon apiece, I must count it a miracle."

"You have the temerity to criticise my driving, too?"

"You were not driving those cattle, madam. You were slaughtering them!"

A tide of angry red flooded the classic features and a snarl of rage contorted the fine lips. "You may go to the devil!" She spat the words and began to tug at the reins.

"Miss Winsford!" Fitz called out. "Miss Winsford, wait!"

"And take your friend there with you!"

Then the lady whipped up her horses and the phaeton leapt forward in a swirl of dust.

Fitzwarren gazed after it in blank amazement. "I wouldn't have believed it."

Chiddingly ground his teeth. "If I could but get my hands on her! Look at that reckless pace. She will kill those horses."

"Gammon," said Fitz, reviving. "It may be a wicked pace, but by heaven she is an excellent whip. Why, I have not seen even you do better, Chid."

But Chiddingly was in no humour to give credit to the lady's undoubted driving skill. "And the violence of her temper! Do you see? Where is the vaunted charm of manner now?"

"Come now, Chid, you did set up her back. Though I confess she proved somewhat volcanic. I can see it might be a trifle uncomfortable to be married to such a female. You would never know when she might erupt."

"Married to her? Why, I should never know a moment's peace. Nor, more importantly, should my horses."

They had turned their own nags by now and were riding at a steady pace towards the gate.

"Still, I am intrigued," Fitz said, the amusement creeping back into his face. "She did not recognise me, you know. An extraordinary girl. Full of surprises, even if some of them are less than pleasant."

"Ah, so you did not like it any more than I," Chiddingly said, not without a touch of satisfaction.

"I did not like her temper. You know, she said to me something of the sort." Fitz grinned. "It is my belief she is an incorrigible little prankster. She told me she wants to cut a dash. I wonder if perhaps all these equestrian larks are expressly designed to that end."

"Larks? I hope you are still so complaisant when she breaks her neck. In any event no one is about, so I fail to see how she could achieve her objective if that were the case."

"There is that. This becomes more and more fascinating."

"Oh, let us have done with Miss Winsford!" They had left the park and were riding down Piccadilly. Chiddingly grinned at his friend. "I have a far more fascinating female for you to meet. To tell the truth, it was for that I dragged you out this morning and not for an infernal witch whom I don't care if I never meet again."

If Viscount Fitzwarren found these words cryptic, he did not remain long in ignorance of their meaning. When he would have gone home to change, Chiddingly prevented him.

"Premature, Fitz. The lady I spoke of is of the four-footed variety."

For a moment, the viscount was puzzled, then his brow cleared. "Not another new horse?"

"Another? A boatload! Come back to my lodgings for breakfast and we will set off as soon as may be."

Fitz was willing enough to accompany him, but he thought it proper to scold. "Here you are whistling a fortune down the wind, and you tell me you have purchased another string of bloodstock. Where have they come from?"

"I purchased them from a trader when I was in Constantinople last year. Mostly Barb and Arab. At least that is what the rascally fellow promised he would send. I had to take a job lot to get the filly."

It was no surprise to Fitzwarren that Chiddingly was again importing horses. The best champions came from mixed Arabian and English stock, and Chiddingly had made several trips to the Arab lands and the countries of the North African Barbary coast. Between Barb and Arabian there was little to choose. Both were compact horses, with short backs, arched necks and fine, small heads. Large, expressive eyes and full and flaring nostrils were characteristic, as were their sensitivity and intelligence. The Arabian had perhaps a little the advantage of speed, the Barb of endurance. But either provided any breeder with a quality animal to inject fresh blood into his stock to try to improve his chances.

By the time they had partaken of a hearty breakfast, his lordship's man came to tell them that the team had been put to and his lordship's phaeton was at the door.

Fitzwarren's quizzical gleam came into his eye as he saw the horses that awaited them in the street. "Ah, the magnificently unmatched team. Now, I wonder what a certain young lady might say if she witnessed this partisan flying in the face of convention."

The baron ignored this provocative remark. Unlike his fashionable acquaintance, he had no patience with matched horses, which he regarded as an affectation. Yet as Fitz was quick to point out, this team was beautifully toned.

"Toned how?"

"A grey, a dapple grey, a black and a blue roan."

"Coincidence."

"I suppose it is coincidence that your favourite pair are a bay and chestnut so light that the one is almost gold and the other as bright as an orange sunset."

Chiddingly had the grace to blush, but said defensively, "Well, there is nothing in choosing a pleasing colour, after all. I own I am partial to greys above all."

"A pity, then, that nearly all your blood horses are of darker hue."

"Not at all. This very filly is a grey, and she is pure Barb."

So indeed it proved. It took some time to reach the Legal Quays hard by the Tower, and the wharves were so crowded there was nothing for it but to leave the phaeton in the groom's charge and proceed on foot. They had to push their way through hawkers and porters with loads rolled along, yoked across shoulders, or wheeled on a handcart through the press of persons clamouring for each other's attention.

"I wish I had waited until I might see this Barb in comfort," Fitz complained.

But when they finally caught sight of a string of horses being walked off a couple of barges about fifty yards down the quayside, he forgot his woes, catching something of his friend's enthusiasm.

"There they are! Good grief, Chid, there are enough to equip a company."

If this was an exaggeration, there were certainly a good five and twenty horses.

"Tidmarsh!" called out Chiddingly, catching sight of his trainer. Along with Clatterbridge — the baron's head groom who had arranged to meet him here — Tidmarsh moved about the group, organising the unloading of his cargo and going from horse to horse, keeping them calm.

"Tidmarsh!"

He looked round, saw his master and waved. It was a surprisingly young face that was turned towards them. A good-looking lad in a brown scratch wig and a dark old-fashioned frock, he did not look at all like a man to whom one would entrust the delicate business of training a racehorse. But Tidmarsh had been around racing stables all his life and had come to Chiddingly two years ago, chock-full of revolutionary ideas which had tallied so exactly with his master's own thoughts that he very soon took over the entire conduct of the training routines for the baron's stud.

"What have we got, Tidmarsh? Anything promising? And my Barb — you have her safe?"

"She's here right enough, my lord. I brought her off myself."

He led them between the flanks of two large bays to where the filly stood, not, like the rest, roped up in twos or threes, but alone, her bridle held by a small boy who was ready enough to earn a couple of shillings. She was a superb animal. Almost pure white, she was close coupled and at a year old already well ribbed-up, with good let down hocks and plenty of bone. She had the Barb's small head and great velvet eyes.

"What a beauty!" Fitz exclaimed, running a hand down the sleek neck.

"Gentle as a lamb, too," put in Tidmarsh. "Sweetest tempered little thing I ever saw. No vices, I'd stake my life, my lord."

Proving the truth of his assertion, the filly nuzzled at Chiddingly's hand as he put it up to stroke her, and stood quietly while he examined her legs and checked the hoofs.

"Perfect," he said with satisfaction as he stood back at the end of this exercise. "Now, what of the rest?"

It was then he became aware of an air of suppressed excitement that hung about his trainer. His breath caught and he felt a pulse beat in his throat. He spoke almost brusquely.

"We have something?"

Tidmarsh drew a breath and his eyes lit. His voice was calm, however. "Yes, my lord. We have something."

Without another word, he turned and moved back towards the barges. Chiddingly exchanged a glance with Fitz and recognised an echo of his own rising excitement.

Most of the horses had been unloaded by now and were being shunted, under the direction of Clatterbridge, through the press on the dock to a yard behind some warehouses hired for their temporary accommodation.

Chiddingly and Fitzwarren reached the edge of the quay and followed Tidmarsh's pointing finger to the first barge, where a single horse had been left to stand alone.

As if to emphasise the supreme importance of this moment, the sun, which had been playing at peek-a-boo amongst the clouds, chose this instant to plunge a shaft of light out of the sky. Silhouetted in the rays, Chiddingly beheld the inky black outline of a magnificent stallion.

"Fitz! Oh, sweet heaven, Fitz!"

Chiddingly put out an unsteady hand and grasped his friend's arm. His eyes still on the horse, Fitzwarren clapped his own hand over his friend's.

"I know, Chid, I know."

In a moment the grip left his arm and he turned his head in time to see Chiddingly dash a hand across his eyes. He was not surprised at his friend's emotion. Even he, mediocre judge of horseflesh that he was, could tell at a glance that here was something quite out of the ordinary. How much more must it mean to Chid, whose sole ambition was centred on the search for just such a creature?

It still remained to be seen whether the conformation was perfect, but it was to be supposed that Tidmarsh, whose enthusiasm had been patent, was enough of a judge to tell if anything had been amiss. It did not take a genius to wonder whether such an apparently excellent piece of horseflesh might have faults, considering he had been despatched as part of a job lot.

Tidmarsh and Chiddingly were even now moving on to the barge to take a closer look. Fitz followed and stood watching while the pair walked round the stallion, arguing his merits. They agreed that he filled the eye, but Tidmarsh held that he looked to be too heavily built for a sprinter.

"Yes, but I will lay you odds we have a stayer here," Chiddingly countered. "Look at those long muscles. And his shoulders are deep enough."

"For my part," Tidmarsh argued, "these strong gaskins are of more moment. I'll warrant he goes well at the gallop."

"The hocks! I cannot wait to see him run!"

But both parties were at one in their satisfaction that the great barrel of a chest showed the stallion to be deep through the heart, which was, they asserted, all that really mattered. The horse fidgeted and tossed his head, blowing and stamping as if he resented this discussion of his points.

"Perhaps it is his temperament that led your scallywag of a dealer to dispose of him?" Fitz suggested.

"If it was, the more fool he. To my mind, this display of attitude is but proof of his mettle and not to be deprecated."

Tidmarsh was in fervent agreement, and the two men continued to eulogise over the horse, to the animal's obvious disgust.

By the time they had done, Fitz's interest had long turned to boredom. He thought the stallion exceptional and would certainly be willing to see him show his paces, but he could not share this wholehearted absorption. His attention wandered about the busy dock, and he amused himself by watching the press of persons there.

As his eyes flitted across the sea of faces, one seemed suddenly familiar: a gentleman of middle years, engaged in haranguing a set of porters who were manoeuvring some heavy trunks towards a cart drawn up close by the warehouses. Next to this stood a coach with its door open wide. Fitz glanced again at the man in charge of these proceedings and noted, with abrupt realisation, the deep colour of his features. The nabob!

As the thought came into his head, movement in the coach doorway caught his eye. He saw a lady's feathered hat poke out, charmingly framing the features of Miss Penelope Winsford.

"Good grief! Here, Chid!"

He had to call again before Lord Chiddingly's attention could be dragged away from his new acquisition.

"Chid, look there. Just climbing out of the coach there. It is Miss Winsford."

Chiddingly looked, but it was plain that Miss Winsford's appearance could not rival the attractions of his horse.

"Shall we not go over?" Fitz suggested. "After this morning's meeting, I'll warrant she will be much surprised to see us."

"You may go over," Chiddingly said on a sour note. "For myself, I have better things to do."

"Upon my soul, have you not yet done fawning over that beast?"

"I have concluded my examination, but I must check the others and decide which of them to keep. Those we don't want we will send directly to Tattersall's yard to be auctioned off."

"You may as well sell them all and be done with it. You can surely want no other now that you have this paragon."

Chiddingly gave a short laugh. "Let us hope it may prove so. But I am far too fly to be pinning all my hopes at this juncture."

If Fitz was unconvinced he did not say so, merely adjuring his friend to follow him when he had concluded his business.

"No, let us meet at the phaeton. I shall not be above ten minutes."

"Ten minutes? I dare say I may count myself fortunate if you reappear within the hour!"

Chiddingly laughed and promised to be as quick as he could, and Fitzwarren made his way alone across the dock to confront Miss Winsford. She stood on the steps of the coach, peering over the many heads to see what progress her father was making.

He was agreeably surprised by her greeting. Her eyes lit and she smiled warmly as she gave him both her hands.

"Why, Fitz, what in the world do you here?"

"I might ask the same of you. Allow me to assist you to alight, Miss Winsford."

"Oh, thank you." She stepped down and he released her. "We are fetching some of the trunks. They have been brought down here by barge from the warehouses at Blackwall. Such a muddle they seem to be in! Poor Papa is growing quite outraged."

Her laughter trilled and once again Fitz found himself amazed at the change in her demeanour. She hardly seemed to be the same girl.

"I was afraid you would not recognise me, Miss Winsford," he said, his tone playful but his eyes watchful for any sign of guile.

"Fiddle, why should I not?"

"Well, after this morning."

"This morning?" Her brow wrinkled. Then she gasped, widening her eyes. "Don't say you went looking for me in the park?"

It seemed such an extraordinary thing for her to say that he was struck dumb for the moment. She read the answer in his face and he felt something of Chid's annoyance as her eyes began to dance.

"Oh dear. What did I —? Was it —?" A giggle, hastily choked, escaped her, and she tried to prim up her mouth. "I owe you an apology, I dare say."

"Not me," he returned, unable to withstand her charm.

"Not Lord Chiddingly again? Oh, don't say so."

But her laughter bubbled up. As the bell-like peal tinkled pleasurably in his ears, he reflected it was just as well Chid had refused to accompany him.

He smiled in spite of himself. "Miss Winsford, you are an abominable little devil. But I confess I cannot be angry with you."

"I am glad of that." She twinkled at him. "I am dreadful, I know. But not as horrid as you might suppose. Truly."

"I don't think you horrid at all."

"Thank you."

"What I do think…" he began, and hesitated.

"Yes? Don't spare me."

"Very well, Miss Penelope Winsford, this is what I think. You are either an unmitigated rogue and an accomplished liar —"

He paused as the grey eyes darkened and all the light died out of her face. In the silence that followed, though she did not flinch from his gaze but met his eyes squarely, it was as if he had dealt her a blow as painful as that she had given to Chiddingly's hand. A dart seemed to pierce his breast.

"Or else," he continued in a softened tone, almost without knowing what he said, "you are an innocent little darling."

The grey eyes wavered a little and a tremor disturbed the corners of her mouth. But the sweet, musical voice was quite steady. "Well, when you have discovered which, don't neglect to inform me."

For a moment longer the look held between them. Then Penelope seemed to wrench her eyes away. A laugh escaped her. Not the spontaneous peal of silver bells. A brittle sound, harsh, like the voice she had used to rate Chiddingly earlier in the day.

"I must go and assist Papa. Good day, Lord Fitzwarren." She began to move away.

His heart cracked. "*Pen!*"

She looked back. "Yes, Fitz?"

His smile was rueful. "Am I still invited to your debut?"

"Of course." She turned and retraced the few steps that lay between them. There was a trace of the old warmth as she gave him her hand to kiss. "I am depending on you, Fitz. Don't fail."

A moment later she had vanished into the quayside throng.

Lady Rossendale's saloons were as full as they could hold. It was a triumph so early in the season. But her ladyship had timed it well. Any earlier and many of the notables would not yet have come to town. Any later and their diaries would be too full to accommodate her.

She had wisely forborne to send out her cards of invitation until interest in the nabob and his family was aroused. Then she had offered her guests a mere five days' warning so that no other matron had a chance to nip in and snaffle the most favoured society dignitaries, a practice not uncommon among rival hostesses anxious to have their functions voted the success of the season.

Viscount Fitzwarren was one of the stars in the *bon ton* firmament for whose arrival her ladyship kept out a jealous eye. But she need not have worried. Fitz would not have been absent for a fortune. Penelope had bade him not to fail her and that was enough. What was more, he dragged the unwilling Baron Chiddingly along with him, saying that he would spread the news of his wonder horse among his racing cronies if he did not come.

"They will hear of it soon enough, I dare say," Chiddingly said indifferently. "These things are bound to leak out."

"Leak out? I shall shout it from the rooftops and ruin all your chances."

Chiddingly smiled, but persisted in his refusal. "I have no desire to meet Miss Winsford."

"Do you mean to shun fashionable circles?"

"Of course I don't."

"Then you are bound to meet her. You may as well do so at this ball."

But in the event he was not called upon to do so, as the guests of honour did not appear to be present. Though a steady stream of fashionables were set down at the door of the great mansion, there was no sign of the nabob or his family.

Mrs Harraton, still anxious for Chiddingly to claim a share of the nabob's coffers, sought out her friend Lady Alice Chumleigh.

"Alice, where are they?" she asked, coming upon her friend at the dais where that lady was conferring with the musicians on her mother's behalf.

Lady Alice turned, a worried frown creasing her plump countenance. "They will be here presently."

Though she tried to infuse conviction into her voice, she only succeeded in conveying her own doubts. She was a dumpy young woman whose recent pregnancy had rendered her a trifle stout. Like her brother, she had taken after her father in stature, though inheriting Lady Rossendale's nervy disposition.

"But I thought the Winsfords were staying with you."

"They were, but my Uncle Archie took a house. In Hanover Square, you know."

"Bought a house in Hanover Square?" echoed Cordelia, her eyes popping.

"He might have done so, but no. He is the oddest man, Cordelia. He says he may never have use for a town house again, and why go to such extravagance?"

"You mean he has hired it?"

"Yes, indeed. Was ever anything more shabby? Though he may purchase an estate, he says, when he should have leisure to look about him and decide where to settle. It is Mama's belief, however, that he is waiting to find out where the girls will be, for he dotes on them, you must know. I am sure he will never bear to be far away from them, even when they marry."

"Girls? Oh yes, I recall now you said there was a sister. I had gathered she must be too young to come out, however."

"Oh no, she is to be here tonight. At least we hope —" Alice broke off in consternation. "I should not have said anything. Pray do not regard it."

Mrs Harraton was looking at her reddening cheeks in the liveliest astonishment. "What in the world —?"

"Pray excuse me, Cordelia. I must go to Mama."

Her friend almost dashed away, leaving Mrs Harraton somewhat puzzled, though she could see that most of the guests seemed to be well enough entertained, and undismayed by the possible defection of the Winsford clan. Her brother particularly so, she noted in disgust.

In fact the baron, in the thick of his racing cronies, was trying to ward off the burgeoning interest in his latest acquisition.

"Come now, Chid, no need to be shy. All friends here, ain't we?" one gentleman offered, his jovial laughter very much at one with the bulk of his protruding stomach.

"In breeding for the turf, there is no such thing as friends, Billy," said Sir Charles Bunbury with austerity. "If there were, we'd have no need for the Club."

Lord Egremont, who boasted at Petworth the biggest stud in the country, agreed with him. "You keep your own counsel, Chid. I would."

"Lord, yes," Clermont put in, shuddering. "The qualms I suffered over Aimwell until I had him safely on the ground!"

Aimwell had won the Derby for Lord Clermont the previous year. His fears were not without foundation. The turf was by no means free from dishonesty and cheating, or even downright crime.

"Stuff and nonsense," scoffed Billy Bolsover. "There'd be no racing at all if we all went in fear of our entries. Why, I have never had an instant's concern over any of my nags."

"You've never had an instant's concern over anything, Billy," Chiddingly said, grinning, "bar what you put in your belly."

There was a shout of laughter in which Bolsover himself heartily joined. He was almost as short as he was stout and presented so comical a figure in his tight breeches and his long bob wig that he was obliged to endure much chaffing. But he did so very good-naturedly and never took offence; none ever had a bad word to say of Billy.

This did not prevent Bunbury, the perpetual president of the Jockey Club, from setting him straight. "All very well, Billy, but Clermont's in the right of it. You would not credit the complaints we get, of grooms riding on the wrong side of the post, or a jockey crimping his mount to throw the race."

"Yes, by God," averred Egremont. "What of Miss Nightingale at Boroughbridge? Died the Sunday before the race and they found two pounds of duck-shot in her stomach."

Several men nodded, and Sir Charles, who had a longer memory, reminded them of earlier atrocities. "There was Tosspot given a dose of physic at Scarborough, and Rosebud poisoned at York."

"Yes, yes, but these are isolated cases," Bolsover objected, still smiling. "Great God, there is not one of us here who would dream of such a thing."

"Oh, isn't there just?" muttered Chiddingly, casting a darkling glance across at another group.

On the fringes of this, one man, tall, with a hawk-like countenance, hovered as if he did not belong. The other men had no difficulty interpreting this cryptic remark. Lord Goole's racing career had been summarily terminated by the Jockey Club committee only last year for cheating practices, and this hard core of turf notables cast repulsive looks at the man whom they had cold-shouldered into seeking other company than their own.

"Come, come, you are all very gloomy," chided Billy in heartening tones. "For all that Chid may choose to say nothing, it is very evident we all know *something*."

His little baby-blue eyes twinkled merrily at the baron, and there was a general laugh and an easing of the atmosphere.

Chiddingly sighed. "I suppose you could not help but do so, though I'd give a monkey to know how you came by your knowledge."

"What do you take us for, Chid, a parcel of noddies?" laughed Bolsover. "Can't send a whole collection of Arab horseflesh off to Tatts without raising a lot of questions."

"Clatterbridge!" Chiddingly said in disgust. "What a blabbermouth the man is. What did he say?"

But it appeared the head groom had been discreet, though he was usually given to chatter easily about his master's stables. Only his firmly closed lips had led everyone to suppose there must be something to hide.

Chiddingly, finding Bolsover disinclined to drop the subject, inadvertently lent colour to this belief by making his excuses and going off to find Fitzwarren. He left behind him a speculative group who began to murmur among themselves.

Viscount Fitzwarren had meanwhile become the centre of an animated circle of fashionables like himself. He was, when Chiddingly joined them, engaged in examining a snuff box presented for his judgement by Count Leopold, an impecunious runaway from the Hanoverian court whose high rank and engaging address had secured for him a place in the *beau monde*.

"Fitz, *liebchen*, you say nothing," he complained in an agony of apprehension. "But speak, I pray you."

The viscount did not raise his eyes from the object resting in his palm. He traced a finger across the surface of the delicate box, made of translucent shell with a pinkish pearly sheen, and set in a silver filigree frame.

"Ten guineas you gave for it, you say?"

"I say he was robbed," commented Lord Buckfastleigh. "What is the use of such a thing? It would break in an instant."

"Hush," reproved his lady. "You are not asked for your opinion, Buck."

"No, veritably," agreed the count, rolling a fiery eye at him. "*Mein Gott*, that one should seek from you the eye of beauty? Change first the tailor!"

As his lordship's abominable taste in dress was well established, his over-embroidered suit of a garish hue being no exception tonight, this insult provoked a deal of hilarity.

"I'll lay a pony Fitz condemns it, then."

"No one would take you, Buck." Chiddingly had entered the lists. "Fitz never condemns anything. You should know that."

"Oh, you're there, are you? Well, I'll thank you to stick to horses and leave beauty alone." Buckfastleigh grinned. "Unless you care to furnish the name of *your* tailor to Leopold."

The count shuddered eloquently, but Chiddingly merely smiled at the titters about him. He was too used to Fitz's comments on his careless dress to take offence.

Fitz himself, though smiling at the raillery of his friends, had continued to scrutinise the snuff box. At last he raised his head and everyone fell into respectful silence.

"Well, Leopold."

Count Leopold held his breath. The last time he had presented a very unusual fan to Fitz, the arbiter had smiled faintly, said, "Enchanting!" in a bored tone and walked away, leaving the crestfallen count to the comfort or laughter of his friends. Leopold had ripped the offending fan to shreds.

"Name your price," Fitz said softy.

Leopold flung up his hands with a joyous shout and there was a spontaneous outbreak of applause. The count named no price, but took back the box and turned to relay his excited triumph to the confounded Buckfastleigh. For Fitz, as was well known, never bought anything. No matter the price named, he would insist the owner kept it on the score of not wishing to deprive them of it.

"You know, if I ever did buy one of those things," he murmured as he strolled away with Chiddingly, "I have a strong suspicion my opinion would be severely devalued."

"What opinion? And where is your precious Miss Winsford? I thought this was to be her debut."

"I am at a loss to account for her absence," frowned Fitz, looking towards the big double doors at the end of the ballroom.

The room was so large it was not difficult to see them, in spite of the mass of persons in the way, and the bobbing of feathers, fringes and ribbons on the ladies' overlarge hats which were *de rigueur* even with full dress.

"It would scarce be a wonder if you had missed her in all this crush," Chiddingly commented.

"I have not missed her," Fitz muttered, in what was for him a testy manner. "She is not here. Nor are her parents. Everyone is talking of it."

But at that very moment Lady Rossendale's major-domo thumped the floor for attention and announced the arrival of Mr and Mrs Archibald Winsford — a formal proceeding necessitated by the fact that the hostess and her son had already left their post by the door.

The nabob came briskly in, the lady on his arm a neater, younger and more rounded copy of Lady Rossendale herself.

The hum of voices in the room was dying away as the major-domo made his second announcement.

"Miss Penelope Winsford and Miss Persephone Winsford."

The two Misses Winsford entered and paused on the threshold to stand framed in the double doorway. A startled hush fell upon the ballroom and everyone stared.

From the toes of the yellow kid shoes on their feet, and their full-skirted gowns of apple-green taffeta with quarter-length sleeves and sprays of yellow roses fastened low on the bosom, to the crowning glory of their frizzed gold locks dressed wide and high under neat chip hats, beribboned and feathered, and their classic features and sculptured lips, Penelope and Persephone Winsford were exactly alike.

CHAPTER THREE

Alone, a single Miss Winsford had been a sufficiently pretty picture. Together, they were a sight to take the breath away.

After the first stunned moment, a kaleidoscope of memories tumbled through Chiddingly's mind. Golden hair flying, and a snarling lip as a whiplash rose and fell through the air; a violent ride and a thundering team, with a husky voice in passionate rage; sparkling eyes and lips that trembled on a silvery laugh; and questioning eyes in an innocent face and a sweet, musical voice.

So it was Penelope, mischievous Penelope, who had not known him, and yet had known enough to make a game of him. And it was Persephone, of the wild ride and blazing eyes, who had flung insults in his face and dared to whip at his hand.

Then Fitz's laughter and the uproar in the room penetrated the flood of his chaotic thoughts and he saw the twins engulfed in the press of persons that surged forward.

"Thus all is explained," Fitz gasped, hardly able to speak for laughing. "Now I see why — why she was so much enjoying her mischief. Upon my soul, I cannot blame her. What a rich jest! How I shall scold her for this."

He sobered a little, remembering he had his peace to make with Penelope first. But his delight in the masquerade knew no bounds until he saw that Chiddingly was not similarly elated.

"Now what ails you, Chid? If there is anything in this revelation to send you up into the boughs, beyond the fact we have not a notion which is which, I should like to know it."

"I am not up in the boughs. I am happy to think Miss Penelope Winsford was able to amuse herself at my expense.

And even happier that Miss *Persephone* Winsford is ready to abjure society. I will thus be spared another encounter."

"Does it look as if she intends to abjure society?"

"She has done so up to now. I dare say she may do so again."

"Obviously she has done so in order to achieve this *éclat*."

Chiddingly threw him a scornful glance. "I shall be much surprised if we find that to be the case."

"I will lay you a monkey it is."

"Done," said Chiddingly promptly.

Fitz grinned. "Thus, dear boy, you are committed to another encounter. Try at least for a little conduct."

But there was no getting near the Winsford twins, besieged as they were by one group of persons after another. Fitz was in despair until he conceived the happy notion of enlisting the services of the nabob himself. It was not such an easy matter to detach Mrs Winsford from the eager young men who were anxious to secure an introduction to her daughters, but Fitz at length managed to make his way to her side. She recognised him after a moment.

"Of course, Lord Fitzwarren, you must forgive me. With so many new people, I am quite at a loss."

"Never mind it, ma'am. Allow me to present Lord Chiddingly to you. You may forget him again at once, and so be comfortable."

A trill of laughter very like that of Penelope escaped her lips. "No, how can you say so? Do not heed him, Lord Chiddingly. I recall now Pen saying he was a dreadful tease."

"Would you think me very saucy, ma'am," Fitz said, smiling, "if I were to suggest that, coming from Miss Penelope that is a case of the pot calling the kettle black?"

"Very true, indeed. She is a sad romp."

"Unusual manners, ma'am?"

She tutted. "You have been talking to my sister."

"Not at all. It was Miss Penelope who told me of them."

"Really, I am ashamed of her. What a very odd idea she must have given you of the company with whom we shared our pleasures. If the girls are free-spoken, I am afraid it must be laid at the door of my husband. He would encourage them."

Fitz seized the cue. "Speaking of your husband, ma'am, we are anxious to make his acquaintance."

"My husband? Oh, I quite thought —"

"No, no. Recollect that we have already had the felicity of meeting one of your daughters."

Stifling her surprise, Mrs Winsford led them over to where the nabob stood, chatting easily to a group of older men. Archie Winsford was a bluff, hearty man of an outgoing disposition, who was very pleased to meet anyone at all. His friendship was not, however, bestowed indiscriminately. One did not acquire a fortune in business without a deal of shrewd judgement. But he had a large tolerance, and did not mind a man's being a fool provided he did not have to do business with him, nor consider him in the light of anything other than a passing acquaintance.

He had an unfortunate trick sometimes of peering under his brows at people, which gave him a quite unfounded look of ferocity. He directed this stare at the young men when his wife introduced them, but Fitz dispelled it with his first words.

"How do you do, sir? Did you manage to sort out the jumble of your trunks at Legal Quays the other day?"

The nabob was so surprised he burst into laughter. "Now, how the deuce do you know anything of that, young feller?"

"I met your daughter there, sir, and she told me of your troubles."

51

"Ha! Trouble a-plenty. These officious porters of yours are not worth a straw. Give me the wallahs back in India any day. Still, we got there in the end. So you know my Penelope, eh?"

"An entrancing young lady, sir. May I say the picture your daughters present together is quite the most ravishing I have seen?"

"Ha!" The nabob rubbed his hands in glee. He glanced at his wife. "Did I not say so, my dear? Clarissa wanted me to force that girl of mine into the picture at the outset. But no, I said. Let her have her way. No sense in a pitched battle. Turn it to good account, I said. Let her play least in sight as she wishes and then — boom! And you see I was right."

Fitz's eyes were alight with laughter, but before he could speak Chiddingly intervened, casting him a glance of triumph.

"In fact, Miss Persephone had no wish to come out?"

"Pooh, not she. Hated the idea from the word go. In fact, she'd a deal rather have stayed —"

"Archie!"

The nabob turned to his wife. "Yes, m'dear?" He caught the unmistakable signal in her eye and recollected himself. "Ah, quite so." Then he laughed heartily. "Never could keep my tongue between my teeth about my girls. Why, they are the best little daughters a man ever had."

"I am sure they must be, sir," Fitz said, smiling at his simple enthusiasm.

Satisfied of his discretion, Mrs Winsford went away. But the nabob leaned confidentially towards Fitz and Chiddingly.

"You know what females are. You'd think three of them in the house would drive me to distraction, but not a bit of it. My girls are the most engaging little rascals. Always were. For all they are like in looks, you know, they are quite different. Mind you, I am the only one who can ever tell them apart. Fact." His hearty laugh rang out again. "I call them my *little peas*, you know, but I can tell you at once which is which and before either has opened her mouth."

Fitz pounced on this. "No, can you indeed? I own I should like to witness your skill, for I confess myself to be completely baffled."

"Ha! Nothing easier, my boy. Come along."

The nabob marched off and Fitz, pausing only to wink at Chiddingly and jerk his head for his friend to follow, trailed after him closely.

Such was the force of the nabob's personality that he shouldered a path through the throng with the greatest of ease, the crowd parting before him. Before long, Fitz found himself confronting the Winsford twins, who turned together as their father hailed them on his approach.

"Pen! Seph!"

The gentlemen monopolising them fell back and the newcomers took their places. Fitz noted the baron's eyes travelling from one classic face to the other, his expression inscrutable.

"Now, then," Archie said with authority.

The twins looked at him in mute question.

"Have to prove my mettle, my little peas. Not a word now, either of you."

Obediently they stood silent, their faces in repose quite indistinguishable one from the other. The nabob took hold of Fitz's arm and drew him forward a pace.

"Take a good look, young feller. You've met Penelope. Now what d'ye say?"

Fitz looked ruefully from one to the other, half hoping for a sign from Pen. That give-away sparkle in her eyes, perhaps. But there was nothing in either pair of cool grey orbs to help him.

"Upon my soul, sir, I cannot tell in the least."

Obviously pleased, Archie Winsford looked around the interested circle about them. Then he turned to Chiddingly, without even glancing at his daughters.

"You, sir?"

"By no means," Chiddingly responded, though he too looked into their eyes, sure some echo of Persephone's fury must creep into them. But both pairs were coolly impersonal and, like Fitz, he had to acknowledge defeat. "No, sir. You will have to tell us."

"Ha, ha!" laughed the nabob, plainly enjoying himself. "Then you shall have it without further ado. To the right is Persephone. Penelope is to the left."

At once the classic features on the left broke into the warm smile Fitz remembered, and the characteristic laugh rippled from her. "Well done, Papa!"

There was instant hubbub, and a chorus of congratulation.

Persephone's eyes, however, now held a militant sparkle and she compressed her lips as if she despised this charade. Chiddingly found himself quite unable to take his own eyes off her. As if she sensed his scrutiny, she met his glance and he thought he detected a challenge in the grey eyes. Nor was he mistaken.

No sooner had the nabob left them with a passing adjuration to his daughters to "Take care of these fellows, my dears, grant them a dance or some such thing," than Persephone's husky voice addressed the baron directly, the underlying steel apparent.

"I fear I must decline taking care of you, sir. I am but a novice in the art of dance, and would doubtless call down your freely worded criticisms upon my head."

"They cannot dance with either of us, Seph," said Penelope, intervening in haste. She turned her eyes to Fitzwarren, and he saw they had lost a little of their sparkle. "You are tardy, Fitz. I regret that both of us are already engaged for every dance."

But Fitz was ready for this. "My dear Miss Penelope, there was no getting near you."

Persephone's fine lip curled. "It seemed to me enough gentlemen managed it." She flicked at Chiddingly a glance of contempt. "But of course they had address."

"It may have escaped your notice, ma'am," Chiddingly said through his teeth, "but neither of us has in fact requested a dance."

"We had already resigned ourselves to the fact that we must forgo the pleasure," Fitz cut in adroitly. "However, might we perhaps be permitted to take you in to supper?" He saw refusal forming on Penelope's lips and added, "Now, don't say you mean to disobey your papa, Miss Winsford. Remember that he bade you take care of us."

Penelope's lips twitched and some of her stiffness evaporated. "Very true. What do you say, Seph? Do we relent?"

Her sister shrugged an indifferent shoulder. "One must eat."

"Do we take that for gracious consent?" Thus Chiddingly.

Her eyes flashed, but Fitz quickly intervened.

"We will come to claim you." A wicked gleam invited Penelope to share his amusement. "It promises to be fraught with interest."

The musical peal of Penelope's laughter rewarded him and, seizing Chiddingly's elbow, he marched him away before he could provoke either sister into cancelling the arrangement.

To his surprise he found his friend ready enough to fall in with the scheme, even if the light in his eye was less than amiable. "She shall not snub me so easily, I promise you. I shall soon show her what I think of her insufferable conduct."

At eleven o'clock the musicians were granted a respite. The company began to file out of the ballroom to partake of a succulent supper laid out upon a buffet, which they consumed sitting about at a number of small tables spread over several of the saloons.

Fitzwarren had filled in the intervening period by dancing with several young ladies, but Chiddingly, finding everyone had nothing better to talk about than the remarkable twins, sought refuge in the card-room, where he watched the play and exchanged idle conversation with some of his racing cronies.

He joined his friend in a mood of hostile anticipation, ready to do battle at the slightest provocation. But when the twins were discovered seated in attitudes of exhaustion in two chairs by the wall, and fending off belated requests to take them down to supper, Chiddingly's ire melted as they looked up and he discerned relief in both pairs of grey eyes, though he was not immediately able to tell which twin each pair belonged to. He was not left in doubt for more than a few instants.

"Oh, here they are," cried the melodious voice of Penelope. She rose at once, scattering apologies about the crestfallen losers.

Persephone said nothing, but, with a palpable effort, she too got up out of her chair. Fitzwarren, with the idea of forestalling unpleasantness, stepped forward and offered his arm, leaving Chiddingly to escort Penelope.

"You look as if you could use some refreshment, ma'am."

"I could more readily use a bed," Persephone told him roundly. "How people can bear to comport themselves in this tiresome fashion night after night is beyond me."

The viscount hid a smile. "You are not enjoying it?"

"No, I am not. I knew how it would be. Nothing but sighing and simpering silly females and foolish men, who suppose the paying of fulsome and empty compliments may put them in the way of helping themselves to the contents of Papa's purse."

Fitz's eyebrows flew up. "You are very frank."

She turned her fine grey eyes upon him and he saw with misgiving that the militant sparkle had returned. "Why should I pretend we are here for any other purpose? I promise you, I am almost ready to accept the first man who offers only to be rid of the business. Then perhaps they would all of them leave me in peace."

"Seph!" Penelope protested from behind her. She left the baron and came to clasp and shake her sister's arm, murmuring, "Drat you, Seph, you promised, you know you did!"

Persephone halted and the two identical faces looked into each other's eyes for a moment. Then Persephone sighed and an apologetic smile flitted across her mouth "Yes, I did. I shall say no more."

"It is uncanny," burst from Chiddingly. Two pairs of enquiring grey eyes turned towards him. He laughed. "It must be like looking into a mirror."

Penelope tinkled. "Oh dear, not at all. To us the similarity is minimal, I assure you."

"How can that be?"

"If you were to give your brain the indulgence of a little thought," Persephone said, "you would see at once it must be so."

Chiddingly bridled. "Indeed, ma'am? Then perhaps —"

"You may explain it presently," Fitz interrupted. "Let us first sit down and partake of some supper."

By the time the ladies were settled at a table in a corner of one of the saloons, which buzzed with the laughter and chatter of many tongues, and the gentlemen had procured for them plates of choice viands and glasses of a strawberry cup, Chiddingly had recollected the impropriety of indulging in a quarrel in public. As it was Penelope who referred to the matter, he inferred that Persephone had reached the same realisation — though more likely prompted thereto by her shrewder sister, thought the baron cynically.

"You see, unless we are both looking into the same mirror," explained Pen, "the face I see on Seph is that seen by others."

Fitz shook a puzzled head as he raised his glass of claret to his lips. "I don't follow you."

"Oh dear, I do not explain it very well. Seph, you try."

Persephone shrugged. "It is very simple. Any portrait painter will tell you that no countenance is symmetrical. One side must always be different from the other. Therefore, in a mirror one sees the opposing sides reversed from the way one is seen by others. The result is markedly different. Now do you see?"

Chiddingly looked struck. "Of course. Small wonder sitters are seldom satisfied with their portraits."

"Or that there is so much argument over the likeness between them and their relatives," Persephone added, and, for the first time, she laughed. A slow, deep gurgle that left her eyes warm.

"But that does not help us," Fitz protested. "All very well when you talk, for your voices are pitched so differently, but —"

"Oh, you must not depend upon that," Penelope cut in, twinkling. She looked at her sister, the mischief dancing in her eyes. "Do me, Seph."

"Oh no, Pen. Folly! You are as bad as Papa."

"If you *please*, Seph. Or shall I do you?"

"Spare me!" Persephone cast her eyes heavenwards. Then, as her sister began to draw herself up, features pulling taut and eyes narrowing quite in Persephone's own manner, she flung up a hand. "That will do. Very well, if you insist."

Then, before the two gentlemen's amazed eyes, the stiff and husky-voiced Persephone seemed to melt away. In her place were the sparkling eyes, the warm smile and the tinkling laughter that characterised Penelope.

"Oh dear, oh dear," gushed Persephone, aping exactly both her sister's manner and the sweet musicality of her voice. "You must not mind my sister, dear sirs. She is the naughtiest, most teasing little baggage imaginable."

Both gentlemen burst into laughter, in which Penelope merrily joined.

"There," said Persephone, reverting to her usual manner. "Now, if you dare to do me, Pen, I will not ride with you in the park."

"I won't," Penelope promised.

"But how is this?" Fitz asked. "I had thought it must have been you, Miss Persephone, who had need to persuade your sister to ride with you."

"Oh dear, no," Penelope said, "for I mean her to come out at the fashionable promenade — not at the crack of dawn. Tonight has shown me that I need her with me to cut a dash. Do you not agree, Fitz?"

"Indeed. The two of you on horseback must gladden every eye."

"Which of you is the elder?" asked Chiddingly.

"We have no idea. It is the most diverting thing," Penelope said. "Mama will have it I was the first."

"But Papa holds that it was I," put in Persephone.

"They have never ceased to argue the point, and so we are both styled Miss Winsford." Penelope's laugh pealed again. "I tell Papa it is as well we were not boys."

"That would have meant the devil to pay," Persephone agreed.

"You mean as regards your fortunes?" Chiddingly said. A slight flush reddened his cheeks as her eyes narrowed in suspicion.

"Yes." Her lip curled with disdain. "As things stand, they are exactly equal. So you may as well have one of us as the other."

"I knew how it would be," seethed Persephone, striding up and down the Persian carpet in the rather old-fashioned parlour that had rapidly become the family headquarters.

"Seph," begged Mrs Winsford, in despairing accents, "strive, I do beg of you, for a little control."

"My control, Mama, was exhausted the other night," said Persephone, glancing across to the table in the window embrasure where her parents and sister were still seated, finishing off an informal breakfast. "Ask Pen if I did not hold myself well in hand."

Penelope nodded, but her eyes teased her sister over the cup of sweetened chocolate, well laced with butter and cream. "Barring one or two near misses, you were very good, Seph."

"Yes," Persephone said in triumph, "and if it had not been for that hateful —" She broke off, catching Penelope's warning frown.

Mrs Winsford did not appear to notice the slip. "Archie." She leaned across the table to call out to her spouse, who was buried in the *Morning Chronicle*, apparently divorced from the chatter of feminine voices, a habit he had long since perfected. "Archie!"

The nabob looked up, peering at her over the top of the reading spectacles perched upon his nose. "Yes, m'dear?"

"I wish you will put down that paper. Your daughter is like to ruin all with her stubborn ways, and all you can do is sit there muttering of that Hastings man as if he were of more account than your own family."

Archie looked across to where Persephone was still walking to and fro, kneading her unquiet hands. "Seph? Pooh, nonsense! Why should she ruin anything?"

"Can you not see what she will be at, marching about in that unbecoming fashion?"

"Seph, sit down," barked the nabob, with an assumption of severity. "Your mama is afraid you will wear a hole in the carpet."

Penelope laughed, and Persephone's stern features visibly lightened as she bit her lip on a rueful smile. Clarissa Winsford was too thankful for these signs of softening to take exception to her husband's banter. Archie stretched out a hand to his wayward daughter and she came across and laid her fingers in it.

"Oh, Papa, why could you not have left me in India?"

"Now, Seph, you know that would have been quite ineligible," Clarissa said.

"Moreover, you would have had to marry dreadful old Colonel Drummond, who had no more notion of a good horse than our ayah," Penelope put in, twinkling.

The nabob pulled his daughter down to him and gave her a kiss. "Sit you down, Seph, and be still. I'd a deal rather have stayed in Bombay myself, as well you know. But it couldn't be done."

"No, and thank heaven for it," Penelope exclaimed. "For my part, I am ready to embrace Mr Pitt."

It had been the introduction of the Prime Minister's India Bill two years ago —forcing the East India Company to accept a Board of Control in the Government that had power over the directors themselves — which had been the ruling factor in the nabob's decision to leave. While it was not quite so drastic as the earlier bill, introduced by Fox and rejected by Parliament, which would have deprived the company of all its power and trading privileges, the new Act threatened to severely curtail the perquisite of trading on the side — and other more questionable practices — that had enabled the company's servants to accumulate their vast personal fortunes. Archibald Winsford, along with others of his colleagues, had seen the writing on the wall and expressed himself as now being willing to gratify the dearest wish of his wife and one twin by resigning his post and coming home to England.

Clarissa and Penelope blessed Mr Pitt, breathing sighs of relief, and plunged into the business of packing up with unadulterated enthusiasm.

Not so Persephone. Informed of the approaching change in their lives, she had gazed at her father aghast, tears in her eyes. "Leave Bombay? Leave India? But my horses! Oh, Papa, no!"

She saw the regret in her father's eyes, the jubilance in her mother's, and knew it was true.

"But Shiveen —" She whispered the name, the vision of her favourite mount filling her mind.

"You may take Shiveen," her father said at once, "but for the rest…"

He did not finish the sentence. Grief flooded Persephone's heart. Tears spilling over, she fled the house and ran to the stables.

Ufur, the old Indian martinet who ran the stables and had taught her to ride almost before she could walk, was not there.

A sleepy groom, dragged from his afternoon slumbers, saddled the grey, while his mistress's clouded eyes wandered from one beloved glossy head to another and she fought down the lump in her throat.

Her horses. They were her friends. Her world, her *life*. Now she must leave them. Ufur, too. How could she bear to part from the grumbling, scolding old man to whose strictures and blandishments she owed everything she knew of horseflesh?

She rode out of the Fort and down to the bay where she had ridden all her horses across the sands. Her distress communicated to Shiveen, and the mare bounded forward under the unconscious pressure of her hand, hurtling over the beach at the water's edge, kicking up sand and spray.

Wind whistled past Persephone's face, streaking the hot salt tears across her cheeks, catching at the loosened golden locks and whipping them about her head.

But after a few moments of this heady pace, long habit reasserted itself. Even through the desolation in her breast, Persephone knew the heat of the afternoon was too much for Shiveen. It did not need the heaving flanks of her mare as she slowed her to a walk to tell her she had been imprudent. Ufur would be furious.

At that thought, a fresh deluge of tears coursed down her cheeks and she bent her head over Shiveen's silky mane and wept as if her heart must break.

Ufur, her beloved mentor. Under his stern rule, Persephone had grown up to have a respect and care of her horses which far surpassed anything she might feel for people, with the exception of her immediate family, and of Ufur himself. Though she no longer needed his guidance, she could not bear the thought of going out of his sphere of influence, far away to the other side of the world.

Her first grief spent, Persephone turned the mare and trotted her gently home. Back at the stables, a familiar turbaned figure awaited her, arms folded, arrogant head thrown back, on his wrinkled brown features a fierce frown.

Ufur seized the bridle, glaring up at his mistress. "Miss Sephy," he growled, "I am taking my stick to your back, never mind that you are a big girl now."

"Don't scold, Ufur," Persephone begged, slipping out of the saddle. "Please don't."

He saw her ravaged face as she slid down and his dark eyes softened. "*Salla*, Miss Sephy! Time is coming now. I've been waiting many moons, knowing this time is coming."

Persephone looked at him. "Ufur, I think I shall die."

His mouth split apart, showing his remaining teeth in a cackling grin. "No, Miss Sephy. I am dying soon. I am an old man. You are a young lady. You will live many years, and know many horses before you die."

Persephone's lips trembled on a smile, but her eyes filled again. "Oh, Ufur, I shall miss you."

"I will also miss you, Miss Sephy. But you are not forgetting old Ufur and the lessons you learned."

"How could I forget?" She stood gazing at the old man, trying to visualise a life without him. "How will I bear it?" she cried, and, bursting into fresh sobs, she fell upon his chest.

He patted her, muttering soothing phrases in his own tongue, but his stern eyes were moist.

In the end all the horses were sold, with the exception of Shiveen. Persephone, finding she could not bear to subject her ageing mare to the rigours of a long sea voyage, and feeling a complete break would be marginally less painful, gave Shiveen to her old mentor, who had been provided with a home and a generous pension. At the final moment of parting, Ufur told her with determined cheerfulness that Shiveen would grow old and they would die together.

Once in England, Persephone had been agreeably surprised at the quality of the English cattle, but the foul weather and the cold had produced a resurgence of her loss and she refused point-blank to appear in public with a view to finding herself a husband. Thanks to the nabob, she had been allowed to have her way, seeking solace in flinging herself into violent exercise on her cousin Rossendale's horses.

But the debut had inexorably arrived, and she had perforce given in at last to Penelope's entreaties.

"Dearest Seph, I know you don't care for socialising, but it is my heart's desire to cut a dash. Papa is so clever to have sworn us all to secrecy about there being two of us, and to have hit upon us wearing the exact same ensemble when we appear at last together. What is more, I might have betrayed you, but I did take the blame for you, you know I did."

"Yes, I know, but —"

"I never said a word to let either Chiddingly or Fitz imagine that it was not I, but you who had behaved so very badly."

"They will know soon enough it was I."

"Yes, but not if you don't come tonight and — oh, drat you, Seph, I am depending on you! I am nothing without you, you know I am not."

"Devil take you, Pen, that is nonsense. You would charm a snake."

"But I can't throw a thunderclap on my own. You are my twin, dearest. I *need* you."

So Persephone had capitulated, promising to behave with all the propriety in the world when her mama had begged her, almost tearfully, to remember her company manners and refrain from putting them all to shame.

A taste of fashionable London life, however, had confirmed all Persephone's worst suspicions. She had not minded the dull and uncomfortable parties in Bombay that drove her sister to screaming boredom, for it was a highly parochial milieu which demanded no social graces. The *beau monde* of England was altogether different.

The worst aspect of the whole enterprise, to Persephone, was her father's accursed fortune. Bad enough in Bombay, where they were naturally enough sought after by every bachelor, whether eligible or otherwise, but here it was infinitely worse.

"Mark my words," she told Penelope, as soon as her parents had withdrawn, "that abominable Chiddingly is after a fortune."

"Well, and why not? I must say, Seph, we are extremely fortunate. If our portions were merely respectable, we would be obliged to accept almost anyone who offered and be thankful. As it is, we may please ourselves."

"If I pleased myself, I would have none of them."

"Fiddle." Penelope's eyes danced with mischief. "Ten to one you will end by bestowing your hand and heart upon Chiddingly, for by all accounts he is as horse-mad as you."

"I? Marry that — that insolent knave? That hectoring bully? That — that devil? I would rather die!"

Penelope twinkled. "So would he, I dare say. I must ask Fitz."

"If you dare to do anything of the sort —"

"Don't put yourself about," recommended Penelope, smiling. She rose from the table and crossed to the door, casting a disparaging glance over her sister's attire. "I hope you mean to change your dress. That old habit is positively shabby,

Seph. It may do well enough for your dawn antics, but it will not pass muster in the fashionable promenade."

"I have a very good mind not to come with you."

"If you cry off now, Seph, it will be the most abominable thing in the world."

"Oh, very well, but it is a great bore."

"Fiddle. I dare say you will meet all manner of useful persons. Any number of fashionable gentlemen are addicted to sporting pursuits, Cousin Alice tells me. You may hunt and see the racing. I am certain you will soon find yourself mightily at home."

Penelope ushered her reluctant sister out of the room, adding naughtily as they went along the corridor, "Moreover, if you are desirous of entering that set, let me recommend you get upon terms with your hectoring bully. An acknowledged nonpareil, they tell me."

She then whisked into her bedchamber before her incensed twin had a chance to express again her undoubted preference for death.

CHAPTER FOUR

"Daisy cutters!" said Persephone in disgust, looking about at the sedately high-stepping mounts chosen by the *bon ton* for hacking in the park at the fashionable hour of the promenade.

She was herself bestriding a raking bay, whose sidlings and tossings evidenced his uncertain temper. The Winsfords were still borrowing from Lord Rossendale's stables, until, as the nabob expressed it, his experienced daughter should have learned her way about and might choose her own cattle.

Penelope, thankful for the ill opinion of her skill held by her sister that had prompted her to pick for her use a well-mannered, quiet horse who could give her a comfortable ride, saw nothing amiss. "They look perfectly well to me."

"That is because you know nothing of the matter," said her twin, controlling the plunging progress of her own mount with an effortless grace that won the admiration of the new groom riding behind. "For the most part, they are peacocky specimens, obviously meant only for show."

Her eye then fell upon a grey trotting towards them. She pointed with her whip. "Now, *there* is a fine horse. Pure Arab, I would say at a guess."

"And guess who is riding it?" Penelope gurgled.

Looking from the horse to its rider, Persephone drew in her breath sharply. "*Salla!*"

"Seph, you bad girl! Thank heaven no one can understand you." Penelope turned her welcoming smile on Chiddingly and his companion, who were halting their mounts as they came abreast. "Good day, Fitz. How do you do, Lord Chiddingly?

My sister has just been admiring your grey. You must know she dotes upon horses."

"Be silent," hissed her twin.

"Indeed?" said Chiddingly, his gaze travelling coldly and indifferently over Persephone. "I confess I had not observed it."

Persephone's eyes flashed. "Your observations, sir, are quite without interest."

"You look a dazzling sight, the two of you," interpolated Fitzwarren, looking them over.

Obedient to her sister's plea, Persephone was clad in a dashing habit of military cut in olive-green with gold braid. Penelope, also in green, had chosen an altogether more feminine garment garnished with a quantity of lace, and her frivolous feathered hat formed a pretty contrast to the stark severity of her twin's unadorned beaver.

"But how rash to speak first, Miss Penelope," Fitz teased, "and so deprive us of the agreeable game of guessing."

"Oh dear, how silly of me. Yet I do not know. You could hardly fail to observe our differences on horseback. Why, I am cast quite into the shade by Seph's skill."

"You seem perfectly competent to me," Chiddingly said, turning his mount and bringing it up alongside. "May I ride a little way beside you?"

"By all means," Penelope agreed, throwing a quizzing glance at her sister's stormy face as she urged her horse forward.

But Fitzwarren was even now taking his friend's lead, and guiding his mount ready to accompany her sister.

"If that is his notion of gallantry," Persephone sneered, "he will not go far with Pen, I promise you."

Fitz laughed but made no comment on this. "Your sister was in the right of it, you know. You have the best seat I have ever seen. You will take the shine out of all our equestriennes."

Persephone's fine eyes met his in a straight look. "I am no target for gallantry, sir, so pray do not trouble yourself to invent pretty speeches for my benefit."

"I spoke nothing but the truth. As for gallantry, I am afraid you will have to accustom yourself to that." He read a retort in her eye and added, "But let us not talk of such trivialities. Tell me instead how you come to be so excellent a horsewoman."

Persephone thawed a little. "I had an excellent teacher."

"Your father?"

"No, indeed. Papa has little interest in horses. My mentor began as my father's head groom, I believe. But latterly he had overall charge of the stables." Her eyes softened. "And me, of course."

"Good grief, was he a native, then?"

"Certainly. Do you imagine the Indians to be savages, untutored in such arts?"

"Not at all. I was surprised just for the moment."

"I can assure you, my lord, a great many of our friends were Indian. Besides, there was in Bombay an ease of social intercourse which I dare say you would deprecate."

"Not in the least. I imagine it was inevitable in such a small community. Upon my soul, Miss Persephone, we are not so high in the instep. You will find the racing fraternity, for example, hobnobbing with all sorts and conditions of men."

"Racing! How much I should like to see your famed courses. I have heard much of Epsom and Newmarket. We had some racing, naturally. Paltry affairs, mostly, but nevertheless exciting."

Her eyes warmed and Fitz was reminded irresistibly of Penelope as the classic features lit with a glowing animation.

"We used to get up the meetings among ourselves. On the Esplanade behind the Fort, stretching to Back Bay. There was a race course of sorts out by the Dongri on the flats. But our own meetings were better, for I was permitted to take part." Her deep gurgle of laughter came. "Until they complained I could not lose and no one would be fool enough to bet against me. Ufur, needless to say, would not allow it to be so. And he was right."

"Ufur?" Fitz was fascinated by the change in her as she spoke of what she patently loved.

"Yes, my tutor. He was himself a notable horseman. They hated him to ride at the Dongri, too. For no one could touch him, even at the last. He was near seventy years old by then."

"He sounds a very paragon."

"Oh, past price!" Persephone's eyes clouded and the distress in her face smote Fitz to the heart.

"You miss him very much."

She nodded, her trembling underlip gripped between her teeth.

"Well, if we cannot offer you such a paragon, I'll wager Chid would come a close second. He does not ride his own racehorses, naturally, but even his peers acknowledge him an undisputed virtuoso in the saddle."

This observation had the effect of wiping the woe from her countenance. She stiffened alarmingly. "Indeed?"

Perhaps fortunately, they were at this point interrupted by Count Leopold and Lord Buckfastleigh, who were in attendance upon his lady wife, sitting sedately in an open carriage with a companion.

"Ah, the lovely Miss Winsford," shouted his lordship, and pointed an accusing finger at Fitzwarren. "Might have known we'd find you monopolising her, Fitz, you dog." He bowed, tipping his hat to the lady. "Which one of them are you, if I might be pardoned the liberty?"

Persephone accorded this sally the barest modicum of a smile.

"This is Miss Persephone, Buck. Pray allow me to present Buckfastleigh to you, Miss Winsford. And this —"

"No, no, already I have had the pleasure," Leopold said in a tone of reverence. "Though I dare not hope a place to hold in the memory of such incomparable beauty."

This time Persephone did not even smile, casting him instead a glance of scarcely veiled contempt.

"I should warn you, Leopold," put in Fitz, with an irresistibly quivering lip, "that Miss Persephone has no taste for gallantry. If you wish to win her esteem, you must talk of horses."

"Horses? But the horses I care nothing about."

"I'll talk to her of horses," said Buckfastleigh. "Give place there, Fitz, and don't be a dog in the manger."

"For shame, Buck! And you a happily married man," teased Fitz. But he allowed himself to be ousted from Persephone's side and trotted ahead to see what had become of Penelope and the baron.

Buckfastleigh and Leopold, receiving only monosyllabic replies to their inane attempts to excite Persephone's interest, exchanged glances of mutual understanding and cast about among the fashionables present for urgent relief.

"Ah!" cried Leopold, spying Lord Goole. "There someone is who will be happy to converse on horseflesh. Frederick, *mein freund*!"

Goole turned his hawk-like countenance, and, seeing the count's wave, rode over. Adroitly, Buckfastleigh and Leopold performed rapid introductions, extricated themselves with aplomb and cantered after Penelope, now some way ahead, leaving their victims equally hostile at this high-handed manipulation.

Then Goole's eye fell upon Persephone's horse. "Thunder and turf, you are riding one of Rossendale's ugly customers!" He cast a knowing eye over her competent hands. "You can hold him, too. Egad, ma'am, you are a capital horsewoman, then."

His blunt surprise appealed to Persephone far more than flattery would have done. She relaxed, smiling. "Thank you. You know something of cattle, I take it."

"I know enough to beg you to abandon Rossendale's brutes. Oh, you can clearly handle them. But they are unworthy of you, ma'am. You deserve better."

Persephone laughed. "I don't know that. My cousin, I will admit, is a poor judge of a horse. Though he has one superb team. Bays. Light-mouthed, easy goers, all of them, and so fast!"

Goole gave a short laugh. "You need not applaud your cousin on their account, Miss Winsford. They are out of Chid's stables."

"They were Lord Chiddingly's horses? They would be. Devil take the man!"

"You don't like him?" Goole asked. His brow lowered, and the impression of some bird of prey became pronounced. "No more do I. But there is no denying he has an eye for a horse unequalled in these times. Except for Tattersall, of course."

Persephone forgot about the baron. Here was a mine of information. She had naturally heard of Richard Tattersall, the chief and most respected of the horse dealers, whose yard was a fashionable haunt. He had also provided the Jockey Club with its present premises, where the gentlemen members could place their bets and settle their debts in comfort.

She pelted Goole with questions, learning where and when the principal race meetings were held, and having a number of turf notables pointed out to her. She wondered why none of these gentlemen approached to converse with Goole, such an habitué of the turf as he appeared to be. She never dreamed that Sir Charles Bunbury, having noted her incomparable seat, was regretting that Goole's unwelcome presence precluded his effecting an introduction.

Further along the Rotten Row, another pair of eyes glanced back and observed with austere disapproval the apparent easy intimacy of Miss Persephone Winsford with Lord Goole.

"Upon my soul, Chid," said Fitz, noting this surreptitious examination and the subsequent drawing down of the corners of Lord Chiddingly's mouth. "What the devil ails you? At least the fellow has something in common with the poor girl."

"He cannot add to her consequence."

"Gammon. You only say so because he has offended on the turf. No one else cares a straw."

"Well, if she wants to be accepted by the horsemen who matter, she would do well to be more careful of her company."

"Why do you not tell her so?"

Chiddingly shrugged. "It has nothing to do with me."

"As you were at pains to demonstrate. Not that it did you much good. Could you not hold your own against Leopold and Buck, my poor Chid?"

"I wish you will have done!"

Fitz grinned. "Do you? Now, why are you so ready to be at outs with me? I believe it is Miss Persephone's fault, after all.

She put you out of temper at the outset, and no amount of Pen's charm has succeeded in mending it."

"Oh, be quiet! You were well enough entertained, I dare say."

"Surprisingly well, as it happens. She is an odd sort of a girl, it is true. But there is far more to her than you would at first suppose. Also a vulnerability that is positively touching."

There was a short silence.

Chiddingly broke it, his voice harsh. "Do you mean to prose on forever about the Winsford twins, or is it too much to ask you to give your attention to a different matter altogether?"

Fitz's unusually serious expression was dispelled by one of his twinkling looks. "I am all attention, my oh, so amiable friend."

"I am trying out the paces of my new stallion the day after tomorrow," Chiddingly told him, choosing to ignore this gambit. "Do you care to come and watch?"

"What, the wonder horse? You perceive me positively agog, dear boy." He paused as a thought struck him. "Unless you mean to hoist me from my bed at some damnably unseasonable hour?"

"You must expect to rise early for a try-out. I mean to use Epsom, and I dare not attempt the issue later than six. You know what these devilish touts are. One word and I may kiss goodbye to all my expectations."

There was every need for caution in such a case, Fitz was aware. If Chid hoped to make a killing on the horse's first appearance — given that he proved to be of championship calibre — no hint of his prowess must leak out. Knowing the matter was of great moment to his friend, Fitz kindly forbore to tease him further.

"Very well. Epsom, you say? Well, then, I shall meet you at the Cock at half-past five of the clock. None of our friends is likely to be found at such an unfashionable inn at that hour."

Chiddingly agreed to it. He then moved to hail an acquaintance, unaware that Lord Goole and Persephone Winsford had closed up so much of the distance between them as to be in a position to overhear.

"I am determined to go, if only I can find someone to show me the way," Persephone said with resolution.

Penelope stood frowning before the pier-glass, trying out the effect of a ravishing new hat of white beaver with an enormous brim that had just been delivered by an exclusive milliner.

"I am not so certain this white is truly becoming." She glanced briefly at her sister, restlessly pacing the floor as usual. "Why do you not simply ask Chiddingly if you may go?"

Persephone halted. "I would not ask anything of that hateful man."

"It is his horse, after all."

"Yes, and everyone is talking of it, convinced it is something special. At least, so Goole informs me."

Her twin, apparently preoccupied with her search for the right provocative tilt to her hat, spoke absently. "Well, if you don't care to ask Chiddingly, you may try Fitz."

Persephone bit a pensive lip. "It is an idea. He is an excessively good-natured man; far more the gentleman than his odious friend."

Her sister agreed to this, her tone a trifle distant. "Though I dare say he would refuse if he thought Chiddingly might not like it. He seems overly fond of promoting the man's aims and objects."

Catching the acid note in her twin's voice, Persephone looked at her closely. "What's this, Pen? Are you jealous because Fitz took pains to entertain me? I assure you I have no designs upon him."

"Dear me, Seph, how you do take one up," said Penelope, shifting the hat about with agitated fingers. "Why in the world should you think I care for that?"

"Because I have seen how your eyes light up whenever he comes near. Besides, you are blushing."

"I wish you will not be so absurd. Drat this thing!" Penelope snatched the hat from her head and threw it aside. "I made a mistake ever to suppose I could wear white with these yellow curls. I shall have to take it back."

Persephone watched her sister's petulant action without further comment. "I dare say you are right, in any event," she said, reverting to the original subject of her discourse. "It is more than likely your Fitz will not take me. It would be unfair to ask it of him. I shall have to think of something else."

She moved to her sister, who was plucking at the disarranged coils of her hair, crimping them back into shape. Putting an arm about her, she smiled at their joint reflection in the mirror.

"Take the hat back, dearest. It is perfectly insipid." She reached for the offending white beaver and placed it on her own head. "You see?"

The unusually sober expression on Penelope's face gave way to her sunny smile. "Hideous! I must have been mad."

An hour later, Penelope was stepping out of the milliner's door in Bond Street, a perfectly charming feathered hat of dark beaver set at a rakish angle upon her elaborate coiffure, when she came face to face with Digby Norton-Fitzwarren himself, as *point-device* as ever.

A look of sparkling pleasure leapt into Penelope's eyes. Then, as she remembered her sister's words, the light quickly died again and she gave him an uncharacteristically prim nod.

"Miss — Penelope?" Fitz asked, doffing his own high-brimmed hat. He peered somewhat anxiously at her unresponsive features. "It is you, is it not, Pen?"

His intimate use of the short form disarmed her and she smiled, unable to prevent the twinkle from creeping into her eyes. "Yes, Fitz, it is I. Don't you know one has to positively drag Seph to visit a milliner?"

"So I should imagine. You are not alone, I trust? Where is your maid?"

"No, no, Mama is with me. She will be here presently. I stepped out merely to go to the perfumiers across the road."

"Pray allow me to escort you," Fitz said, promptly offering his arm.

Penelope hung back. "But you are occupied. I must not keep you."

"Gammon. My whole desire is to visit the perfumiers. I have just recollected I am in need of some — er — jessamine drops."

Penelope broke into her trilling laugh. "To sprinkle upon your hands? For shame, Fitz. Am I to think you a very fop?"

He gazed with apparent solemnity upon her, but the quizzing gleam was in his eye. "Madam, you mock me!"

"Sir, you began it!"

He laughed. "Come, that is better. I had begun to think I had offended beyond forgiveness."

"I — I don't know what you mean," Penelope stammered, blushing.

He took hold of her gloved hand and raised it to his lips. "I did offend you. That day at the docks."

"Not at all. I — I —"

"Dear Pen, we began as such friends. I have so much missed that easy, confiding air. May we not begin again?"

Penelope stared into his smiling eyes, aware of a fluttering in her breast. She had liked him on first acquaintance. Very much. Then he had appeared to doubt her integrity. She was still a little afraid to trust, but this was an olive branch. If she refused it, he might withdraw altogether. That she could not bear.

Her smile was a trifle tremulous. "I think there is something melancholy in second beginnings. As if the first had gone awry. Let us say we are still friends."

"Indeed we are." He pressed her hand slightly before releasing it. His eye gleamed again. "Thus, in a spirit of true friendship, I will offer to show you far more entertaining marts than these."

"But I thought Bond Street was the most fashionable place to shop."

"So it is. But on the dull side, don't you agree? Do come with me. Tomorrow?"

"But where?"

"Let that be my secret. I will call for you at eleven. If you are thinking of the proprieties, we will invite your mama to go with us if my groom is not chaperon enough."

But Penelope was not at all in favour of her mama's presence ruining what promised to be a delightful *tête-à-tête*. "Fiddle. I am not so missish. If anyone should remark upon it, we will tell them the customs obtaining in Bombay are markedly different."

"Unusual manners, Miss Winsford?"

"Of course," she agreed, twinkling.

When Mrs Winsford presently came down and Fitz took his leave, she went off with her cheeks aglow and her head in the clouds.

Persephone, meanwhile, determined to see Lord Chiddingly's horse, had bethought her of the one person whom she could ask about Epsom without further betraying the baron. For, hate him though she might, she could not reconcile it with her conscience to speak of this secret trial to anyone who might use the knowledge for some unscrupulous purpose.

She was not so lost to all sense of propriety as to think she might with impunity visit a man at his home. Besides, she had no idea where Lord Goole lived. She wrote a note, therefore, requesting him to visit her, and directed one of the footmen to deliver it.

His lordship, caught on his way to conduct some business of his own, arrived at the Winsfords' house in Hanover Square in no very amiable mood. He could not imagine what Persephone wanted of him, having no illusions about his conspicuous lack of attraction. When she bluntly asked him how to get to Epsom, his jaw dropped.

"You are not thinking of crashing this trial?"

"Yes, I am. Why should I not? You said yourself the horse must be worth seeing."

"I know, but —" He stopped, frowning in suspicion. "Why come to me? I had supposed you to be upon good enough terms with Chid, or even Fitz, to permit of your securing an invitation."

"You supposed wrong. I did not ask you here to question my actions, but to provide me with information. If you decline to do so, it is all the same to me."

"Egad, ma'am,if this is your manner of obtaining favours—"

With a strong effort Persephone controlled her rising temper. "Will you have the goodness, sir, to help me, or will you not?"

"I will not," snapped Goole, who had his own reasons for not encouraging this interest.

"Obliging of you. Obviously it is useless to request you to escort me."

"Quite useless. If you can afford the loss of reputation, ma'am, I certainly cannot."

Persephone stared at him in surprise, her anger forgotten. "What can you mean?"

"Never mind," he said hastily. "Let me assure you, you had as well ask Laetitia Smith to escort you as myself."

"Laetitia Smith? Who in the world might she be?"

"She is — well, a — a friend of Sir John Lade. You will recall I spoke of him yesterday."

"Oh yes, the notable whip." The grey eyes were intent suddenly. "Is he not a racing man?"

"Among other things," Goole said on a dry note. For Sir John Lade's vulgarities and the reckless nature of his gambling propensities had led the *beau monde* to regard him with disgust.

"It makes no matter," Persephone said. "I dare say it will be better for me to remain here, after all."

She had an idea, and was now as eager to get rid of Lord Goole as she had been to see him, in order to put it into execution. He was glad enough to go, and she waited only until the front door shut behind him before running upstairs to fetch a hat, gloves and an outdoor garment. Warmed by a thick spencer over an old habit, she walked round to the mews where Rossendale stabled his horses, reflecting that no one would look twice at her in such a garb.

While a groom saddled the big bay for her, she engaged him in conversation, taking the precaution of sliding a gold coin from her pocket and rolling it ostentatiously between her gloved fingers. She had not lived in India, the daughter of a wealthy merchant, without learning the power of money.

"Do you know of Sir John Lade?"

"Aye, miss, that I do." The groom licked his lips as he eyed the flashing coin.

"You are familiar with his doxy, too, I dare say?" suggested Persephone, betraying her understanding of Goole's veiled conversation.

The groom might have become more used to the peculiar conduct of his master's cousin, but this patently shocked him. He stared, mouth agape.

"Come, come," Persephone said, digging her hand into her pocket and bringing out a second gold piece.

The groom's eyes glistened. "I know her, miss, if it was that there Letty Smith you was meaning. Smart little house he give her, up Bloomsbury way."

"Good. I wish you to guide me there. But say nothing of this to anyone, do you hear?"

The groom nodded his agreement. "Mum as an oyster, miss." Who was he to quibble when the lady was so open-handed?

Laetitia Smith, however, when informed of the identity of her unconventional visitor, was moved to bluntness. "Plaguy odd it is in you, ma'am, and I don't know what people might say, but I'm very happy to meet you."

Persephone took the outstretched hand and shook it warmly. "Thank you. I don't know why you should be, however."

"Ha! Miss Winsford, I myself am accounted something of an equestrienne. I am naturally agog since all the world is talking of your skill."

"The devil it is. I had no idea of it. Word spreads fast in London, I perceive."

"Don't it, ma'am? All the faster when the word is blameful."

Persephone gave a scornful laugh. "I don't fear critics."

"Well, you should, if you'll pardon the liberty, ma'am. Lord knows I've had a bellyful — I mean, I've had my share of them," Miss Smith corrected herself.

"Don't put yourself about. No one knows I am here. Besides, we are accustomed to treat very differently those ladies less fortunately circumstanced than ourselves. In Bombay, if you could but come by a ring, you would very soon be accepted." Her gurgling laugh escaped her. "Bored to death, too. I'll wager you relish doing the pretty as little as I."

Laetitia laughed. A great, raucous belly-laugh that indisputably stamped her origins upon her. Persephone had a fleeting vision of her aunt Rossendale's face, if she could see her now, and hid a mischievous smile.

"Right you are, ma'am. More at home in the saddle than a drawing-room. Though, for my part, I'll take the ribbons for preference any day."

"I, too, am partial to driving, but as yet I have not set up a stable and my cousin Rossendale has only one team of decent cattle for the purpose."

For a few moments the two ladies fell deep into conversation and discovered in each other the same fanatical devotion to horseflesh. Formality went by the board, and within a very short time they were addressing each other by name, like old friends. They sat together in Miss Smith's cosy parlour, its inelegant and old-fashioned chairs and sofas built more for comfort than for show — like the hostess herself.

Laetitia Smith was a handsome woman, who affected a mannish diction and whose career had spanned dubious connection with a highwayman and a number of other unsavoury characters before she had fallen in with Sir John Lade. She was fully alive to the dangers for Persephone in association with a woman of her class.

"Well, Seph, I'm bound to say I'd give a pony to see you with even a pair in hand," she said at length, "but I don't for the life of me see how it can be managed, situated as we are."

This was Persephone's cue. "Letty, I have now to confess my whole reason for coming to see you."

"Ah, thought we should come to it. Tell me it all."

Persephone complied and found Letty to be as keen as she was herself.

"I heard Chid had something under his belt. So he means to try at Epsom. Lay my life Derby has no notion of it. He's a house there, you know. The Oaks. You might say Epsom was his own ground, for he and Bunbury between them established several races there."

"You will not tell him?"

"Lord, no, shouldn't dream of it. I won't even tell Johnny what I see, for I can't abide cheats. Won't be able to bet myself, of course, and nor will you."

"Can't abide cheats?" echoed Persephone unguardedly.

Letty's cheeks coloured. "You need not think my way of life means I've no honour, Miss Winsford. I'll have you know there's some codes as even a thief won't break."

Persephone begged her pardon. "I could not imagine anyone who cares so much for horses behaving with dishonour."

Mollified, Letty calmed down and graciously forgave her.

"Will you tell me how to get to Epsom?"

"I'll do better than that. I'll drive down with you. Won't meet a soul so early. At least no one you know, which is all that signifies."

Letty was as good as her word. When Persephone crept out into the cold at half-past four the following morning, wrapped up in Lord Rossendale's greatcoat with a fur-lined bonnet and muff to keep out the frosty night air, she found Miss Smith walking her horses. Only they were found to belong to her lover.

"Borrowed John's greys," she said by way of greeting, gesturing at the team harnessed to her carriage. It was a light affair with a hood, built for speed, Letty told her. "A curricle, they call it. It is well sprung and therefore good for long journeys. I thought we'd make better time in it."

It was still dark and the way only dimly visible by the light of the flambeaux in the street and the lanterns bobbing on the shafts. Thus, although Persephone was itching to drive, her companion wisely forbore to test her skill just yet.

"Shan't put you at such a disadvantage," Letty declared handsomely. But once they were clear of the town and on a straight road, with the grey light of dawn just beginning to lighten the sky, she handed over the reins with a single adjuration. "Don't spring 'em!"

"Not in this light," Persephone agreed.

Letty watched with interested eyes her competent handling of the ribbons and said she would dearly love to engage in a race with someone so obviously accomplished. Persephone enjoyed herself very much, and was quite sorry when Letty announced them to be approaching Epsom and suggested she should take over since she knew the route and Persephone did not. It was well she did so, for, their mission being secret, they had to approach the Downs by a circuitous route, conceal the carriage with the groom in charge in some trees hard by the course, and make their way on foot to a vantage-point from where Letty said they might expect to see without being seen.

They had arrived in good time and had some while to wait. Persephone grew chilled and hungry, and began to fret, convinced that six o'clock had come and gone, or else they had arrived too late and missed the trial. Or even that Chiddingly had somehow got word of her intended exploit and cancelled just to spite her.

Letty, producing a fob watch from one capacious pocket of the thick travelling cloak she wore, announced the hour wanted but ten minutes to six. Persephone cursed and was just resigning herself to a further uncomfortable wait, when the sound of flying hoofs became audible across the green of the Downs.

Both ladies straightened up, cold and hunger forgotten, and craned their necks.

In the distance they saw it, pointing excitedly. A single horse, his rider bent so low in the saddle as to be almost invisible, his head and neck well up, the distinctive features becoming every instant clearer as he covered the ground in a matter of seconds.

Then he was almost upon them. A black stallion moving like a thunderbolt, strong legs a blur as he seemed to fly past at heart-stopping speed.

Persephone watched him out of sight, unaware she was holding her breath.

"Well!" burst from Letty behind her. "I am lost for words. Did you ever see the like?"

Persephone shook her head dumbly, her eyes still on the diminishing figure in the distance.

Letty was still a-bubble. "With Siegfried up, too! I'll warrant Tidmarsh is in high croak. How I will keep my tongue between my teeth I don't know."

"A horse in a million," breathed Persephone.

In a daze, she followed the still exclamatory Letty towards the place where they had left the curricle.

Suddenly Letty stopped mid-sentence, seizing Persephone's arm in a vice-like grip.

"What in the world —?" began Persephone.

"Hush!" hissed her new friend. She pointed away from the trees. "See there! Some others have had the same notion."

Persephone followed her pointing finger to where three men stood in close conversation. Even at this distance she could make out one set of hawkish features. "It is Goole!" So this was why he had refused to help her.

"No, is it indeed?" Letty peered. "A plague on it, I can't see! Who is that with him?"

"I don't know, but it is certainly Lord Goole. One is dressed like a groom. The other is a short gentleman, extremely stout."

"Not Billy Bolsover?" Letty looked as closely as she dared. "I believe you are right. He certainly has the figure of old Billy. Well, I wouldn't have believed it! Depend upon it, he has come like us, out of curiosity. Goole, however, is another matter."

"We had better go before they see us," Persephone said, and they moved quickly and quietly into the trees, where, safely concealed, they watched the men until they began to move off.

The third had been largely concealed by Bolsover's bulk, but as the group broke up and shifted, and his face turned momentarily in their direction, Persephone noted a livid white scar running from the man's forehead, across his face to the corner of his mouth. It gave him a sinister look and Persephone shivered. As he walked away behind the gentlemen, she saw he had a pronounced limp. She was just about to ask Letty about him when she found her friend had already moved towards the carriage and was calling to her to hurry.

They were soon bowling back along the way they had come. "Ten to one we will run smack into Chid if we take the usual route," Letty said. As she drove, she gave vent to her disgust at the presence on the ground of Lord Goole. "He means mischief, I'll be bound. That plaguy man is not to be trusted."

"What makes you say so?"

"He's a cheat, that's what."

"A cheat?"

"I dare say you might name any foul trick a devil might play on the turf to win his bets, and you will find Goole has done it. Why, Charles had him thrown out of the Jockey Club, and a good thing, too."

Once she had heard how Goole had paid off jockeys to lose races, had caused his own riders to trip their fellows, had in a word used every means in his power to nobble the opposition in order to avoid losses, Persephone heartily agreed with her.

But, with the excitement over, the ladies found the pangs of hunger began to be too insistent to be ignored.

"I wish I had thought to bring a basket," Letty said in a fretful tone. "I am like to expire."

"I am very hungry, too," Persephone confessed, "but it was worth it."

This did not satisfy Letty, however. "Now what is to be done, Seph? For let you go all the way back to London empty-bellied I won't. Yet we can't eat in a public inn. Anyone might see us."

"Do not concern yourself over me, Letty, I beg you."

"I have it," exclaimed her companion, unheeding. "We will go to the Oaks and knock up Lizzie Farren. She will be glad to give us breakfast."

Nothing Persephone could say would move her from this plan. From what she said it was to be inferred that Elizabeth Farren, an actress of some note, had taken up residence at the Oaks under the Earl of Derby's protection, his wife having left him for Lord Dorset some time previously. In vain did Persephone try to tactfully convey to her friend the impropriety of her breakfasting with two notorious gentlemen's mistresses, even in private. Letty was in fine fettle, so pleased with her ready solution to the dilemma Persephone felt it would be churlish to persist in refusal.

On arrival at Lord Derby's house, the ladies were ushered into a cosy breakfast parlour where Elizabeth Farren soon joined them.

"Lord a' mercy, Letty, what are you about?" she scolded on discovering the identity of her visitor. "Sir Charles in the house and all! What if he were to come down?"

"Plague take it, Lizzie, we are starving! You may lock the door if you choose."

But this Miss Farren would not take it upon herself to do, for fear of her Ned coming down. "Not that it is likely at this hour, I admit. But he would be bound to suppose I was in here with some man and break the door down. He is quite vilely jealous."

Persephone, having abandoned her scruples, was highly amused by this disclosure and demanded to know more. Nothing loath, Miss Farren launched into a graphic description of Lord Derby's marital difficulties, and was only brought to desist upon the arrival of a dish of coddled eggs, freshly baked bread and a pot of steaming chocolate. The two guests fell upon the meal with voracious appetites and no early risers entered to mar their enjoyment of it.

As ill-luck would have it, however, just as Miss Farren was escorting them across to the front door, Sir Charles Bunbury came yawning down the stairs. He glanced idly at the ladies and his eyes widened.

"Good Lord!" He stared at Persephone.

"Oh, the devil," she swore, biting her lip on a rueful grin. "How do you do, Sir Charles? We have not met, but you were pointed out to me the other day."

He came down the stairs and crossed the hall, holding out his hand. "So you are Miss Winsford. What a piece of luck. I had been wanting to meet you excessively. Such a notable horsewoman."

Persephone shook his hand and thanked him. "Coming from you, sir, I gather that is high praise."

"A notable whip, Charles, too, as I live," Letty put in. "I am on my mettle, I can tell you."

"Well, well," laughed Bunbury. "If only we allowed females to join the Jockey Club, ma'am, I should certainly support your membership."

Lizzie Farren, quite scandalised by the easy camaraderie they were all adopting, almost thrust Persephone out of the house.

"Have no fear, Miss Winsford," she whispered. "He will not mention your having been here. I shall see to that. There are things he would much dislike to have known, you know, so I have the means to compel his silence."

But Sir Charles, following them out of the house, had overheard this speech and was chuckling. "No need to compel me, Lizzie. I should not dream of putting such a tale about. I have too much respect for Miss Winsford."

Persephone could only thank him as she turned to follow Letty to the curricle which, in the charge of a groom, awaited them at the bottom of the steps. She then stopped short, almost cannoning into Letty who was standing stock-still, staring aghast at a second vehicle drawn up beside it.

Standing next to it, his greatcoat hanging negligently open, his hat on his head and his whip in his hand, clearly having just alighted, was Lord Chiddingly, his outrage patent.

CHAPTER FIVE

Shock rooted Persephone to the steps, all coherent thought suspended.

But Letty Smith was on the move, gruffly scolding. "Lord, Chid, what the plague brings you here just at this moment? What a curst mischance!"

Chiddingly turned on her. "Have you run mad, Letty? What can have possessed you to bring Miss Winsford here, of all places? And how do you come to be upon terms at all? I suppose you inveigled yourself into her way, like the grasping self-seeker you are."

Letty fairly gasped under this attack, eyes popping with indignation.

"How dare you?" burst from Persephone, low-voiced, as she ran down the steps. "Letty has shown me nothing but kindness, and I will not suffer you to speak to her so. I sought her out, if you must know. Not that it is any concern of yours."

"Don't fret yourself on my account, Seph," begged Letty, grasping that lady's hands as they reached protectively towards her, and returning their convulsive pressure.

"Very affecting," said Chiddingly. "You are both of you out of your senses. As for your conduct, Miss Persephone Winsford —" he began, apparently in no doubt of her identity.

"Don't dare to criticise my conduct yet again, sir," flashed Persephone, turning on him in fury. "I will not bear it! You have no right."

"None but the decency of a gentleman. I have enough of that, ma'am, at least to —"

"Oh, *please*," begged Miss Farren from the top of the steps. "If Ned were to come down! His room overlooks us here."

The three looked up to see her standing in an agony of apprehension, quite alone. Sir Charles Bunbury had disappeared, clearly having no wish to participate in the brewing storm.

"Plague take it, she's right," said Letty, her indignation giving place to lively apprehension. She turned to the baron as to an ally, her tone hushed almost to a whisper. "I'd better get her out of this, Chid. You know what Derby is. We can trust Charles to keep mum. But let Ned get in his cups and it will be all over town in a twinkling. Come on, Seph."

She began to push Persephone towards the curricle, but Chiddingly intervened, his angry tones also lowered.

"Wait! She had better come with me."

"Come with you?" echoed Persephone in accents of loathing. "I had rather be ruined tenfold than travel one yard in your company!"

"Don't think it will be any pleasure for me to take you," retorted Chiddingly. "But as your reputation will be far less at risk, I shall have to swallow my dislike."

"What is my reputation to you? If you imagine, sir, that —"

"For pity's sake!" hissed Lizzie Farren, running down the steps. "Go, go, *go*!"

"He's right, Seph," Letty said with regret. "We have left it too late. It's already long past eight, and by the time we get to town there will be any number of persons abroad to see us together."

"I don't care! I am not going with him!"

"You have no choice, Miss Winsford." Chiddingly advanced upon her. "And I am not staying to argue the point."

Then, before the women knew what he was about, he had seized Persephone in his arms, lifted her bodily and swung her up willy-nilly into his phaeton. His victim, deposited in considerable disorder on the seat, was so surprised she had only time to utter a muffled shriek of protest before the baron had leapt nimbly up to take his place beside her and set his team of mixed greys in motion.

Persephone's first thought was of Letty. Hoisting herself upright, she turned in her seat, and craning dangerously over the back of the carriage, called out to her. "Letty, Letty, I have not even thanked you! Lizzie, too! Letty, write to me. Be sure I shall see you again."

"Oh no, you will not," Chiddingly said. "What in Hades were you about, you stupid little fool?"

Persephone turned back in her seat to confront him. "You will be sorry for this, my lord. How dare you take it upon yourself to abduct me in this high-handed fashion?"

"Abduct you? That is rich. Believe me, Miss Winsford, nothing could be further from my intention."

"Well, if you think my reputation will be safe driving about the countryside alone with you, you have even less understanding of the conventions than I."

"Have no fear. We will be picking up my groom at the Cock. In an open carriage, he will be chaperon enough."

This piece of information enraged Persephone further. "Very clever, my lord. You need not think I don't realise why you are so mindful of the proprieties. I do not flatter myself you have the least interest in saving my reputation, but for one circumstance."

"Spare your breath, Miss Winsford," he said, though a tinge of red crept into his lean cheek. "You may need it to explain yourself to your parents."

Persephone drew in her breath. "You would tell them of this? The devil take you, but I believe you would. You despicable cur! Distressing my mother with such a tale. My father, too."

"You should have thought of them before you embarked upon this crazy adventure. Not that I suppose even the nabob capable of controlling your extraordinary quirks."

"How dare you sneer at Papa?"

"I did not do so. He has all my sympathy, I assure you. Were I in his place, there would be nothing for it but to cut my throat. That, or regularly administer a salutary whipping."

"You — you scoundrel! You savage! *Ooloo*!" she spat, reverting to the Hindi curses culled from the lips of old Ufur. She threw at him the word that in India was the deadliest insult. "*Kuta*! Dog!"

It was wasted on Chiddingly. But he lost no time in adding fuel to the flames. "Rail and rave as you please, Miss Winsford. It but confirms me in my opinion of you."

Breathless with rage, Persephone lost command both of her voice and her senses. "I w-will not — stay to be — so insulted!"

Then she launched into the air, with the idea of throwing herself from the fast-moving carriage.

In instinctive reaction, Chiddingly let go the reins and grabbed for her, catching at her clothing and seizing hold of one arm in a painfully violent grip.

Next moment, the horses were bolting, the phaeton careering off the road, Persephone hanging hazardously over the side, her fingers clawing frantically at the leather seat and the baron's person, desperate for a purchase.

"Hold on!" yelled Chiddingly, panic rife in his voice.

She had left off her heavy greatcoat, which had been forgotten in Letty's curricle, and Chiddingly had hold of a handful of the skirt of her habit. Holding on to the one arm he had safe, he leaned over as far as he dared, let go the skirt and seized Persephone under the armpits. Exerting all his strength, he dragged her back into the phaeton where she ended up splayed half across the seat, her hands locked on his coat, her limbs still trailing out the sides.

For a few hair-raising seconds, the carriage rocked dangerously on one wheel, as if the overbalanced weight on one side might cause it to overturn as it swayed and bumped over the turf at the edge of the road. Letting go of Persephone, Chiddingly struggled to retrieve his reins. In a few moments, the horses were under control again and he had brought them to a floundering standstill.

Pausing only to tug Persephone fully into the phaeton, where she knelt on the floorboards, her body heaving with panting breaths, Chiddingly leapt down to go to his horses' heads.

In the time it took to soothe them into a calmer frame of mind, Persephone managed to painfully haul herself upright and sit on the seat, where she remained, clothes and bonnet awry and shoulders hunched over her lap. She was shuddering uncontrollably.

But when Chiddingly called to her to take the ribbons so that he might leave the horses standing, she pulled herself erect and did so at once. As he leapt back up into his seat and snatched back the reins, the natural reaction to the frantic anxiety of the last few moments bubbled up and a stream of invective poured from his lips.

"You crazy little fool! Do you want to get us both killed? You are, without exception, the most totty-headed, addle-brained, lunatic virago that ever drew breath! It was clear from the outset you have a reckless disregard for life and limb, but I had not until today realised you were bent on self-destruction one way or another. I almost doubt the evidence of my own eyes. An act of such foolhardiness passes belief!"

He stopped at last, quite out of breath, as he saw the misadventure was having its inevitable effect. Slow tears were trickling down Miss Winsford's wan cheeks. He felt his anger draining away, and reminded himself it was no thanks to her that the phaeton had not overturned and broken his horses' legs.

"Well may you weep," he said in a savage tone, whipping up his resentment.

Persephone dashed impatient hands across her eyes. "I'm n-not weeping." Reaching up to straighten her bonnet, she hissed in a breath and stopped. Then she put a hand to her shoulder, biting her lip and wincing.

"Are you hurt?"

"Not in the least," she lied.

"Well, you damned well deserve to be!" He pulled her hand away and reached to feel for the injury.

"Leave me alone!" Persephone jerked away too precipitately, inducing her to cry out in sudden pain.

"Let me see! I should not be surprised if I had wrenched your arm quite out of its socket."

With surprisingly gentle hands, he explored her upper arm while Persephone endured in silence.

"It is a trifle swollen about the shoulder," he announced presently. "I think you have strained it pretty severely. You will have to rest it for a day or two. Does it pain you anywhere else?"

Persephone shook her head, determined not to admit to any other hurt, though she felt bruised and battered from head to foot. "Aside from that, I am perfectly well."

"Don't lie to me," Chiddingly said, his eyes on her white face. "You are all but at the point of collapse."

"I am nothing of the sort," she retorted in a stronger voice. "You should be the more concerned to know whether your horses have taken any sort of hurt."

"I am. But as they appear to be as good as ever, I have leisure to attend to you."

Persephone's lip trembled. "You are the most loathsome, boorish, unmannerly —"

"Excellent. That is much more like you. A period of rest in a bedchamber at the Cock and I am sure you will be so much recovered as to be able to think of a great many more forcefully abusive adjectives."

A low gurgle of laughter escaped her, and was instantly suppressed. She was not going to be beguiled into forgetting her grievances. This hateful man had not only interfered with her actions in a very high-handed way, she reminded herself, but had taken it upon himself to reproach her. Moreover, she was certain she knew why. Her reputation would have meant nothing to him, were it not for the fact he had designs upon Pen. She had suspected it from the first night at the ball, and nothing in his conduct since had led her to change her opinion. Well, if Pen was fool enough to marry him —!

The phaeton had for several moments been in motion, and now came within sight of the hostelry where Chiddingly's groom awaited him. Persephone, walking with some degree of caution, was conducted by the landlady to a small bedchamber where she was thankful to remove her bonnet and lie down, more shaken by her ordeal than she had been prepared to admit, even to herself.

An hour's rest followed by a cup of strong tea did much to revive her, and she re-joined the baron in a much better temper, determined to avoid any further quarrel, at least before his servant.

Chiddingly having made a similar resolve, the first few miles were accomplished in stiff silence, neither trusting themselves to speak without giving way to one of the many complaints they had both stored up against each other.

At length Chiddingly asked a question that had been lurking at the back of his mind, though thrown to one side by the excitement and consequences of Persephone's mad action. "What were you and Letty doing at Epsom in the first place?"

Coming out of the blue, the query caught her unprepared. "We came to see your try-out," she blurted before she could stop herself.

Chiddingly turned to her, his eye kindling all over again. "You did what?"

Persephone was aware of the flush rising to her cheeks and took refuge in defiance. "It was my idea. I overheard you and Fitz talking of it in the park and determined to see for myself."

"Why in the name of Satan could you not have asked me like an honest woman?"

"Nothing would have induced me to do so. Don't dare to pretend you would have permitted it, even if I had."

"So instead you took a course liable to land you in the suds, together with your family," he said, ignoring the obvious truth of her remark.

"Thank you, you have said enough on that head."

He bit his lip on a sharp retort, remembering both the groom on his perch behind them, and the previous appalling consequences of driving this madcap female to go her desperate length.

"Am I to have the benefit of your doubtless expert opinion on the stallion?" he said instead, with a sarcastic inflexion.

"Since you clearly do not value it in the least, I shall hold my peace."

"No, I beg of you, Miss Winsford," he said with exaggerated courtesy, "I should count myself honoured to be favoured with your thoughts, even though they were formed clandestinely."

"I will suffer myself to be whipped at the cart's tail before I utter a syllable about your devilish horse!"

"An apt punishment for your misdeeds."

Persephone was so much infuriated to have fallen into a pit of her own digging she clamped her lips on further speech and turned her face away.

Chiddingly gave a short scornful laugh, but refrained from further comment.

In spite of herself, Persephone found her thoughts running on the trial, and she recreated in her mind's eye the picture of that magnificent animal flying across the turf like some great velvet bird. In the keen brightness of the sun labouring behind a bank of cloud, his inky black coat had reminded her of something that at the time had eluded her memory. Now it floated into her mind.

"Indigo."

"I beg your pardon?"

Her quarrel with Chiddingly was forgotten. On impulse she turned, her grey eyes warm. "Indigo. It is a plant used in India to make a dark dye. A blue-black with a velvety appearance. They use it for ink. Here, too, perhaps. I dare say it is imported from there."

"So, and what of it?"

"Your horse. That is his colour. Indigo." He stared at her, plainly at a loss. "There is no need to gape at me like a dolt."

"Yes, but — out of nowhere —!" He broke off and a sudden grin lightened his features. "You are the most unaccountable girl."

"Thank you, I have had my fill of your opinion of me."

He was silent, and she said no more until he deposited her on the doorstep of her home in Hanover Square.

"I shall not thank you, my lord, for I consider your actions unpardonable. What is more, I know very well you have but one reason for having rescued me from my own folly."

"At least you have the grace to acknowledge your fault."

"I acknowledge nothing. But mark this. You are wasting your time."

His brows rose. "I have not the remotest conjecture as to your meaning."

"Have you not?" Her lip curled. "Well, then, you can have no objection to hearing your quarry is even now enjoying an outing with your friend Fitzwarren."

Chiddingly drove back to his lodgings in a mood of deep chagrin. The intelligence that his friend had left him immediately after the trial, with the flimsiest of excuses, only to return to London to steal a march on him with Penelope, was less than welcome.

Almost from the moment of discovering the Miss Winsford whom he had thought volatile beyond belief was in reality two people, he had been toying seriously with the idea of trying for Penelope's hand. That Persephone had divined his purpose annoyed him. That she recognised his motive, as he could not doubt, infuriated him. She would throw a rub in his way if she could.

Yet was he quite wise, he wondered, to contemplate a marriage which would saddle him with a sister-in-law whose activities were to be counted upon to sour his existence? Today had shown him how unbridled were her passions. Could a man be comfortable closely tied to a female who had proved herself a candidate for Bedlam?

A memory crept into his mind unbidden. That whimsical idea of hers about indigo dye. Really, when she was not baying like a hound in full cry, there was something quite taking about her. And he had to confess a sneaking admiration for her courage.

He caught himself up. Fiend seize it! It was Penelope who concerned him. Not Persephone. To hell with that troublesome wench! No, he must think of Penelope and the perfidy of his friend Fitz.

When Fitz returned to his house later that day, he found Chiddingly awaiting him.

"Why, Chid, you are back betimes," Fitz said, the good humour in his face leaving Chiddingly in no doubt of the success of his engagement. "I had expected you would remain all day at Derby's place."

"Ha!" exclaimed Chiddingly on a bitter note, the evils of the morning rising forcibly to his mind. "I did not get within Derby's doors."

Fitz's brows rose and he smiled quizzically as he stripped off his gloves and threw them, together with his beaver hat, on a convenient table in his library. "Now what has occurred to put you all on end, dear boy?"

"Never mind that," Chiddingly said, driven to impatience by his friend's cheery manner. "I shall tell you presently. At this moment, I have something of more importance to discuss with you."

"I am entirely at your service, my dear Chid. Let me but request that fool of a butler to bring us some refreshment and I shall be with you. Why he could not think of serving you himself, I do not know."

So saying, he stepped out into the hall and gave an instruction to someone outside the baron's line of vision. Coming back into the library, he flung himself down in a comfortable armchair and bade his friend do likewise.

Chiddingly took a chair opposite and regarded Fitzwarren in frowning solemnity. "Fitz, I would not do this if we were not such old friends, for it is not an easy question to ask a man. But I must know. Have you any serious intentions towards Miss Winsford?"

Fitz sat very still for a moment, but something of his teasing gleam was in his eye. "Which one?"

"Don't be a nodcock. Penelope, of course."

There was a short silence. Fitzwarren, having inspected his friend's compelling stare without any apparent change in his own expression, fell to contemplation of the toe of one shining top boot. "Now, that is a question which demands some thought. No doubt a glass of wine will aid concentration, if only the man will bestir himself." He looked up again. "I might ask, have you?"

"Yes, I have. But though I would scorn to consider Leopold or Rossendale, I would not for the world tread on your toes, Fitz."

His friend smiled. "I thank you."

He rose as the butler brought in a tray with a decanter and two glasses, which on the viscount's signal he left on a table. Pouring Madeira, Fitz tried to put his thoughts in order. Until Chiddingly had put it to him so bluntly, he had not thought about matrimony.

Years of agreeably untrammelled bachelorhood had rendered him unused to considering the question. Unlike the baron, he was neither in need of funds, nor was he the last of his name. There were brothers and nephews enough to succeed to his dignities. While he might flirt, he had long perfected the trick of remaining sufficiently aloof not to raise expectations which he had no intention of fulfilling.

But Penelope Winsford, he was now forced to realise, had seriously disturbed his habitual egotism. Her spontaneity, her zest and sparkle, had enchanted him, together with that unconventionality which so amused him. When he had hurt her that day at the docks, the dimming of her lustre had cost him a lasting pang of conscience.

But then, so too had Persephone touched him. They were a unique pair, not only in the undoubted attraction of their identical appearance, but in their refreshing lack of artifice.

He emitted a self-conscious laugh. "To tell you the truth, Chid, I have not the least idea. I dare say I shall never marry. At this present, though I will admit the charm of Penelope's society is vastly appealing, I am not contemplating spending the rest of my life basking therein."

Chiddingly heaved a sigh of relief and tossed off his wine. "So you have no objection to my pursuit of her."

"None whatsoever, dear boy," Fitz said, with determined cheerfulness, ignoring an uncomfortable sensation at the pit of his stomach. "Heaven speed your wooing!" His eye gleamed mischief. "You will allow me to suggest, however, that you would suit far better with Persephone."

"Persephone be damned!" Chiddingly exploded, shooting from his seat as if the thought of her set off a firework inside him. "I would not marry that girl if you were to put a pistol to my head. Do you know what the infernal little fiend did today?"

Fitzwarren grinned at him. "No, tell me."

Chiddingly told him. The recital took all of fifteen minutes and the consumption of two more glasses of Madeira, embellished as it was with his lordship's freely expressed opinion of Persephone's conduct and general character.

Fitz shouted with laughter. "I tell you what, Chid. You may marry Pen and do away with this tiresome Seph and so come off with twice the fortune."

"There is not the slightest necessity to do away with her. I have no doubt at all she will break her own silly neck without any assistance from me."

Unaware of the fate thus prophesied for her, Persephone was at this moment relating her own highly coloured version of her adventures to her sister, with quite as venomous a tongue as Chiddingly himself. It was the true version on this occasion, for she had been obliged to concoct a tale to account for the injury to her shoulder that would satisfy her parents.

Fortunately, they were so well used to her wild ways that neither was surprised she had come to grief, as she told them, over the head of one of Rossendale's raw hunters. She said she had been rescued by a kind couple passing by, whom to save investigation she had designated of humble origin. This fictitious pair had insisted on bringing her back to their modest establishment to rest before sending her home in a hackney, which accounted for the lateness of her return.

Both parents exclaimed at the mishap, and a surgeon was sent for. He confirmed Chiddingly's diagnosis, applied some liniment to the inflamed shoulder, fashioned a sling for her arm and bade her lie up for a day or two.

"At least I shall be spared appearing at these horrid parties," Persephone said, sitting up in bed and leaning comfortably against a bank of pillows.

"I think you must have taken leave of your senses, Seph," said Penelope. "You might have been killed!"

"Do not you begin. I have had quite enough scolding from that boor of a Chiddingly. Which reminds me," she added, frowning direfully at her sister, "if you accept an offer from him, I shall never speak to you again as long as I live."

Penelope's mouth fell open. "Accept an offer from Chiddingly? I think you must indeed have taken some sort of knock on the head, Seph, which has driven your wits quite out of it."

"I thought as much. I told him so, too."

"Do you say he told you he intends to make me an offer?"

"He did not admit as much, but I guessed at the outset. He is bent on enriching himself out of Papa's coffers. I dare say those horses of his are costing him a pretty penny."

"Seph! Never tell me you were so lost to all sense of decorum as to discuss the subject with the man. You are quite incorrigible. As well ask Fitz if he — I mean —"

Her sister eyed the flushing cheeks with interest. "I shall, if you wish it. I have no missish scruples."

"Seph!" gasped Penelope, bouncing up and down in agitation where she sat on the edge of the bed. "You would not! Promise me you will not. I should die of mortification."

"Very well, I shan't, then. There is no need to behave like a cat on a hot bakestone. You are jogging my shoulder."

Subsiding, Penelope begged pardon. "Besides, I am not in the least sure that — that — I mean, he has shown me no sign of —"

"Naturally not, he is a gentleman. But he was attentive? You had an enjoyable day with him?"

"Oh, it was famous." Her eyes sparkled. "He took me to Temple Bar, you know. Quite unfashionable, but so amusing. Such a rush of people. It was like the bazaars in Bombay where Ayah used to take us, remember? Except that the wares in the shops were of far higher quality."

"So I should imagine. You always were an acquisitive soul, Pen. Confess now. What monstrously useless items have you purchased?"

"None, upon my honour. But I could well have spent a fortune. There was anything you could wish to buy, and the shops so opulent and splendid. Only in the linen-drapers was I perhaps a trifle disappointed. For so much of their cloth is from India, you know. You would not credit the outrageous prices. Fifteen shillings per yard for a muslin for which I would not give fifteen rupees!"

"No!"

"Yes, indeed. Though Fitz said it was to be expected. Such a long way to come, and the taxes imposed, you know, are quite iniquitous. Why, he tells me there is talk of a tax on hair-powder."

"Outrageous," Persephone agreed, but with a twinkle in her eye.

"Well, it is," insisted Pen, but with a quivering lip. "I know you take no interest in such things, but you would sit up fast enough were horses in question."

"Yes, I confess I am bowled over by the quality of the English cattle." She reached her free hand out to clasp her sister's fingers. "I am very happy for you, Pen. You are plainly in alt to be here. Now, if we can but nudge Fitz on —"

"Don't be absurd. Oh dear, I wish you were not so acute."

"We are twins, dearest. I can't help but be attuned to your emotions." She noted the clouding of Penelope's eyes and added, "Do you care so much?"

"Oh no, indeed I don't. I — I like him very well and — and I will confess I do think about him rather. But I can't altogether trust him. Oh dear, that sounds churlish after his kindness to me. But it is true."

"Trust him how?"

"Oh, in his expressions of friendship. I suspect he is amused by me for the moment, you know. And — and perhaps when he has grown used to my odd ways, he will seek another source of entertainment. Do you see?"

"Very well indeed. This is the penalty of fashion. Everything must be *de rigueur* and *á la mode* for the time. Until some new quirk arrives and all that is *passé*."

"And Fitz is in the forefront of fashion."

"Until some other gifted upstart ousts him."

"Yes, but if I must wait for that, Seph, I shall very likely be an old maid."

"Not you. Papa has already turned away any number of *prétendants*. There will be Cousin Rossendale and that foreign idiot."

"Count Leopold," her sister put in, "and I doubt if he is in the least bit serious."

"Is he not? He is as poor as a church mouse by all accounts and must be only too ready to line his pockets. Like Chiddingly. Mark my words if he is not knocking on Papa's door within the week."

But, before Chiddingly found an opportunity to put in his bid, another would-be suitor had gone to see the nabob, and put him in a most unaccustomed rage.

A few mornings later, the Winsford twins were sitting cosily in the small shabby parlour when they were interrupted by the eruption into the room of their father.

"Ha! You're both there, are you? Well, I'll thank you to tell me who the deuce is this Bolsover? I'll Bolsover him!"

Two sets of grey eyes regarded him with astonishment.

"Don't stare at me like a pair of noddies! Who — is — he?"

Penelope shook her head dumbly, but Persephone frowned, recalling the day of the baron's horse trial. Had not that been the name Letty had mentioned? Billy Bolsover, was it not?

"A little man? Tubby?"

"Tubby? As broad as he is long. Impertinent jackanapes! So you know him, do you?"

"I have seen him, I think. But we have not been introduced."

"As I suspected. As I suspected, by Jupiter! The infernal impudence of the man!"

"Why, Papa, what has he done?" quavered Penelope.

"I will tell you what he has done," the nabob said, in a tone of suppressed passion that showed plainly the origin of Persephone's volatile temperament. "This man has been here to request permission to address my daughters."

"What?" gasped the twins in unison.

"To address my *daughters*," repeated the nabob with emphasis. "I assumed it was a slip of the tongue. 'Sir,' I said in a jocular tone, 'surely you cannot mean to marry both of them?' He laughed. Very merrily, I thought. So I asked him, 'Well, which one, sir?' as would anyone have done. 'Which one?'" Here the nabob's tanned features darkened as his eye kindled again. He blew out his cheeks.

"Well, Papa?" prompted Penelope.

"Do you know what the roly-poly, squat-faced, pig-eyed, swag-bellied pork hog had the audacity to say to me?"

Two golden heads shook from side to side.

"Either," announced the nabob dramatically.

The twins gazed at him, stunned.

"'Either, sir?' I roared," continued their father. "'Did I hear you aright? You said *either*?' He had the temerity to repeat himself. Well, I told him what I thought of him, you may be sure of that. Deuce take it, I know there are bound to be bloodsuckers after my blunt, but let them at least go about the business with a little finesse! Either, indeed!"

He was seriously discomposed. The more so when Penelope went off into a peal of laughter. He glared at her.

"You find it humorous, do you? Well, I do not."

"Nor I," Persephone agreed. "It is the outside of enough."

"I b-beg your pardon, Papa," Penelope gasped, making valiant efforts to contain her amusement. "It is very bad indeed. But I confess I find it droll, nevertheless. Don't mind me, Papa. I am dreadful, I know."

The nabob's hostility began to melt. "Well, well, I shan't scold you. Always were a frivolous little puss. Merry at the slightest thing. But mind this, both of you. If you take it into your heads to marry any such pork-bellied jack-pudding, not a farthing will you get from me!"

With which valedictory utterance he stalked from the room, leaving Penelope to have her laugh out in comfort.

It was with some misgiving, therefore, that he received from Lord Chiddingly a couple of days later a request for the hand of his daughter. Looking suspiciously at him, the nabob asked in a somewhat belligerent tone, "Which one?"

"Miss Penelope, sir," said Chiddingly, without hesitation.

"Ha!" barked Archie, visibly relaxing. "Well, sit down, my boy, sit down, and we'll discuss the matter."

He motioned his guest to one of the strawberry damask-covered chairs which his wife had caused to be re-upholstered upon their taking up residence, declaring the original covers to be shabby beyond belief. Once Chiddingly and his host were seated either side of the wide fireplace, Archie bade his guest say why he had fixed upon Penelope.

"Seems an odd choice for a man of your tastes," he said, looking at him rather hard.

Chiddingly was annoyed to feel himself reddening. Damn the man! Did he mean to insinuate, like Fitz, that he would be better suited with Persephone?

"I was attracted to your daughter at the outset of our acquaintance. I find her … exquisitely … charming."

"Hm. Not one for pretty speeches, are you? Can't think you'll make much headway with my Pen," the nabob said with devastating frankness. "But my little peas will decide for themselves. I have nothing to say to it, so long as they take care to choose an honest man." He held up a hand as Chiddingly made a move to speak. "No, I don't mean to imply any criticism, young feller. Nor I don't expect any romantical nonsense that takes no account of my circumstances. When you're as warm a man as I, you must expect it to weigh with any suitor."

"Quite so, sir."

"But an out-and-out fortune-hunter I won't tolerate. It's a tidy sum I'll be leaving my little peas, quite aside from their fifty thousand apiece."

"Fifty thousand?" echoed Chiddingly.

So it was not one hundred thousand, after all, he thought in shock. That was the sum of their combined fortunes. This put a different complexion on the matter.

Fortunately the nabob took his exclamation the wrong way. "Yes, it's a goodly sum. Could have made it more. But as I say, I'd have had every man jack of a self-seeking adventurer after them. As it is, if I'm disappointed in my hopes, I can tie it all up in trust to ensure no husband sees a penny of it. D'ye see?"

"I see, sir, and I applaud your foresight. I believe you will not find me as greedy as that."

"I certainly hope not. But it's early days to be discussing settlements. Better try your luck before we come to terms. I'll send Penelope down to you."

He nodded at the visitor, and went off without more ado. Chiddingly was left to kick his heels, and mentally kick himself for being so precipitate. Fifty thousand was still a considerable sum, and, invested well, would keep him rolling for a few years at least. But was it truly enough to be worth tying himself up in matrimony? And to a female so closely allied to one whom he would be happy never to meet again?

But having gone so far, he could not with honour pull out of it. He caught himself hoping Penelope would refuse him, thinking that if only Fitz had been more *épris* he would have refrained from coming to the point himself. What was more, he would have been able to confound that hellcat, Persephone, showing her suspicions of him to appear unfounded. As it was

—

The door opened, cutting off his thoughts, and Miss Winsford entered the saloon. She was looking remarkably pretty in a chemise gown of soft green muslin with a dainty sprig, her golden curls uncovered and falling loosely about her face and shoulders.

She paused on the threshold for a moment, a look, he thought, of uncertainty in her grey eyes.

"Good morning, Miss Winsford," he said, nerving himself for the ordeal with which he now had to proceed.

She came into the room and closed the door, and Chiddingly, wanting to get it over with, plunged into speech.

"Miss Winsford, I have spoken with your father. He has permitted that I address you, and I therefore have the honour to ask for your hand in marriage."

The lady's cool grey eyes looked him over from his head to his heels. Then she spoke, the husky tones unmistakable.

"Choosing another filly for your stud, Chiddingly?"

CHAPTER SIX

"*Persephone!*"

"Yes, it is I. Now, how do you propose to extricate yourself?"

"What are *you* doing here?"

"I live here, or had you forgotten?"

"No — I mean — I was expecting —"

"You were expecting Pen, were you? What a surprise. I came down to collect a book I left in here earlier, as it so happens. I little thought I should find instead a proposal of marriage."

"I was not — I did not mean —" Chiddingly stopped, flushing as he realised into what a quagmire he was sinking.

"You did not mean to offer for me, is that it?" asked Persephone in a deceptively innocent tone at variance with the militant sparkle in her eye.

"You know very well I did not!"

"No, but you *have* done so, and as a gentleman you are in honour bound to stand by it. You cannot withdraw." She gave a false, brittle laugh. "What a fitting punishment for your misdeeds, as I recall someone once saying to me. To be obliged to marry *me*, that I may make your life a misery to the end."

"Take care! I am not so much the gentleman I will feel myself bound to a contract entered into under patently false pretences."

Persephone gasped and exploded. "Do you imagine for one single instant I would hold you to it, you arrogant barbarian?"

"*Barbarian?*"

"Yes, barbarian! I would not marry you if you were the last man alive."

"Permit me to return the compliment."

"Easy to say now, sir. You were ready enough to marry Penelope and we are so exactly alike, you could not even tell the difference."

Chiddingly gave a scornful laugh. "Alike? I beg to differ, madam. Your sister is a lady, Miss Winsford, whereas you —"

"Don't dare to criticise me, you hectoring bully!"

"Do you imagine you have exclusive rights over insults? You are a vicious little she-devil, and before I married you I would burn in hell!"

"Where you would be mightily at home, my lord!"

"Why, you little cat! I wish you had accepted me, after all. As my wife, you would be obliged to take me for your master."

Speechless with fury, Persephone fought for breath and tottered on her feet. "You — you — *savage!*"

Running to a table, she seized a heavy brass ornamental figurine of Indian origin and hurled it at him across the room. His horror-filled eyes watched it fly over his head to strike the wall behind him. Turning in time to see Persephone pick up a candelabrum from a side table by the window, he ducked behind a chair just as the silver object sailed through the air.

"You raving little bedlamite, stop that!" he shouted from his place of safety. "If I could but get my hands on you!"

As a remark calculated to mollify a raging termagant it left a good deal to be desired, as was evidenced by a third heavy thud behind him. Fortunately, the door opened and he saw Penelope come running into the room before any further missile could be unleashed.

"Seph, have you run mad?" Penelope cried, seeing the wreckage all about one corner of the room.

"Call her off!" yelled Chiddingly from behind the chair.

Penelope had already seized the next object from her sister's hands and set it down, instead holding her twin by the arms. Hearing the baron's plea, she turned her head and, seeing him peeping over the back of the chair, his wig askew, she went off into gales of laughter.

Persephone, still growling imprecations, had reverted to her Hindi curses as usual. "*Salla*! Get him out of here before I kill him. I hate him, I hate him, I *hate* him!"

Chiddingly was edging towards the door, but at this he paused to deliver a parting shot. "Believe me, madam, your sentiments are entirely reciprocated!"

Then he was gone, leaving Penelope doubled up over a chair in convulsive fits of laughter, and Persephone trembling from head to foot, her passion spent.

Lord Chiddingly drove away from Hanover Square, his mission in ruins, thanking his stars to have escaped from a fate worse than death, and determined to forget both twins and concentrate on the stallion who looked set fair to realise for him his driving ambition.

En route to Paddy's to assuage his ruffled temper with a glass or two of wine, he recalled that he had arranged to meet with his trainer, Tidmarsh, at Tattersall's. Dropping in at his lodgings instead, he took a glass of dry sack and straightened his disturbed headwear before setting off again almost immediately in his phaeton.

Arrived at Tattersall's yard at Hyde Park Corner, Chiddingly at once sought out the owner, Old Tatt himself. Richard Tattersall, though he came of Yorkshire yeoman stock, had risen in the world of racing to a position of such prominence that he counted among his regular drinking cronies at his home at Highflyer Hall the young Prince of Wales and the prominent politician Charles James Fox. Himself a past master at judging a horse, he was quick to recognise Chiddingly's ability in that line, and was wont to say he was the only other man he would trust to pick his own nags.

Always pleased to see the baron, he greeted him with a jovial bonhomie. "Chid, you young horse-chaunter, what's this pack of breakdowns you sent me t'other day? Not worth a straw."

"I know," Chiddingly grinned, his mood lightening. "That's why I sent them to you. Done badly, have they?"

"Badly? Dead meat, dear boy, dead meat."

"Penniless, then, am I?"

"Penniless? Am I an apprentice? But it ain't at a price I'd have chosen to get for you, Chid, and that's the truth."

Chiddingly shrugged. "As long as I've covered my costs."

"By all accounts you'll recoup soon enough with this famous young 'un you've acquired."

"Fiend seize it, does the whole world know of it already?"

The old man winked. "Can't expect to keep these things under wraps. Everyone's on fire with speculation. You'll find old Billy down there pumping Tidmarsh at this very moment."

But when they reached the yard, the fat little gentleman spied Chiddingly and instantly deserted the trainer for bigger prey. "Aha, the man himself. Now, tell me true, Chid, is it promising, or does rumour lie?"

Chiddingly's jaw tightened. "Rumour, Billy, is always suspect."

"You see. You knew at once I was talking of your famous new horse." He lowered his voice and winked. "Confidentially, Chid, I've a serious proposition. At least, I'm acting for others."

"Indeed? What is this proposition?"

Billy tucked a hand in his arm and walked him out of earshot of the people about them. The mistrustful Tidmarsh followed closely.

"I've a buyer interested," Billy said. "Wouldn't say anything before Tatt, because I didn't want him to feel cut out. Been entrusted to ask you, privately, of course, if you'd care to sell."

"Sell?" Tidmarsh exclaimed from behind them. "The devil he will!" He saw Chiddingly's stern eye on him and resolutely shut his mouth, but his dark eyes glowered.

"You're mighty cagey, Billy," his master said. "What's to do?"

"Cagey? No, Chid. You take me up quite wrong. No, no. See here, man, my ... er — client, shall we say, for want of a better word? — doesn't want to be seen in the matter."

Chiddingly almost snorted. "Do you take me for a flat? There are only two people who would use a go-between. One is Goole. The other is Florizel. And, as his pockets are to let, I am unlikely to sell him a twenty-pound breakdown, let alone my new stallion."

Florizel was the sobriquet by which the young and very amorous Prince of Wales was widely known after his pursuit of the actress who had so prettily portrayed Perdita in Shakespeare's play. Since his financial embarrassments were common knowledge, Chiddingly's prejudice was understandable.

"It ain't either of them," Bolsover said almost testily.

"Then let him come and make me an offer in person. Or rather, don't bother. I'm not selling."

"I knew you wouldn't, my lord," Tidmarsh said in triumph, though not without a touch of relief.

"Very well, then, when do you mean to put up this paragon?" Billy asked, his smile breaking out again. "Newmarket?"

"Newmarket?" echoed Tidmarsh. "Why, that's only a week or two off. He's barely begun training. Epsom is more like."

"Oh, come, Tidmarsh," the little man laughed. "You're a better man than that. We all know your work. Lay anyone a pony you can have him ready in time."

Tidmarsh shook his head. "No one would take you, sir."

"You see, Billy?" Chiddingly said. "Tidmarsh has spoken. As you know, his word is law when it comes to my horses."

"Stuff and nonsense, Chid. You are the only arbiter of your own stock. Come now, put the stallion in for Newmarket. I'll put my own Magnet up against him, so I will."

Tidmarsh whistled, and other racing habitués pricked up their ears and gathered round. Bolsover's Magnet was a proven champion who had won at Doncaster only the previous month.

"What's this?" demanded Egremont, always ready for a bet. "Billy putting Magnet up against an unknown? Damme, Billy, I like your spirit. Are you on, Chid?"

"I say no, the horse is not ready," Chiddingly said, thrown into ill-humour by Bolsover's inexplicable persistence.

"Fudge," scoffed Egremont. "If he's as good as they say, he can do it."

"Don't you let them push you, Chid," came the voice of Sir Charles Bunbury, who appeared beside him to enter the lists.

Lord Derby, that dissolute earl, was with him, and he dug his friend playfully in the ribs. "Don't spoil sport, Charles. Can always do with new blood on the course."

"Fiend seize you all," Chiddingly cursed. "I'm entering Firefly for Newmarket, as well you know."

"So? No reason why you can't enter another horse," Derby said. "Have a new race. We did it at Epsom. You can, too. We'll even call it *the Chid* after you, old fellow."

There was a general guffaw from those who remembered the discussion at the Oaks when the now well-established Derby had almost been called the Bunbury.

"There you are, Chid," broke in Billy Bolsover. "Can't say fairer than that. It's all set up. My Magnet to your — what the devil is the horse's name? Or ain't you thought of one yet?"

"No, we ain't," Tidmarsh said.

"Yes, we have," Chiddingly said, nettled by Billy Bolsover's manner. "It is Indigo."

Tidmarsh blinked at him. It was the first he had heard of it. Chiddingly saw his puzzled frown and gave him a nod, as if to say it was all settled. With a sinking heart, he listened to his master's next words, knowing what was coming.

"Since you are all so insistent, so be it. I will put up Indigo against Magnet — and any other horse anyone cares to throw in my face — at Newmarket, the distance to be decided."

"Bravo!" shouted Tattersall, among a general huzzah. "I'll fetch the betting book at once."

"Sink me, if this won't swell the crowds at Buckfastleigh's," someone said.

Since Lord and Lady Buckfastleigh had their country estate in Cambridgeshire, close to the Newmarket course, it was their custom to hold a large house party there during race week in early April. It formed a mid-season break from London, and the exclusive invitations were coveted by the fashionable set and racing men alike.

"Trust you'll be one of the crowd there, as usual, Chid?" said Billy, twinkling. "Keep my eye on you. Bring you up to scratch."

Tidmarsh bristled at this slur on his master's honour. But Chiddingly merely said, "I shan't fail. But I shall certainly be at Buckfastleigh's."

"Ah, and — er — the nabob's *little peas*, eh? I must say I'm keen to see this nonpareil of a rider. Going to be there, are they?"

"I have not the remotest guess," Chiddingly said. "You had better ask them." With which, he signed to Tidmarsh to accompany him, and withdrew.

Early the following week, had he cared to enquire into the matter, he could have answered Bolsover's question. The Winsford family were delighted and honoured to receive an invitation to spend race week near Newmarket with Lord and Lady Buckfastleigh.

For once it was Persephone who was over the moon at this treat in store, while Penelope sought the first opportunity of asking Lady Rossendale if it was worth the nuisance of a two-day journey.

"Surely it must be the dullest party in the world, Aunt?"

"One would say so, but no," responded her ladyship, shifting on the damask sofa and readjusting the skirts of her open robe about her. "I must say, Clarissa was clever to choose this strawberry. It is an excellent colour. No, Penelope, you must not think of crying off. I should be mortified. Although you may not enjoy the races, the company is always vastly entertaining. Though I admit the journey is appalling." She glanced across at the stocky figure of her son, who was standing by Penelope's chair, awaiting an opportunity to seize her attention. "Is it not so, Edmund?"

"Vastly disagreeable. But I dare say it may be less so if we all travel together." His prim smile encompassed his cousin.

"An excellent suggestion," agreed Lady Rossendale, and turned to call to her sister, who was conversing with a friend of her husband's while that worthy had gone off to fetch something to show him. "Clarissa!"

Mrs Winsford turned her head. "Yes, Harriet?"

"I am saying we must all travel together."

"Where?"

"Newmarket, of course. It will be far safer. More comfortable, too."

The nabob came back into the saloon at this moment. "Now then, old fellow, I've papers here to prove it." Wholly ignoring the rest of the company, he sat down by his friend and fell into discussion.

Mrs Winsford came to sit beside her sister on the sofa. "I think it an excellent idea to travel together, Harriet. Though we cannot accommodate all of us in one coach."

"Naturally not. We will take two. I hope you will keep me company on the journey, Clarissa, for Rossendale will ride, of course."

"Is that necessary?" her sister asked, with a sympathetic glance at her unfortunate nephew.

"Unless you wish to go to the expense of hiring outriders, most necessary," declared Lady Rossendale. "The roads are positively infested with any number of rogues. I should not dream of travelling without protection."

But the nabob, forcibly dragged from his conversation to be consulted on the matter, was scornful. "Outriders? Pooh, nonsense! Do you mean to say I cannot protect my own daughters after years and years in India?"

"Yes, but this is not India," his sister-in-law said. "We are talking of footpads and highwaymen."

"Ha! We had to contend with a deal worse than footpads, let me tell you, my lady. Why, a bandit would cut your throat for a handful of rupees."

Her ladyship gasped, raising a protective hand to her neck.

"Archie! Don't heed him, Harriet," Clarissa soothed.

"Don't you fret over me and my little peas, my lady. If it will comfort you, I will have a pistol about me, and thus engage to deal with any number of desperadoes."

"Well said, Papa," applauded Penelope. "I am sure you will."

She was so amused by the fuss and bother attendant upon a simple journey she was moved to relate the episode to Fitzwarren when she encountered him at a *soirée* a day or so later.

"One would think this two-day expedition comparable to our voyage from Bombay. Even Mama seems to be carried away by the excitement of it all."

Fitz laughed. "Is she indeed?"

"Ridiculously so," Persephone put in. "We have heard of nothing but trunks and bandboxes, and whether to take our own sheets for the inn where we break the journey, down to which hats to wear and how many shifts it will be proper to take."

"Seph, bad girl, hush!"

"Well, it is so absurd. For my part, a single habit will do. All I want is to get on that course and see the racing."

Fitz smiled to see her eyes sparkle with such unwonted enthusiasm. What a difference in her from the night of that first ball. All because she had at last an opportunity to indulge her preferences. He became aware the girls were both looking doubtfully down at someone standing by his elbow.

"Present me, Fitz, I charge you," said Billy Bolsover. "I have been dying to meet the nabob's *little peas*."

As Fitz introduced them, the twins exchanged glances. So this was the suitor who would have either of them to wife. Seeing Penelope showed a distressing tendency to giggle, and assuming Billy's squat appearance to be the cause, Fitz hastily threw the onus of responding on her sister.

"Billy is another of your horse-mad turf notables, Miss Persephone."

Persephone looked at Billy Bolsover's jovial countenance, the animation dying out of her face. Her voice was cold. "How do you do?"

"Splendidly, Miss Winsford, splendidly. Gather we are to have the pleasure of your company up at Newmarket, eh?" said Billy, impervious to her hostility.

"We are going to Newmarket, yes," she said, unwilling to commit herself to his company.

"Excellent. I've heard a lot about you. Wonderful seat, Charles tells us. Very much look forward to seeing you on horseback."

"Do you ride, Mr Bolsover?" Penelope asked, her eyes dancing. "I have a burning desire to see *you* on horseback!"

But Billy had not endured the roasting of his intimates for years without learning not to take offence. He roared with laughter and Pen could not but warm to him.

"Very droll, Miss Winsford. But you will not put me out of countenance, you know. I see we shall have an amusing time of it with you at Buckfastleigh's."

"Oh, are you staying there also?"

"Certainly, certainly. Mind you, it's a tricksy journey. Good thing there are so many of us travelling up at the same time."

"There now, Seph, you see," said Penelope. "And Mama would have it we needed outriders."

"Stuff and nonsense," scoffed Billy, unconsciously echoing the nabob. "Outriders? Absurd! How do you mean to go?"

Once again the discussion turned on the Winsfords' travel arrangements, Penelope finding an appreciative audience for the joke of the fuss and bother being made, with Fitz joining in amid a deal of hilarity.

Only Persephone was struck by the thought that this Billy Bolsover was showing an uncommon interest in their journey, asking what days they meant to travel and where they meant to put up for the night they must spend on the road.

As it chanced, the journey proved monotonously uneventful until, on the second day, an unprecedented halt was necessitated by the discovery that one of the horses in the team pulling the coach carrying Archibald and the girls was lame. Persephone and the groom conducted an investigation.

"A badly placed nail," Persephone told her relations. "The poor beast must have been in considerable pain all this while."

While they limped the coach on to the next village, she held forth, hot against a smith who could take so little pride in his work as to make such a seemingly trivial, yet disastrous mistake.

The coach bearing the servants and baggage had been sent on ahead so as to be able to make suitable preparations in their employers' allotted rooms at the Buckfastleigh mansion. As time was getting on, Archie persuaded his wife and sister-in-law also to continue on their way.

"For if we should find it difficult to procure another horse, at least there will only be three of us to be incommoded."

There was no denying his good sense and the second coach lumbered off with Rossendale in attendance on horseback, Clarissa taking her place beside her sister once more, having borne her company as requested. They were able to hire a fourth horse from a local farmer without too much difficulty. Arrangements then had to be made for both horses' return, and as by this time everyone was hungry, a little refreshment was taken at the inn, which meant that they were quite late starting off again.

Dusk was falling by the time the coach left the main road to take the rackety pot-holed track that led past Newmarket Heath towards the estate owned by Buckfastleigh. They had rattled and bumped only a couple of miles over this rough way when there was a sudden flurry of thudding hoofs, a hoarse cry, and an explosive crack that nearly deafened the inmates as the coach came to a shuddering halt.

There was a chorus of exclamation within the vehicle.

"The devil!"

"Drat, what now?"

"What the deuce?" cried the nabob.

But before he could indulge in further speculation, the door of the coach was wrenched open and he found himself staring down the barrel of a long pistol.

The inside of the coach went deathly quiet.

"Come on out of that!" ordered the man behind the pistol gruffly, his greatcoated bulk shutting out the last of the daylight.

"Down with you!" he said, sharpening his tone, and stepped back, gesturing with his weapon for the nabob to alight.

"Get down, Papa, for heaven's sake," whispered Penelope.

"Very well, you scoundrel, I'll come down. But be sure you will pay for this!" barked Archie, as he hoisted himself out of the coach and jumped down into the road.

"You too, my pretties," the man said, pointing with his free hand into the coach, while his pistol still covered the nabob.

Penelope hastily jumped out and went to stand by her father, but Persephone, though her heart beat fast, took her time, pausing in the doorway to take in the scene outside.

The man who had now stepped back from the door was masked, with a slouch hat pulled low over his forehead. Another man, also masked and still on horseback, covered the groom on the box, against whom the coachman lay slumped. Then that had been the explosion they had heard. The coachman had been shot. Some yards away another horse stood in the shadows, the rider on its back sitting quietly, not as yet taking part in the scene.

Her dilatory progress might have earned her a reprimand from the highwayman, were it not for the fact he was looking from her face to her sister's in surprise.

"Dang me, if you ain't as like as ninepence," he said, whistling, and then a curse from his companion by the horses brought him to a recollection of his business.

"Get down, missie, before I blows a hole in the old man!"

Persephone jumped down and went to join her father and sister.

"Now then," the man said, waving his pistol impartially at all three, "let's have a look-see what we got here."

"Ha! You'll get nothing from us, varmint!" Archie said.

"Will I not, then? Think I'm a rum pad, eh, a-going to empty your pockets for a few gewgaws? Well, I'm not." He shouted at the groom who was shivering on the box, his eyes riveted on the second man's pistol. "Hoy, you! Get down out of that!"

"Move!" growled the second man, urging his horse closer and aiming his pistol higher.

As the terrified groom scrambled down, the nabob stealthily crept a hand into his pocket, while the highwayman's eyes were off him. The movement caught Penelope's attention and she looked down. In turn, this brought their captor's head sharply round.

"Be still," he barked. To the groom, he said, "There'll be a strongbox under the seat. Get it out."

The nabob muttered an oath and started forward.

The pistol swung to cover him.

"Stand, I said!"

"You scoundrel! Villain!"

"Stow it!"

"Papa, don't," Penelope begged.

Persephone said not a word. Her eyes never left the man in charge. There might be an opening. Any opening. If only Papa would be more careful!

The groom was already in the coach, searching with shaking hands under the seat. His fingers found something hard and he gave a glad cry.

"You have it?" the highwayman called out and looked round to see the groom tug out a large, carved wooden box. "Ah, there's the beauty!"

Seizing his chance, the nabob dragged his pistol from his pocket. He was not quick enough. The highwayman rounded on him, ready to discharge his own piece.

Before he could do so, there was a flash from his right, a loud report, and the nabob gave a grunt, dropped his weapon, and clapped a hand to his arm.

"Papa!" shrieked Penelope, grabbing him as he began to sink to the ground, dazed with shock.

Looking up, Persephone saw the gun in the hand of the mounted man outside the little circle. She dropped to her knees beside her father, and, turning her back on the ruffian who covered them, groped in the grass. In a few seconds, her fingers found steel and her hand closed around the butt of her father's pistol.

The groom, leaving the strongbox, was standing horror-struck in the doorway of the coach. Next moment, he jumped clean into the air as another explosion shattered the night.

Seeing his accomplice pitch forward on to his face, the second ruffian half made to dismount as he saw a slip of a girl had fired the shot that brought him down.

Then the groom sprang into action, dragging him from the horse and grappling with his pistol hand. Wary of his cocked gun going off, the highwayman had little attention to spare for the fight and so was overpowered and the gun removed from his hand. Not staying to recover it, he leapt on to his horse and made good his escape.

The third man paused, his eyes on the girls, one of whom was helping her father to strip off his coat, the other staring down at the man she had just killed.

As if she felt his eyes on her, Persephone looked up.

At that instant, the moon, which had been obscured by cloud, shone out, and she was just able to glimpse the man's face, down which ran a livid white scar. Then he turned his horse and rode off.

"Seph, help me," cried Penelope. "Papa is almost fainting."

"Drag this villain off the road," Persephone ordered the groom. Then she dropped again to her knees, and helped Penelope to tie strips torn off the hem of her under petticoat about their father's arm to staunch the welling blood. Then she glanced up at the box where the coachman had fallen on to the seat. "Is he dead?"

"They shot his brains out," the groom told her with a shudder.

"Oh, dear heaven, no!"

129

"Be silent, Pen!"

"But how shall we manage if he is dead?"

Persephone paid no heed to her sister's words. Bidding the groom assist her, she managed with his help to pull the coachman's body off the box and stow it in the boot behind the coach. Setting her teeth, she returned to Penelope.

"How is he?"

"I will live, my peas," the nabob uttered with determined cheer, but his voice was faint. "I will live. Good girls, both of you. Now, help me into the coach."

But it was the groom who had to hoist the nabob to his feet and half carry him to the coach. Penelope pulled from inside, and they dragged him in, but the exertion brought the wound to bleed again and Archie fainted away.

"Seph, what shall we do? We must get him to the Buckfastleigh place and to bed."

"Seems I'd best ride there and bring back help," the groom offered.

"Nothing of the sort," Persephone said. "Get up on the box. Don't fret, Pen. I will drive us to Buckfastleigh."

"Oh, how silly. I never thought of that. Quickly, Seph!"

Persephone shut the coach door and, retrieving the coachman's whip from where it had fallen, purposefully mounted on to the box.

"You ain't never going to drive us, miss?" gasped the groom.

"Certainly I am."

"Lord a' mercy!"

But when he saw how competently she took the reins and with what ease she managed the horses, he was struck dumb with awe. He was not so enamoured, however, of the cracking pace she set, which resulted in considerable jolting.

Inside the coach, Penelope had much ado to keep her small hands tightly clasped about the bandages covering the wound in her father's arm and several times cursed her sister freely. But at length they arrived within sight of a large country estate which had to be the Buckfastleigh residence, as they had been told it was the only house of any size in the district.

So indeed it proved, and since the drive, in contrast to the rutted road, was very well-kept, Persephone was able to whip up her horses, which arrived at the magnificent Palladian frontage in a lather of sweat.

Under her orders, the groom jumped down and ran to the front door to give the alarm. Within minutes, people came streaming from the house and the twins were able to relinquish their responsibilities, the one into the competent hands of several grooms, the other into the care of their mother. Clarissa Winsford came rushing out and, smothering her shock, immediately took charge of her husband's person, bidding Lady Rossendale take care of the girls.

But her ladyship was already in a way to having a spasm, as she assured the assembled company. "Did I not say so? Did I not warn him? Outriders, I said. Highwaymen and footpads, I said. Would he listen to me? Now see what has come of it!"

"Yes, indeed, Harriet, it is very bad," agreed Lady Buckfastleigh, her eyes on her husband and butler who were bearing the nabob up the stairs, his wife in close attendance, "but just at this moment we have more important things to think about."

Then she turned from her guest and directed a servant to ride for the surgeon. Following the cavalcade upstairs, she prepared to render all the assistance in her power, despatching maids for hot water and towels, and her hovering housekeeper to run ahead and open up the bed for Mr Winsford.

The twins, beginning to look worn down now the emergency was over, found themselves surrounded by a vociferous crowd.

"How could this happen?" Count Leopold demanded. "Villains! An escape so fortunate."

"It was not luck, Leopold," Penelope said on a weary note. "It was Seph who saved us. She shot the blackguard."

Into the sudden hush came Persephone's husky tones. "No, Pen. You saved Papa's life. It was you who staunched the blood."

"Well, well, you are plainly a pair of heroines," came Billy Bolsover's jovial voice.

Something clicked at the back of Persephone's mind. Something about this man that connected with what had occurred today. But she could not place it. She sank into a chair, the discussion of their adventure still raging over her head, as each person related to his neighbour what he had been told. Voices grew louder, unnatural, a cacophony of disconnected sound.

Through the milling press of persons she saw her sister, Fitz bending solicitously over her. She saw blood on Penelope's gown and the face of the man she had shot floated into her mind, his mouth gashed wide in a look of utter disbelief as he gazed down at the red-rimmed hole in his chest before he fell.

Spots began to dance before her eyes, colours jumping, as a whoosh hit her ears.

CHAPTER SEVEN

Persephone felt herself lifted and heard the harsh tones of a familiar voice from somewhere far above her.

"Make way, there, make way! Miss Winsford is exhausted and in need of rest. Make way, I say!"

Her head spun giddily and blackness threatened to claim her. She clutched at the solid body which supported her and moaned softy. "My head swims."

"Don't try to talk," the same voice said, unwontedly gentle. "You will be better directly."

The dizziness began to recede, and as her eyelids fluttered open a little she became aware she was being carried up a sweep of staircase in unknown surroundings. Yet the voice had been reassuringly familiar. All at once she realised who it was and her eyes flew fully open.

"Chiddingly?"

His gaze flicked downwards, but he neither loosened his hold nor slowed his progress up the stairs. "You swooned."

Persephone could only gaze up at the line of his firm jaw in wonder. The oddest sensation was succeeding the faintness. A slow spread of warmth seemed to glow and tingle in her veins. Her heartbeat, already fast, began to race, thumping so strongly she was vaguely surprised he could not hear it.

Chiddingly bore her down a corridor and through an open doorway, and Persephone saw, with a sense of shock, that they had entered a bedchamber. The wildest notion crept into her brain and her cheeks began to burn with the shame of it, until she saw Lady Buckfastleigh was present.

Chiddingly laid his burden carefully on the bed and stood for a moment, looking down at her and frowning.

"I am sorry to have put you to so much trouble," Persephone said in an unusually subdued tone.

He shrugged this away. "It is of no consequence at all."

Lady Buckfastleigh was at the windows, drawing the drapes against the darkness.

Chiddingly lowered his voice. "Whatever our differences, Persephone, permit me to say that your valour commands my deepest respect." Upon which he executed a small bow, and, turning, left the room.

The grey eyes followed him, in them a strange perplexity.

They were closed in sleep, however, when Penelope tiptoed in a short time later. She crept under the covers, trying not to wake her sister, for with so many guests in the house they had been assigned the same room.

But although Penelope was tired, sleep eluded her. She wanted to toss and turn, but was afraid to wake Persephone. The day's adventures had taken their toll, but it was not so much this that was keeping her awake. A picture kept forming in her unwilling mind. One that might have been. So horrible was it she kept trying to push it away. As fast as she did so, however, it forced its way back.

In the end, she got up out of the bed, and, without troubling to dress her hair, donned a chemise gown and slid silently from the room. Slipping down the stairs, she avoided the big saloon into which they had been swept on arrival, from which she could hear talk and laughter, and darted past the open door.

Across the hall were several rooms. After peeping into a dining-parlour and a library, she found a small music-room in which there was a harpsichord by an uncurtained window.

There was only one candelabrum alight on the mantel, but the moon was bright, affording a silvery glow through the glass.

Penelope slid on to the stool and opened the harpsichord, letting her fingers play idly over the keys. The desultory plucking of the strings soothed her. Her fingers picked out the tune almost at random, her tension eased and tears began to trickle down her cheeks.

She was unaware when the door opened and only the shadow looming up behind the harpsichord caused her to glance up with a gasp of fright.

"I startled you," Fitz said. "I beg your pardon."

Penelope shook her head, unable to speak for the sudden constriction in her throat.

"What is it?"

The gentle note caused her voice to become husky. "N-nothing."

Fitz smiled, and, drawing up a chair, came to sit beside her. He reached for one hand and held it imprisoned between his own. "Come now. It is a tidy thing, this nothing. You have had a severe ordeal, but it is over."

She looked at him then, and he saw the trace of tears on her cheeks. "It is just that I keep thinking if — if that dreadful man had aimed just a fraction further to one side, or if Papa had been standing more to the left... It was so close. He might have died, Fitz!"

She was sobbing, and found herself cradled to a broad chest, strong arms comfortingly close about her.

"Hush, child, it is nothing but a bad dream," Fitz murmured into her hair. After a moment, he spoke in a stronger voice, the teasing note apparent. "Never mind. Tomorrow you will be in your element watching the horses and will forget all about it."

Penelope was so surprised she sat up in a bang, pulling herself from his hold, and dashing at her wet cheeks with her fingers. "In my element?"

Fitz frowned, but the gleam in his eye told its own tale. "Do not tell me I have the wrong sister?"

"Oh, you are quite abominable," Penelope said, breaking into laughter. "You know very well it is I."

"Pen? Good grief!"

"Drat you, Fitz, I wish you will have done! You will not, I can assure you, find me in the thick of things tomorrow. I shall be content to watch sedately from a carriage."

Fitz laughed. "Now I know it is you, Pen. As for your sister, if I am any judge, we shall be hard put to it to stop her from joining in the race."

There seemed little doubt Fitz's prophecy would prove true, as the company gathered on Newmarket Heath the next day. Persephone seemed to be everywhere at once, riding hither and yon on one of Buckfastleigh's hacks, in a state of unprecedented elation.

"This is capital, Pen," she called out happily to her sister as she passed by Lady Buckfastleigh's open carriage. "I shall see you presently. I must go and inspect Egremont's entry."

Then she was off, cantering over to where a knot of racing notables were discussing the points of several horses being walked around preparatory to the next race.

"Come now, Miss Winsford," Egremont said, "what think you of my Galway Wonder? Is she not a charming piece?"

"Very pretty, my lord," Persephone conceded, riding around the grey filly to take an overall view. "But she looks to be over at the knee, and I frankly would not back her against that little lady." She pointed with her whip to where a jockey was leading a small chestnut into the circle.

"Siegfried!" Sir Charles Bunbury called out. "Over here!"

The little man leading the horse looked round, saw who hailed him and waved. He was a bow-legged individual, spare of body, with a wizened, monkey-like face.

"Extraordinary little varmint, Siegfried," Bunbury told Persephone. "Polish, he claims. Though you would never think it to hear him. Pure London in his speech, is Siegfried. But rides like a demon."

"Well, he will not beat my Galway Wonder," said Egremont with grim determination. Nevertheless he greeted the jockey as he came up. "Hey, there, Siegfried, Miss Winsford here fancies your lady against mine. On form, is she?"

"Lord luv yer honour, would I tell yer if she weren't, then?" grinned the jockey cheekily, turning his eyes to Persephone. "Not but what the missie has more sense in her knowledge-box than wot you has, putting up that great Irish fussock agin our Firefly."

The gentlemen about him roared with laughter, Lord Egremont showing no offence at this outspoken insolence. Persephone, seeing the truth of Fitz's assertion that the racing aristocracy were easy with their fellow men, smiled warmly at Siegfried.

"I take that to be a great compliment, and must congratulate you on this Firefly. She carries a good head, and I make no doubt we'll see true action when she's on the move."

"That you will, missie. But you lays your blunt where you chooses. Don't go a-blaming of me if it don't come back to yer."

"Don't heed him, ma'am," said a new voice, and Persephone turned her head to see a fresh-faced young man on horseback by her side. "He cries like a baby when he loses a race."

"That I don't neither, you fibbing Tidmarsh," cried the jockey in shrill tones. "Nor I don't need you a-coming chivvying of me. I knows how to do."

"Then keep the filly on the move, you misbegotten whelp," ordered the harsh voice of Baron Chiddingly.

"*Salla!*" muttered Persephone, startled into forgetting the proprieties.

Siegfried's bravado collapsed as he recognised the voice of authority. "Aye, aye, master. I'm a-going, I'm a-going."

"She is your horse, then," Persephone said, flushing a little at the memory of the previous night when he had carried her upstairs.

Chiddingly bowed his acknowledgement. Persephone watched the jockey begin to walk the filly round to keep her muscles warmed.

"She is a fine little lady, sir. I will offer my Lord Egremont very good odds against his Galway Wonder beating her, I assure you."

"I'll take you, never fear," Egremont told her.

"I am flattered," Chiddingly said, amusement in his voice.

"You are a good judge, sir," Persephone said, and her low gurgle of laughter rippled from her. "I will concede you that much."

"You positively overwhelm me," Chiddingly said, but there was an answering gleam in his eye. "You should rather put your faith in Tidmarsh, however. His is the hand that guided Firefly to her present skill."

He waved an introductory hand at his trainer as he spoke, and Tidmarsh, rather red about the ears, pressed his mount civilly forward as Persephone spoke to him.

"You trained her, then?"

He nodded. "I did, ma'am."

"So he does all my horses," Chiddingly said. "No doubt he will delight in telling you all about it."

There was a chorus of groans.

"No, for pity's sake!" cried Egremont.

"Not a Tidmarsh lecture!" exclaimed Derby.

The young man grinned sheepishly. "Have no fear, my lords. I am silent as the tomb."

But their lordships were edging their horses apart.

"My poor Tidmarsh," laughed Chiddingly with real amusement. "Let us take ourselves off before we empty the course."

The baron rode away, and Tidmarsh rather shyly made to follow him.

"No, don't go," Persephone called. "I would love to talk of training."

"I'll tell you anything you wish to know, ma'am, but his lordship was funning. His friends all complain I have but one subject of conversation, and I disapprove of this custom of sweating their horses to get their flesh off."

"Oh yes, barbarous." She gestured at the horses being walked apart by grooms. "I am reminded of nothing so much as a row of toast racks."

They talked for some time and Persephone acquired, insensibly, a better opinion of Chiddingly, who could encourage improvements in his stables. But the signalling of the imminent start of the next race brought the conversation to an abrupt end.

The three-year-old fillies were gathering at the post for the two-mile sweepstake, Siegfried, up on Firefly, sporting Chiddingly's colours of peacock-blue. There were three other runners besides Egremont's Galway Wonder, and Persephone joined the crowds converging on the starting post with a flutter of excitement in her breast and her grey eyes alight. Here she encountered Letty Smith, and, although they did not speak, a conspiratorial smile passed between them and Letty winked before turning her eyes back to the five horses straining at the leash.

There was a moment of hushed expectancy. Then the steward's handkerchief fell and they were off. Galway Wonder set the pace, proving her reputation and her worth. For the first mile the huddle of five fillies held well together, accompanied by the shouts of encouragement all about them, from the watchers in the carriages on the hill above and the populace on foot beside the course.

Alongside and behind, only just out of the way, a knot of hardened turf-goers swept along, riding from vantage-point to vantage-point to get at every thrilling moment the best view of the race. Of this company, breathless with excitement, Persephone made one. Straining into the second mile, the lesser contenders began to fall behind, leaving Galway Wonder and Firefly struggling for supremacy.

Every muscle and sinew stretched, every breath a gathering of fresh power, they flew down the makeshift track, now neck and neck, now one a short head before or behind. But as they approached within a few furlongs of the winning post, where stewards waited to give judgement, Siegfried applied his spurs and called out hoarse blandishments to urge his mount to greater effort.

Firefly began to creep ahead, her long muscles flexing as her speed increased. Head up, she hoisted her courage for a final burst of energy, and, passing the post at the gallop, took the race to a roar of applause.

Persephone, her attention wholly concentrated upon the filly, was unaware of having ridden with the others, until she found herself hard by the winning post and crying out in triumph as Firefly shot by. She was calling out to every face, an indiscriminate smile of exultation creasing her countenance. There was an instant of vague recognition of the faces of both Letty Smith and Lord Goole.

Next moment, without knowing how it had come about, she felt her fingers gripped in a strong hand and found herself looking into the glowing blue eyes of Baron Chiddingly.

"Oh, Chid, it was a capital go!"

"Was it not?"

"Beyond anything!"

His grip tightened, drawing her in. In automatic response, her knee guided her mount closer and the two horses stood nose to tail, side by side. Their riders were now face to face, a bare foot apart. Their eyes locked.

Persephone was conscious all of a sudden of an intimacy that held them frozen in time, and her lips parted, unaware that her fingers returned his pressure. She knew only that her heart had ceased to function and her breath was trapped in her throat.

Then the pain in her fingers from the forceful grip of his hand made itself felt.

"You're holding too tight!" she gasped.

"I want to," he said, an odd roughness in his voice. "Deeply." A vision of what he meant sprang full-blown into his mind. Shocked at the enormity of his thought, he released his hold abruptly and jerked his horse back.

A tide of crimson flooded Persephone's cheeks, and he could not doubt the answering fire in her that made her fully comprehend what had been expressed so curtly and with the utmost spontaneity. Unable to utter a single word for the confusion that swept over him, Chiddingly merely stared at her, unaware that his stern features grew grimmer by the second.

Persephone, utterly shamed, both by what she had said and the surge of heat that had engulfed her at the words, wanted to revile and curse him. But her tongue had become leaden, the thunder of her heartbeat filling her brain and making it impossible to think.

There was only escape. Pulling at her reins, she turned the horse and cantered away to the relative calm and safety of the bubbling fashionables in their carriages on the hill.

By a fortunate chance, she ran into Lord Buckfastleigh, who had arrived late on the ground, having spent the early part of the day in settling the aftermath of the hold-up that had marred the Winsfords' journey. His report on his activities so successfully diverted her chaotic thoughts she did not notice Lord Chiddingly ride up to the hill.

He signed to one of his grooms, and, dismounting, gave the horse into his charge. As he did so, he heard Penelope's tinkling laughter and looked over to where she stood, flirting impartially with her cousin Rossendale and Count Leopold.

Watching her, he found himself subject to a strange phenomenon. His eyes saw Penelope, and knew by both mannerisms and voice that it was Penelope. But his mind insisted on superimposing the voice and deep gurgle of Persephone's laughter. Yet there was nothing in him that responded to the sight of her.

By turning his head, he could see Persephone herself, also now dismounted, clad in a habit of blue with lace at her throat and wrists. At once, his betraying pulses quickened and his loins ached.

Confused, Chiddingly glanced from one twin to the other, unable to comprehend how one such face and figure could have so unsettling an effect, while the other left him cold.

He heard Penelope's melodic laughter again and winced. He could not have borne that for the rest of his life.

"Changed your mind?" said an amused voice behind him.

"Long ago," he said, turning to look at his friend. "The field is clear, Fitz. I have no further interest in the Winsford fortune. Besides, it is only half what we had thought. But that is of no consequence to you. So you may safely woo Penelope."

"I have no mind to cut out our assiduous Leopold, dear boy," Fitz said, shrugging. "Though I fancy Rossendale will win the day."

As he spoke, he looked round at the group and caught Penelope regarding him. Rather wistfully, he thought. Quite mesmerised, he left Chiddingly without a word and strolled over to her, ignoring both Leopold and Rossendale's claims to her attention.

"Miss Winsford, you look fatigued. Allow me to escort you back to the carriage."

Penelope smiled, but fleetingly. She gave him her hand, however, and allowed him to tuck it into his arm.

"But this is barefaced piracy," Rossendale protested.

"Assuredly. Think you I should send my seconds to wait upon him?" added Leopold.

Penelope twinkled. "No, no, Leopold. If you fight Fitz, everyone will think he has condemned some item you think beautiful."

"*Mein Gott*, you are right! A misapprehension insupportable."

"But all too believable, dear Leopold," sighed Fitz.

He then adroitly removed Penelope, ignoring the inevitable outburst behind him. Once out of earshot, he leaned close to murmur, "Are you feeling quite the thing?"

"I was never better, Fitz." She glanced up at him in frowning surprise. "Why do you ask?"

"You looked at me so oddly."

Her gaze dropped. "Did I do so?"

"Yes. I felt impelled to come to you."

There was no peal of silvery laughter, and her eye, as it flew to meet his, held no twinkle.

"Did you?" she asked. Then, before he could answer, she removed her hand from his arm. "You must excuse me. I see Lady Buckfastleigh signalling. She is ready to go, I believe."

Turning from him, she walked to the carriage and accepted the arm of Lady Buckfastleigh's footman to assist her to climb up. A moment later the carriage moved off and Fitz was left to gaze after it, perplexity in his head and an unexpected hollow feeling in his chest. It was a moment or two before he identified it.

The race parties were breaking up, and as he joined the throng leaving Newmarket Heath, the feeling of desolation intensified. It was not dispelled on arrival at the Buckfastleigh mansion, when he discovered Penelope had retired to her room with a reported headache. He was left to join the racegoers who, in jubilant mood, had set up a demand to see Chiddingly's wonder horse. The hue and cry was being led by Billy Bolsover.

"Come now, Chid, you've had mystery enough. The beast is to run tomorrow. It is high time we had a sight of this famous Indigo."

Persephone, who was removing her leather gloves, jerked her head up to stare at him. "Indigo?"

"Don't blame me, Miss Winsford," said Billy. "That is what Chid calls him."

Persephone's eyes sought and found the baron's. For a fleeting instant as they met she read the rueful acknowledgement in his. She could not but be gratified he had picked up her random thought, and a warm glow pervaded her veins.

Others were taking up the cry.

"Billy's in the right of it, Chid. There can be no need now of secrecy," said Clermont.

"You'll get no peace, Chid, until you show him," declared Fitz, "and so I warn you."

"Very well," Chiddingly sighed, with an air of weary boredom. "Let us all repair to the stables."

But when presently he brought Indigo out of his stall and led him into the yard, his pride in the animal was evident. Of the really knowledgeable men only Lord Clermont and Lord Egremont were present, but everyone was naturally staggered by the beauty of the dark stallion.

"No longer surprised at your caution, Chid," said Billy Bolsover, looking the horse over with obvious approval. "I don't wonder you wasn't interested in selling."

"Did you want to buy the stallion, then, Mr Bolsover?" Persephone asked, low-voiced, her suspicions aroused. For why had he been so hot to view a horse she knew well he had already seen?

Recognising that dangerous note, Chiddingly glanced at her. What in Hades was she getting at?

"What is your opinion, Miss Winsford?" asked Billy, successfully deflecting attention from himself.

"Yes, ma'am, tell us," Clermont said eagerly. "You were right about poor Egremont's Galway Wonder, it seems."

"Miss Winsford is obviously expert," smiled Egremont, a good loser. "I'll warrant she'll favour this Indigo, however."

"I wonder?" Chiddingly murmured, unable to resist casting her a challenging look. He had not quite forgiven her for sneaking a preview of his horse at the trial at Epsom.

Indigo, who, due to Tidmarsh's ministrations, was less mettlesome than at first, was still inclined to sidle and toss his head. The baron, finding he could not both control him and participate in the conversation, handed over the reins to a groom.

"Well, Miss Winsford?" He was finding the desire to goad her quite irresistible. "Your opinion, I beg of you."

Persephone, with the memory of the violent quarrel provoked between them upon the last occasion she had seen the horse vibrating in her mind, recognised his veiled taunt, but had difficulty in refraining from rising to this obvious bait. "I cannot think you need my opinion, being yourself so competent a judge of a horse."

"No, no, ma'am, I positively insist."

Persephone recognised a malicious glint in his gaze and her own eyes flashed. "Very well, sir. He looks well, I grant you, but he shows too much muscle."

"Too much muscle?"

"Far too much," Persephone lied recklessly. "Oh, I make no doubt he will be a front runner and lead the field at first. But he will probably blow up at the second mile."

After seeing him in action, this was sheer heresy, but Persephone did not care. Doubtless Chiddingly had expected to confound her, trip her into saying something which would show plainly she had already seen the horse in action. Well, she was not such a fool to be embarrassed so easily. Let him be confounded by the condemnation. On his own head be it.

Chiddingly was not confounded. He was furious. Forgetting his own challenge as well as the dangerous glitter he had seen in Persephone's eyes, he at once took this ridiculous indictment to be her considered opinion. After he had begun to believe her knowledgeable, too. And she had seen this horse run.

"You cannot know what you are saying," he said, with careful restraint.

"On the contrary. You have but to look at the beast."

In fact, most of the rest of the company were indeed looking at Indigo, and with questioning eyes. Could Miss Winsford be right?

"Stuff and nonsense," said Billy Bolsover, who had good reason to know. "The animal is clearly a stayer. See but his girth."

Chiddingly pounced on this. "Precisely. Plenty of heart there, you may depend upon it."

"I'll warrant you," said Billy. "Why, I'll stake my oath, I am in a veritable tremble for my Magnet. And he is a champion."

They both glared at Persephone, but she hit back with defiance.

"He is too short in the back, and Roman-nosed to boot. Likely he will drag his jockey all over the field, if he is not left at the starting post."

Indigo's ears flicked and he tossed his head fiercely, showing his teeth as if he resented these insults. His owner's sentiments were in no doubt.

"Oh, indeed? Let me tell you, ma'am, I will back this horse against all others, at any price you care to name."

There was a concerted gasp of shock from the onlookers. This was unprecedented. With these words, Chiddingly threw to the winds the killing he had hoped to make on Indigo's first run. If he was this certain, no one would bet against him.

Billy Bolsover grinned. "Well said, Chid. But damme, you've put me properly on my mettle. Well, well, nothing for it but to hold by my entry. Gentlemen," he added, addressing the company at large, "I am in honour bound. I will cover all bets against Magnet, at whatever the odds."

Fitz whistled. "Upon my soul, Billy, you will be all to pieces by tomorrow's eve."

"Not I. I've faith in Magnet yet."

Chiddingly stood silent, his jaw tight. Livid that he had allowed Persephone to prick him into that imprudent challenge, he gave her one scorching glance and turned to his groom with a curt order to return the stallion to his stall.

Persephone, dismayed by the outcome of their stupid argument, felt his burning glance like a whiplash. She turned to eye Billy Bolsover with acute suspicion. He must have known of what Indigo was capable. What had possessed him then to open his mouth so strongly in the stallion's favour? Now here he was faced with a vast loss of capital. Was he stupid, or merely improvident? Unless — Persephone's eyes narrowed — could he have done it by design? But to what purpose?

Puzzling over it, she edged out of the crowd who were vociferously laying bets, and made her way back into the house. She did not reappear that evening, but Penelope, her headache apparently better, came down to dine and to join in the impromptu dance got up by the other guests.

As she came off the floor after an energetic gavotte, shaking out the skirts of her pink tiffany overdress in an attempt to release the petticoats which had become entangled about her ankles, Fitzwarren stood in her way.

"The next dance is mine," he said, in a tone that brooked no argument.

Penelope looked up. She had never heard him speak so. Her own voice was sharp as she answered. "Indeed, Fitz, I am engaged with Leopold."

"No, you are not. You are engaged with me."

Her mouth fell open. "Have you run mad?"

Suddenly Fitz's eyes lit and he laughed. "Yes, I have run quite mad. Dear Pen, do dance with me. Else I shall be wretchedly cut up."

At that she gave a crow of laughter and twinkled. "In that case, what can I do but acquiesce? I could not have that on my conscience."

She turned to look about for Leopold to make her excuses. But Fitz took her hand and led her on to the floor.

"I have already sent Leopold about his business. For the next half-hour at least, you are entirely mine."

She looked up at him, and saw behind the smile an expression in his eyes that was very disturbing indeed. A little flutter began in her breast and, as she took up her position next to him for a fast minuet, she was aware of her fingers trembling in his light hold.

As they went down the dance, she stole a glance at him and found his eyes fixed on her, still with that look in them of something more than friendship. Penelope could not tear her own eyes away. They performed the steps of the minuet with automatic grace, turning and twirling each about each, both pairs of eyes split by necessity apart for the barest minimum of instants, only to meet again and stare intently one into the other. They danced in a silence fraught with unspoken dialogue that set Penelope's head in a whirl and her cheeks aglow. For those precious moments, she was certain the answer to her questing heart reposed in Fitz's bosom.

But when the minuet at length concluded, though he bowed over her hand and kissed it, thanking her prettily, he released her into the company of others and did not seek her out again.

CHAPTER EIGHT

Penelope attended the races the next day in a mood of somewhat brittle gaiety that fooled everyone but her twin. Persephone glanced narrowly at her once or twice, resolving to tackle her at the first opportunity. But when Fenwick, Chiddingly's personal groom, came riding hell for leather on to the Heath, he brought tidings that banished all thought of Penelope from her mind.

"Sir Charles! Sir Charles!" called out the groom, as he urged his mount to where Bunbury and his friends were milling about, waiting impatiently for Chiddingly to arrive on the ground with his new stallion.

"What is it, Fenwick?" Sir Charles demanded, riding forward to meet the man.

"My lord — bade me ask you to — to tell the stewards, sir," Fenwick panted. "Indigo cannot run!"

"What?" shouted Billy Bolsover, cantering over. "Does he dare to default?"

"No, sir. Indeed no, sir. But the horse is sick."

"Oh my God," said Bunbury. "Tell Chid to have no fear. I will square the stewards."

"But what ails him?" came Persephone's fearful voice.

Fenwick looked at her, at them all, and it was plain the news was bad.

"Well, man, out with it." Thus Sir Charles Bunbury.

Fenwick licked his dry lips, and then out it came. "Indigo is dying, sir. My lord believes he has been ... poisoned."

"*No!*" Persephone wailed in horror.

Next instant she was streaking away, galloping back towards the track that led to the Buckfastleigh mansion.

Shock held the rest of the company still, staring after her, until Viscount Fitzwarren, his voice curt, took command and galvanised them all into action.

"Get after her, Rossendale! You will not catch her, but at least if she takes a rattling fall, which is not unlikely, you will be at hand."

Lord Rossendale nodded and took off after his cousin. He was soon followed by one or two others, after a quick consultation among them about who should stay to see the race and bring back the result. Sir Charles Bunbury went off to see the stewards and Fitz rode over to tell Penelope what had transpired.

"I must go back," she said with urgency, all thought of her own troubles swept from her mind. "If that horse dies, Seph will be distraught. She will need me."

"Don't fear, Pen. I will escort you immediately. I cannot myself answer for Chid if the worst should happen."

Persephone, meanwhile, riding as if all the devils of hell were after her, and with a prayer in her heart, made such good speed she covered the distance to Buckfastleigh's place in record time. Cantering up to the stables, she slid from the saddle and called the nearest groom to her, giving him the reins and bidding him rub down the animal.

"Where is Lord Chiddingly's horse?"

The groom was staring open-mouthed at the steaming flanks of her own horse, and she had to rap out the question again.

"Lord Chiddingly, dolt! Where is he?"

Coming to himself, the groom directed her to one of the large stable blocks and she ran across and entered it, searching frantically from one stall to the next, calling out.

"Chiddingly! Chiddingly, where are you?"

In the dim light she saw a tall figure step out into the corridor that ran past the stalls.

"Here," said Chiddingly's curt voice, adding as she hurried up to him, "though what you want here is beyond me."

"Where is he?" Persephone asked, heedless of his words and manner.

Then she looked into the stall and gave a distressed cry. In the pool of light cast by a lamp that had been brought in and hung on a peg on the wall, she could see the great black stallion lying on his side in the straw, his velvet head thrown back, huge eyes rolling as he uttered grunts of protest. His breathing was laboured.

Behind him knelt a middle-aged man in a respectable suit and wig, but with a coarse apron over all. He was feeling for the horse's heart and Persephone took in at once that he must be the local horse-doctor.

To one side stood Tidmarsh, his eyes glowering as he stared down at the fallen horse, beating now and then with a clenched fist against the wall. Near him was Siegfried, his sharp cockney features screwed up in grief, tears coursing down his cheeks.

Persephone turned a haggard countenance to the baron. "Is he dying?"

"I fear so. We shall know more when the doctor concludes his examination."

"Oh dear Lord," she whispered.

Chiddingly's anxiety found expression in a sudden gust of rage. "Why you should look so, I am at a loss to understand. This is your fault! You, with your vindictive tongue, abusing him before the rest so that I felt myself compelled to vindicate his powers. Now see what has come of it. Some unscrupulous blackguard has done his worst. Doubtless to stop him running today. Well, he is stopped, do you see? Thanks to you, he may never run again."

Overcome by emotion, he flung away from her to bury his head in his arms against the doorway of the stall.

Persephone gazed at his back, ashen-faced, as the awful truth of his words struck home. Her voice was a thread of sound. "I did not mean it so. Before God, I would kill myself before I offered such harm to a horse!"

Tidmarsh came up to her and put a hand on her arm, saying in a low tone, "He is overwrought, ma'am. He does not mean what he says."

Persephone looked at him, lips trembling. "But it is true. Heaven help me, it is true!" Then she turned to look again at the suffering horse and a sob tore itself from her throat. "Oh, *Indigo!*"

She fell on her knees in the straw and flung her arms across the horse's neck, weeping into his inky black coat. Her golden hair, loosened by her wild ride, spilled from her shoulders to mingle with the flowing dark mane.

Chiddingly, catching Tidmarsh's words, had turned in time to see her throw herself down and stood for a moment, paralysed with horror at the memory of the things he had said. The anguish of her racking sobs wrung his heart.

Leaving his work, the doctor tugged unavailingly at her shaking shoulders. He looked up, annoyance in his face. "Take her away, for heaven's sake! She is impeding my examination."

Chiddingly started forward, and seizing her about the waist, dragged her up. "Persephone, come away!"

She struggled against him, crying out incoherently, lost in grief.

"*Persephone!*" Chiddingly pulled her bodily away from the vicinity of the horse and turned her about.

His tone penetrated. Her hysteria arrested, Persephone stared at him blankly, her lovely face ravaged and tear-stained.

"Persephone, I did not mean it," Chiddingly said, low-voiced and urgent, his fingers gripping her shoulders. "I was beside myself. Of course you are not to blame."

"I am, I am!"

"Nonsense. In this game there is always a risk, so much money as there is at stake. Anyone might have done it, to any horse."

"But I lied! I never thought badly of the horse at all. He is a — a wonderful horse! The greatest horse I have ever seen!"

In spite of all, Chiddingly felt a grin splitting his face. "Oh, Seph, you little fool."

Her tears spilled over again. "If he dies, Chid, I will never forgive myself."

Chiddingly caught her to him and she wept quietly into his chest, while he held her golden head close.

The doctor's voice interrupted them. "My lord!"

The baron let Persephone go and they turned together, anxiety in both their faces.

The doctor was holding the horse's head still and looking closely into his eyes. "My lord," he said, without looking up, "I dare to hope we may be more fortunate than we expected. I think he is only drugged."

"Drugged?" echoed Persephone.

"Pray heaven you may be right," Chiddingly said.

"The eyes have that look, my lord. The breathing, too, is symptomatic. For all his complaints, I cannot find there is any abdominal pain."

"But drugged how?" said Persephone, reviving fast.

"Opium balls, I suspect," the doctor said.

"I have heard of that," Chiddingly said.

155

"Administered in his feed, no doubt," Tidmarsh suggested.

He and Siegfried, who was once more dry-eyed and listening sharply, had moved close to hear the doctor's diagnosis.

"I'd like to get a-hold of him as done that, so I would," the jockey announced. "Darken his daylights, I will, no question. But who done it, I arst yer? Who?"

"Yes. This wants investigation, my lord."

"Find out what you can, Tidmarsh," his master said, and turned once more to the doctor. "Why is Indigo not asleep, then?"

"No, no, opium does not act as a soporific. It is as if he were drunk, my lord. That is why he cannot stand. His groaning is doubtless in protest against hallucinatory dreams."

"Oh, poor Indigo," Persephone cried, her sympathy stirred.

"Yes, but it is a deal better than poison," Chiddingly said. "At least the villains spared us that."

Persephone was suddenly radiant. "Then he will be well again?"

"With care and due attention, yes." The doctor watched with some indulgence as Persephone fell upon her knees once more, this time to pet and croon over the ailing stallion.

Chiddingly frowned. "You are sure?"

"Certain, my lord. If it were poison, he would be sinking fast by now. If you will but look at his ears, you will see how alertly they still twitch."

It was true. Indeed, Indigo's head was even tossing a little. Finally convinced, Chiddingly breathed an enormous sigh of relief and, hearing running footsteps, turned to find a number of new arrivals crowding into the doorway of the stall. Grinning, he relayed the good news in answer to anxious queries, and on the doctor's acid request herded them all out of the improvised sickroom and into the stable yard.

Bestowing upon Indigo one final pat, Persephone rose up and followed them out. As she stood watching Chiddingly fielding the crossfire of question and exclamation, a movement — somehow familiar and yet alien — caught at the periphery of her vision. She looked round. At the edge of the crowd about the baron, a man with a pronounced limp moved round, craning his neck as if to get a better view.

With a sense of dread rising in her breast, Persephone raised her eyes from the legs to stare at the face. Across it ran a scar, livid and white.

For all the relief of Indigo's recovery, the incident had cast a pall of gloom over the company. Those who had left the racecourse felt no inclination to return there, but stood or sat about in forlorn groups, making desultory conversation.

Chiddingly remained nearly all day in attendance at the stables, but he sent Persephone away, greeting with relief the arrival of her sister and Fitz.

"For the Lord's sake, Penelope, persuade her to go inside. She keeps babbling of some man with a scar and is driving me distracted."

On seeing the scarred man, Persephone had plunged incontinently towards the group, bent on alerting the baron, convinced this villain who had shot Papa must be guilty of the wicked trick perpetrated upon Indigo. But by the time she had managed to get to Chiddingly, pushing through the press of persons about him, the man had disappeared.

"But he was here. I saw him!"

"Miss Winsford, you are overwrought. Besides, I cannot think a highwayman would calmly enter these premises."

"He is not a highwayman. At least —"

She stopped, aware of how foolish she must seem claiming to see here a man who had held them up on the open road, but who could not now be found.

Chiddingly made no attempt to conceal his belief that her imagination was playing tricks. But she had seen him! Unable to rest, and fearful for the horse's safety, she ran back to the stall to check on him and embarked on a search of every nook and cranny to make sure the man had not concealed himself preparatory to committing another assault upon Indigo.

Only when she had been assured not merely by Chiddingly, but also by both Tidmarsh and the doctor, that someone would remain with the stallion at all times, did Penelope succeed in dragging her off to their bedchamber to change her soiled garments and rearrange her disordered locks.

"The villain saw me, of course, and knew I must recognise him," she said, as Penelope relentlessly dragged a comb through her tangled tresses. "You may be sure he has made himself scarce." She shook her head in frustration. "If only I could recall where I had seen him before that hold-up."

"Drat you, Seph, keep still! Unless you wish me to fetch Mama to you."

This threat made her twin groan, but she submitted to her sister's ministrations and presently emerged from the bedchamber freshly clad in a gown of chintz cotton with her hair once more frizzed and curling down her back in ringlets.

In this guise she appeared with the remainder of the guests in the drawing-room before dinner only to hear the startling news that Magnet — who, without Indigo to challenge him, had been expected to walk away with the new sweepstake — had lost the race.

"Most astounding thing I ever saw," said Clermont who, with a horse running, had stayed to see the race. "There was

Magnet, way out in front, with little more than half a mile to the post. When up sweeps Ganymede — eight years old if he's a day — and damme if he don't nick the prize from under Magnet's champion nose."

"Ganymede? Sir John Lade's entry?" exclaimed Persephone, who had studied the form of the opposition. "But he was a rank outsider."

"Indeed he was. Johnny only entered him for a lark. To please his Letty, I imagine, for Ganymede is her nag."

"What, Letty's own horse won the race?" Persephone said, before she could stop herself.

But Clermont, suddenly recalling his company, was flushing vividly. "I beg your pardon, ma'am."

Persephone, brought to an abrupt realisation that her unruly tongue had betrayed her, was also blushing. She could only hope the general embarrassment was at Clermont's slip rather than her own.

Clermont, meanwhile, to cover his confusion, had hurried on. "You might think Billy would be deuced upset over it. But not a bit of it. Well, you know Billy."

He laughed, glancing at Egremont, who nodded, grinning.

"Most sporting fellow I know, Billy. Would have been the same if Indigo had run and won." He looked at Persephone. "How is he, Miss Winsford? Gather you were the only one allowed in the stables."

"Allowed?" exclaimed a jovial voice from behind them. "Couldn't keep her out, they tell me. Ain't that right, Miss Winsford?"

Persephone stared down into the chubby, smiling features of Billy Bolsover and it was as if something kicked her in the stomach as her memory jolted, flashing a picture into her mind: she and Letty under the trees at Epsom, looking at three men. Goole, Scarface and Bolsover!

Some instinct urged her to tread with care. There was danger here, great danger.

"I was very concerned for the horse, yes."

"A masterly understatement," came the amused tones of Baron Chiddingly.

Persephone turned, but she was spared having to reply by the eagerness with which his racing cronies fell upon him, demanding news of Indigo.

"He is, I thank God, on the high road to recovery."

"Excellent, excellent," Bolsover cried happily. Then his baby-blue eyes clouded. "But it's a bad business, Chid."

"It happens."

"Damme, you are mighty cool over it, Chid," Clermont said.

"I am not in the least cool over it. Believe me, if and when I find those responsible, I shall pursue them to the uttermost limits of the law."

"And beyond, I dare say," said Billy, smiling again. "Can't say I blame you, Chid. Out and out villains. You keep your eye on that nag of yours. Haven't given up on our race, old fellow. We'll set it all up again as soon as Indigo is fit to go."

Persephone gazed at him in some awe. How could he talk so? Behave with such seeming solicitude, when all the time … or was she mistaken?

"You are surely not willing to risk another throw," she said, "after today."

Billy's joviality remained unimpaired. "Fluke, ma'am. Sheer fluke."

"But Ganymede, Billy," Chiddingly teased. "Ganymede, of all things."

"I know, I know," Bolsover said, shaking a rueful head, but laughing still. "I shall never live it down."

His friends laughed with him, but, as the gong sounded for dinner and they began to move away, Persephone, still covertly watching him, saw a subtle change come over the chubby countenance. The corners of his little mouth turned down in a petulant pout, and slicing into Chiddingly's back came a shaft from his baby-blue eyes that was positively malevolent.

Next instant, as Clermont glanced over his shoulder with a jovial remark, the look was gone and he was once again the jolly little good-natured friend everyone liked.

For Persephone, however, it was enough. She was not mistaken. But how to convince Chiddingly? Useless to approach him in company, and she could not try to draw him apart without attracting undesirable attention.

Over dinner she pondered her problem, and decided there was but one solution.

Accordingly, she rose very early the next morning, knowing Chiddingly must go to check on Indigo, if nothing else. Equally, they were likely to be the only two guests up at such an hour. But when she arrived at the stables, she found only the trainer and Siegfried in attendance.

"His lordship has been here, ma'am," Tidmarsh disclosed, "but he has gone out riding."

"Better still. Do me the favour of requesting a groom to saddle a horse for me."

"Certainly, ma'am. But you will not find Lord Buckfastleigh's lads equal to your ability. I will ask his lordship's groom to accompany you."

"No, I want no one."

"But —"

"I thank you, Tidmarsh, but I am quite capable of finding his lordship for myself."

"Yes, of course. He is still in the grounds. But surely —"

"I am in a hurry. Don't trouble. I will find a groom myself to saddle a horse."

Then she stalked out, leaving Tidmarsh and the jockey to gape at each other.

"Secret meetings, by gawd," Siegfried said, grinning.

"Don't be a nodcock."

"I ain't neither. I got more sense in me cockloft than wot you has, you Tidmarsh. I doesn't go a-courting trouble with Clatterbridge's daughter."

"You keep your mouth shut. Whatever understanding I have with Cherry —"

"Understanding, is it? A tumble in the hayloft, more like."

"No! Anyway, I'm going to marry her in a year or two."

"Sooner nor that, if Clatterbridge gets wind o' your doings."

"He had better not," Tidmarsh said, raising a threatening fist.

"Keep your hair on, Tidmarsh, keep your hair on. I won't say nothing. But we'd best go and make sure no one else don't know about his lordship and this here gentry mort a-riding about all alone."

This advice seemed sound to Tidmarsh and they hurried out to the stable yard. They were too late. The grooms had been shocked to learn that the lady — who was already long gone — had not only wanted no escort, but had also been so heedless as to ask all about the stable yard which way the baron had taken. As a result, talk of clandestine assignations was already rife among the domestic staff. From the servants' hall to the ears of the gentry above was, as Tidmarsh well knew, but a whisper away.

What to do, Tidmarsh did not know. But he could not stand by and do nothing, that was certain. With a forlorn hope of averting disaster, he went off to find a footman to take a message to Viscount Fitzwarren.

Persephone, intent on her mission, was sublimely unconscious of the storm brewing behind her. She made her way through the grounds to the adjoining park where, a groom had surmised, she would find Chiddingly.

The close trees of the grounds broke out into acres of rolling parkland and after a moment or two of hard riding, she spied a lone figure cantering some distance away. Putting her horse at the gallop, she made for it, and as she neared saw him stop, awaiting her approach. But when she was close enough to see his face, she was irritated to find there a grim scowl.

"In the devil's name, don't ring a peal over me," she called out. "I am here for a sufficient purpose."

"Persephone, are you insane?" he burst out, unheeding. "Where is your groom? You must go back at once."

"Yes, yes, I will do so presently," she said, her need too urgent to waste time in taking umbrage.

"You will do so this instant."

"I cannot. Chiddingly, for heaven's sake, I must talk to you." She read further argument in his eye and hurried on. "It is about Indigo."

Chiddingly's face changed. "He is not worse?"

"No, no, he is well. At least, I have not seen him properly, but Tidmarsh would have said so if anything had been amiss."

"Then what in Hades do you mean?"

"I know who drugged him!"

"How can you possibly do so? If Tidmarsh has been able to glean no information, how should you? Why in the world could it not wait for my return? You are the most rashly behaved —"

"If you will but listen!"

"Very well. But make it fast."

"I came out here because I dare not voice my suspicions where we may be overheard. Besides, on the Heath it would be impossible to find two minutes to converse with you alone."

He could scarcely argue with her logic, but as he was visibly chafing she carried on, speaking quickly.

"I know you will laugh me out of court, but I have every reason to believe the perpetrator of this deed — among others which I shall relate — is none other than Billy Bolsover."

Chiddingly stared. "Billy?" A short laugh escaped him. "Now I know you are raving."

"I knew you would say so. Laugh if you choose, but you will not do so when I have told you all."

"You may tell me on the way," he said, giving his horse a nudge. "For you are going back this moment, Miss Persephone Winsford, and I shall take you."

"You need not speak to me as if I were a child," she threw at him, but she turned her horse to trot beside his.

"When you cease to conduct yourself as if you were not far removed from that state, I shall not do so."

"*Ooloo*! I don't know why I trouble myself on your behalf. You are not in the least deserving of it."

He felt a twinge of conscience. Turning to her, he smiled. "Very true. I beg your pardon. By all means, let me hear more of your theories, fantastic though they may be."

"Well, they are fantastic," Persephone said, mollified, "but I am convinced they are true."

"I am all attention."

164

She was aware he was laughing at her, but she was far too keen to unburden her mind to care. "I did not tell you at the time, but when Letty and I were at Epsom we saw Bolsover there. I did not know then that it was he, but Letty said so and later I recognised him. He was with Goole and another man."

"Goole!" The indulgent look was wiped off Chiddingly's face. "Why did you not mention this before?"

"I had not thought of it. Besides, it is not Goole but Bolsover you have to fear."

"Nonsense. To suspect poor Billy when there is Goole staring you in the face! By thunder, I shall kill him for this!"

"What was *poor Billy* doing there, then? If he is so innocent, how does it come about he must needs beg to see your horse when he has already witnessed precisely what everyone else is anxious to know?"

Struck, Chiddingly stared at her, perplexity in his features.

"You see, now? He forced the bets, playing on our quarrel, which meant he stood to gain more by Indigo's default. Moreover, he had offered to buy Indigo to boot."

"I thought at the time he was acting for Goole. It may still be so."

"But Goole is not here."

"Of course he is. I have seen him with my own eyes."

"I mean he is not at Buckfastleigh," Persephone said with impatience.

"What is that to the purpose? He could have sent over an agent. What could be simpler? There are a score of stable hands here. Who is to notice one more?"

"Oh, I grant you that. But you have not yet heard it all."

"Go on."

"There was another man with them. A groom, as I thought. He had a limp, and an unfortunate scar across his face that gave him a sinister look. Justified, as it chances, for that self-same man shot Papa in that holdup, and —"

"The man you claimed to see in the stables!"

"Exactly so. I could not recall at first where I had seen him. But then, when Bolsover appeared, it all came back to me."

"But — heavens, Miss Winsford, it is fantastic!"

"I told you it was."

They were almost back among the trees and he had unconsciously brought his mount to a halt. He sat staring before him, evidently turning it over in his mind.

"I cannot credit it," he said at length. "Of Goole, yes, but not Billy. How are you to know this man has to do with Billy? He had as well be Goole's associate."

"No, for it was Bolsover who knew the details of our journey. He made a point of finding them out. What could be easier than to bribe the smith and a groom to effect a delay in our journey? You may certainly incriminate Goole, but you cannot exonerate your Billy."

"I don't believe it. There must be some mistake."

"There is no mistake!"

What was the matter with the man? Could not he see how it all fitted together?

"Even if it were so," he went on, "what do you expect me to do about it?"

"Why, call him to account, of course."

Chiddingly gave a short laugh. "Call Billy out? Ridiculous. In any event, even were it true, if I confront him with it, he has only to deny it. Where is your proof?"

Persephone wrinkled her brow over this. "That is difficult. But there is more. He is certainly in want of money, for he asked Papa's permission to propose to us."

"What, both?"

"Yes, both. Or rather, either. He did not care which. Papa was furious. So, you see, there is every reason to suspect him."

"Oh no, nonsense. It is all surmise, Miss Winsford. You may as well accuse myself or Fitz."

"No. There is something about Billy. Oh, I don't expect you to see it. But I am a stranger here, and coming among you I can perhaps see differently what you take for granted."

Chiddingly frowned. "But his motive? Do you say it was all for money? A hold-up, drugging a horse? It does not make sense."

"Does it make more sense for Goole to have done these things? Where is his motive?"

"There is no difficulty in that," said the baron, his cheeks darkening.

"Fudge, you are prejudiced. I can see Bolsover's motive clearly enough, and —" She stopped, striking her hands together. "Of course! I see how ready a solution there may be. You need not call him out, nor trouble to get proof."

"A ready solution? Enlighten me, I beg."

"If our purpose is to keep Indigo safe, then I have only to marry him after all. He will then have sufficient money to —"

"Marry Billy?" Chiddingly interrupted in a stunned tone. "You will do no such thing!"

"Why should I not?"

"Because I say so!"

"*You* say so?" A tide of angry red flooded her cheeks. "How dare you? Who are you to tell me whom I must or must not marry? You take too much upon yourself, my lord!"

"It is time and past someone told you what to do. You are by far too hot at hand."

"And you are an ungrateful, insolent jack-at-warts! I have had my fill of your bullying and hectoring ways."

"Don't call me a bully, you vixen! You are by far more the bully than I, for a more quarrelsome wretch I have never encountered."

"No, for no one has dared stand up to you before you — you arrogant, top-lofty, overbearing ruffian!"

"Oh, this is insupportable!" Chiddingly cried.

"Keep away from me!" Persephone yelled, bringing her whip hand about. The lash flew between them, flicking his cheek.

"Devil take you!" He winced and seized the lash, jerking it to get the whip out of her hand.

But Persephone's grip was so tight that instead she was dragged towards him. The horses clashed together and, losing balance, Persephone slipped from the saddle and disappeared between the horses' shifting flanks to the ground.

"Oh, sweet heaven!"

Chiddingly eased his mount sideways, leaping from the saddle to the rescue.

Persephone, however, was already scrambling out of the way to safety. Her mount, disturbed by all the excitement, ran off a little way into the shelter of the trees.

Chiddingly bent down to help Persephone up and received a box on the ear for his pains.

"Dolt! Imbecile!" she raged, rising unsteadily to her feet. "Look what you've done!"

Chiddingly, his head ringing, lost his temper. "You abominable little shrew!"

"Go to the devil!" she returned shrilly, hitting out as he seized her arm, trying to turn her around.

Lifting her skirts, Persephone thrust a leg behind his knee and shoved with all her might. Chiddingly fell his length to the turf, pulling her with him in a tangle of legs and the heavy cloth of her habit.

The sound of rending mingled with coarse oaths and muffled curses as the two bodies groped for purchase on the ground, and writhed with each other for supremacy.

"I — hate — you," panted Persephone, pummelling at him with her fists.

"She-devil! Vixen!"

Exerting his superior strength, Chiddingly rolled over, trying to seize control, but Persephone fought like a tigress, kicking and biting. Together they rolled on the muddy turf, hurling abuse at each other.

At last sheer exhaustion held both momentarily still, chests heaving with effort, Persephone glaring up into Chiddingly's snarling face above her.

Two pairs of eyes met in hectic hostility, and held.

There was an instant of mutual recognition of an urgent need. Then, with a violence that seemed natural to them both, their lips found each other out.

CHAPTER NINE

Fire enveloped Persephone from head to foot. Hungrily, she dragged with her lips at the mouth fastened to her own and felt the response down the length of her body.

Chiddingly grasped her flesh, powerful arms clutching her closely to him. Her own grip about his back and shoulders was no less tight, and she moaned in her throat as the flame of his passion engulfed her. He came up for air and opened his eyes to see her lovely face wanton with naked desire.

"Oh, *Persephone*," he groaned, and buried his lips in her neck.

She shivered at their touch, and her fingers came up to grasp his face and turn it back, seeking his lips once more, and, as if their lives depended upon it, their mouths clung together.

Persephone felt as if she were drowning, and the sensation intensified as his hand closed over the mound of her breast. A wash of agonising heat swept through her loins and she moaned. Groaning, Chiddingly moved his hand down to drag at her disordered habit, tugging as instinct urged him to seek her naked flesh. At the first tingling touch, Persephone's violent reaction startled her into awareness. Her eyes flew open.

"No, Chid! *Salla*! No!"

His blue eyes met hers with fierce passion. Then he, too, came to his senses.

"In the name of Satan!" Releasing her, he rolled away and sprang up. Reaching down, he seized her hands and dragged her to her feet, letting go again immediately as though he could not trust himself to touch her.

They stood apart, panting, he trembling violently, she dizzy with weakness and hardly able to stand, but their eyes still locked together.

"Savage," she said, her voice ragged. "Barbarian."

"There is blood on your lip," he said on a husky note.

They stared at each other. Then Persephone sprang at him, flinging her arms about his neck, her mouth seeking thirstily for his again. For a moment, he responded with renewed vigour, crushing her against his chest, his lips hard on hers.

Then, with an oath, he wrenched his head away, tugging her arms from about his neck, thrusting her hands away and holding her off.

"*No*, Seph! Sweet heaven, you'd fling away your chastity as easily as your life, you madcap fool. Don't you know what you have done?"

"What I have done? I suppose you had nothing to do with it?"

He looked about and saw the horses were gone. He groaned, releasing her hands. "Now we are in the suds. Fiend seize you, woman, I wish we had never met!"

"You cannot wish it more heartily than I!"

To her indignant fury, he burst out laughing. "In the predicament in which we find ourselves, my girl, that is likely to prove highly problematical."

"Fudge. If I can walk, so too can you."

Without further ado, she picked up her skirts and stepped out boldly. Chiddingly watched her for a moment, a twisted smile creasing his mouth as he realised, with a stab of pity, that she had not yet a notion of how matters stood. The thought of how she would react when she did realise it made him shudder, jerking him into action. As he took long strides to catch up with her, he reflected that if his own appearance in any way resembled hers, their business would even more urgently require despatch.

They were indeed a sorry-looking pair as they came within sight of the stables. Thoroughly dishevelled, muddied and torn, as if they had both taken a toss in a midden, they walked several feet apart, in silence, towards the stable yard and saw Fitzwarren coming out to meet them.

In spite of Tidmarsh's urgent summons, Fitz had been powerless to stop the rapid spread of talk that had already set the house in uproar. Events had marched swiftly, the whisper sweeping like wildfire through the echelons of rank. Already the ladies Buckfastleigh and Rossendale had been in heavy conference. The latter was even now known to be closeted with the rest of her sister's family, while other guests flitted between each other's chambers, gathering the latest details.

"Your horses came in a bare five minutes since," Fitz called by way of greeting. "I was just about to set off myself to find you."

"You had better have done so," Chiddingly said.

His friend eyed his person with unconcealed dismay. "I think so indeed."

Chiddingly saw the rueful look in Fitz's face. "Is it bad?"

"The worst. I cannot think your present appearance will improve matters. You have created a most resounding scandal, the pair of you."

Persephone stopped dead in her tracks and turned to stare at him. "Scandal? But no one knows —"

She broke off in consternation as her eye caught the stares coming from the yard about her. Stable boys, grooms and footmen in livery leered behind their hands, sniggered or whispered as they looked. The grey orbs flew back to flick first at Fitz, then at Chiddingly as the enormity of her position came home to her. Her lip trembled for an instant and then pride came to her rescue.

"To hell with them all!" she flashed, and, golden head high, she marched away to enter the house by the side door.

Chiddingly watched her go, a curious smile in his eyes. "She had no idea, my poor Seph."

Fitz looked at him. "She has all my sympathy. You, too. What will you do, Chid?"

Chiddingly turned his head. "Do I have a choice?"

Persephone, storming up the stairs, was pounced on by her mother in the upper hallway.

"*Persephone*! In here, this instant!"

Dragged into the little sitting-room that had been set aside for the nabob's use, and which adjoined her parents' bedchamber, Persephone found herself the cynosure of four pairs of eyes. Those of Lady Rossendale and her mother were accusing, while her father and Penelope exhibited so much sympathy they almost overset her at once.

"Do you have any idea what has been going on here?" her mother was saying in a furiously lowered tone.

"The whole house has been awakened," announced her aunt Rossendale dramatically.

"Pooh, nonsense," said the nabob testily, glancing at his sister-in-law with dislike. He was considerably recovered, his injured arm reposing in a sling. But although he was permitted to sit up, as now, in an armchair by the window, the doctor had advised him strongly not yet to leave his room. He stretched out his good hand to Persephone. "Come here, my love."

But Persephone remained where she was, ramrod straight, defiant, determined to fight the onslaught of her doom to the last ditch. "Do not fear for me, Papa. I will do very well."

"You will not do very well," Lady Rossendale said. "You will do excessively badly. The house is buzzing with talk, bandying your name, coupling it with Chiddingly as if you were any common harlot."

"Harriet!" gasped Clarissa.

"I knew how it would be at the outset with you, Persephone. For a more unruly, hoydenish —"

"Harriet, that will do," Mrs Winsford said. "Not but what you are in the right of it." She suddenly took in the condition of her daughter's clothing. "For the love of heaven, what in the world have you been about?"

"Mercy on us, child," cried her aunt, "you look as if you had been rolling on the ground!"

Persephone's cheeks burned and she bit her lip, remembering what had occurred when she had been doing exactly that. The two elder ladies, noting these marks of discomfiture, exchanged significant and equally horrified glances.

"So it is true!" Lady Rossendale clutched at her heart. "Upon my word, I am like to suffer a spasm! Lord have mercy! Where are my smelling salts?"

"Oh, Seph, no," wailed her mother. "Never say so! Oh, Archie, Archie, what are we to do?"

"Be silent, Clarissa! I'll tell you what we are to do. Get the poor child fit to be seen again. Pen, take her."

Penelope hurried forward. "Come, dearest."

Clasping her arm about her sister's shoulders, she led her from the room. She hustled her down the corridor to their joint bedchamber and pushed her in. Persephone just stood there and Penelope saw she was shaking.

"Seph, dearest, don't! Let me help you to change."

Unresisting, Persephone allowed herself to be helped off with her muddied habit, and made no protest when her sister brought her to the basin and ewer and instructed her to wash the dirt from her face and hands. But when she was clad in a fresh shift with Penelope tying the laces of her bodice for her, she suddenly threw her hands over her face and sighed wretchedly.

Penelope thrust her down on to the dressing stool. "What happened, dearest Seph? Come, tell me. You will feel better when you have made a clean breast of it."

Her twin raised haggard eyes to her face. "I meant only good, I swear. I never thought — it did not even cross my mind. Oh, Pen, I have made wretched work of it. And Chiddingly —"

"What of him, Seph?"

"He — he knew all the time. He warned me at the outset. He told me to go back. But I would not listen, and now —" She drew a breath. "Well, I cannot blame him. I brought it on myself. If I am ruined, so be it."

Penelope said no more, having a very fair idea of what her sister's fate would be. Ruin was unlikely, if her mama had anything to say to it.

She was quite right. At that very moment, Mrs Winsford was busy enumerating all the ills that would befall the family if Archie did not at once do something about it. "Harriet has already been given to understand there can be no compromise. We are not in Bombay now, Archie."

"No, indeed," agreed her sister. "You will not find the accommodating morality of the colonies here, I am happy to say. The *beau monde* —"

"To the deuce with your *beau monde*! I will not have my little Seph coerced."

"There is no question of coercion, Archibald. There is, very simply, no other way. If, that is, you all of you wish to be received in society. I say nothing of the fact the whole affair will redound unpleasantly on *my* family. But if you are determined to plunge us all into a sordid scandal, I suppose I must learn to bear with it."

"You see, Archie?" Clarissa wrung her hands. "There is nothing for it. You will have to see Chiddingly."

But at this moment there was a knock at the door and Baron Chiddingly himself entered the room. He had changed his clothes, and it might have been the dark sobriety of his blue coat that affected his pallor. However it was, he was certainly paler than usual, but his stern features were set in uncompromising lines. He bowed to the ladies, but addressed himself to the nabob.

"Good morning, sir. I believe we have some urgent business to discuss. You are, I think, the most proper person with whom to settle this affair."

Archie Winsford shot him that unnerving stare from under his brows, but Chiddingly was not noticeably discomfited. "Ha! Very well, sir, very well. My lady, and Clarissa, leave us, if you please."

Lady Rossendale, approval writ large upon her countenance, made a majestic exit. Mrs Winsford, eyeing the baron rather doubtfully, hesitated.

"Clarissa!"

"Yes, Archie, I am going." She drifted towards the door with her eyes still on Chiddingly. "I will fetch Seph."

"Yes, do so."

Chiddingly civilly held the door for Mrs Winsford and closed it behind her. Then he turned to the nabob. "Sir, there is little for me to say. I am fully aware of the compromising nature of this morning's occurrence, and I am … willing to make reparation."

"Pooh, sir!" The nabob rose a trifle unsteadily from his chair. "Don't come that high-flown language to me, young feller, for I won't stand for it. You people and your high *ton*, your precious *beau monde*! I was a victim of it myself all those years ago. Top-lofty lot of fribbles! What a piece of work it is."

Chiddingly could not forbear a smile. "Quite so, sir. It is unfortunately the way of our world, however, and if we wish to survive in it we must abide by its rules."

"What the deuce possessed you to break 'em, then, eh? Eh?"

"Useless, I suppose, to tell you I did not do so?"

"Ha! Do you take me for a nincompoop, sir? I know my daughter well enough." He squared up to Chiddingly, despite the latter's superior height, staring ferociously up into his face. "But let no man dare tell me she had any mind to wanton dalliance."

"Good Lord, no, sir. Persephone is — Miss Winsford is all innocence. And I swear to you I did not take advantage of her."

There was no need, he thought, to take the nabob entirely into his confidence on that subject. It was a matter between himself and Persephone, and the business of no one else.

"Ha! Very well, then," Archie said, visibly mollified.

His outburst appeared to have tired him, for he staggered slightly. Chiddingly slid a hand under his elbow. "You are unwell still, sir. Allow me to assist you."

"Don't fuss, don't fuss!" But Archie allowed the younger man to help him back to his chair. Then he stared up at Chiddingly and sighed gustily. "You be good to her, hey? My little Seph."

Noting his moist eyes, Chiddingly opted for frankness. "Sir, I will not deceive you. It is not what either of us bargained for, and the nature of our relationship has been somewhat abrasive. But I will undertake to care for your daughter as I would any of my horses." He saw a frown in the nabob's eye, and smiled. "If I tell you that on the subject of horseflesh your Seph and I are at one, you may perhaps better understand me."

A short bark of laughter was surprised out of the elder man. "Ha! Well, sir, you seem to have some brains in your head, I'll say that for you. You've given me your word and I accept it. We'll say no more."

There was time for no more for Mrs Winsford re-entered the room then, accompanied by both her daughters, but not, as both gentlemen were relieved to see, by her sister Rossendale, who had gone off to spread the glad news.

It was at once evident that, though Penelope had refrained from telling Persephone what was in the wind, Mrs Winsford had not been similarly reticent. The storm signs were visible, her cheeks flying colour, grey eyes glittering.

Notwithstanding these danger signals, Chiddingly bowed and spoke in formal tones. "Miss Winsford, your father and I have reached the same conclusion. I therefore have the honour to request your hand in marriage."

Persephone tossed her head. "I wish you will not be so absurd. Honour, indeed! If you are stupid enough to engage in this ridiculous charade, I am not. I will not be forced into an engagement just to save face."

"Miss Winsford," Chiddingly said, as if addressing an idiot, "we are not speaking of an engagement to save face. We must and will be married."

"How will that serve? If everyone knows — or at least thinks they know — of our activities, how is marriage going to change their opinion?"

"Don't be stupid, Seph," her mother said. "Within marriage such things are perfectly acceptable."

"That is utter hypocrisy."

"Very true," Chiddingly said. "Unfortunately, it is the code by which we live."

"But it can't be needful!" Her bravado collapsed into plaintive lament. "I won't do it! I won't, I won't."

"You have no option," he said. "Nor, I may add, have I."

That arrested her. Her lip trembled as she stared at him. "But you don't — I don't —"

"Want to marry me," he finished. "Yes, that is understood."

"It is as I told you, Seph," Clarissa said. "Lady Buckfastleigh has made it very clear we will not otherwise be welcome in her house."

Persephone turned to her. "She could not be so uncivil as to ask us to leave."

"Yes, she could," said Chiddingly. "And she would. Make no mistake about that."

"You see, Seph. It is not only you who will suffer. We shall all of us be disgraced. Pen, too. You cannot want that, Seph. I know you cannot."

"No, indeed." Persephone looked across at her sister, half started towards her, and stopped. "Pen — it was you he wanted. Could we not say it was you all the time? Who is to tell the difference? You could do it, Pen."

"I would, dearest, only everyone knows it was you on account of your horsemanship. They would never believe us."

It was true, as Persephone was forced to acknowledge.

"Otherwise," Penelope said, with a glance at Chiddingly's uncompromising countenance that clearly spoke her relief, "I would have been glad to sacrifice myself."

"I thank you," Chiddingly said.

Persephone turned to her father on a last, bleak note of hope. "Papa, must I?"

Archie, looking very glum, nodded. "Sorry to say, but they are right, my love. It is a censorious world. Your engagement will have to be announced before you make another appearance or not a soul will receive you. Can't have all these starched-up tabbies giving my little peas the cut direct."

Persephone drew a shuddering breath. "No, indeed."

Then she turned to Chiddingly and came towards him, walking like a mechanical doll. Her eyes were pools of deep misery. A sharp stabbing pain twisted in Chiddingly's breast.

She held out a hand that quivered pitiably. But her husky voice was steady as a rock. "Here is your filly, Chiddingly. At least she will bring you your gold."

At the end of race week, Persephone, in company with her family, made a subdued return to town. All her pleasure in the excursion had been destroyed.

The day of her fall from grace, followed by reinstatement in society's august eyes as the promised wife of Baron Chiddingly, she had not even ridden on horseback to Newmarket Heath. She had not wanted to make any appearance at all, and none of her mother's representations would have made her relent. But her prospective husband managed to change her mind with one sardonic observation.

"Very well, remain here — that is, if you wish the world to know you are ashamed."

As Chiddingly had confidently anticipated, Persephone's eyes rolled and she tossed her head, for all the world like one of the mettlesome horses she so adored.

"Ashamed? I am not in the least ashamed, and they may all of them go to the devil!"

But, for all her bravado, she had no heart for the company of Chiddingly's racing cronies, and chose instead to accompany her sister in Lady Buckfastleigh's carriage. She was soon regretting this decision, however, for trapped in the carriage she could not escape those who came up to greet the twins, and was obliged to endure a shower of congratulation. Since she could not doubt all these apparent well-wishers must be perfectly aware of the circumstances which had led to her engagement, she received their felicitations in tight-lipped silence.

Chiddingly, who, for the sake of appearances, had remained in close attendance by the carriage, did not long tolerate this intransigent attitude. Waiting only for a convenient interval between visitors, he stepped up to the carriage.

"Persephone, if you do not try at least for an appearance of complaisance," he muttered, "you will, I promise you, presently have good cause to regret it."

As the instant flame in her eyes scorched him, he strode away before Persephone had a chance to utter a word. He left her fuming, Penelope beside her gazing open-mouthed after his retreating form.

"*Kuta*!" Persephone flung after him, but in an under-voice. "How I hate him!"

Penelope seized her hand and held it tightly. "Dearest, I had no notion. Oh, Seph, it is dreadful."

"Of course it is dreadful," her twin said, but more in anger than horror. "Oh, I will teach him to talk to me thus. Only wait until we are married! I will show him."

Penelope stared at her wonderingly. "But — but — are you not afraid of what he may do?"

"Afraid of Chiddingly? I?"

"He was so fierce," shuddered her sister.

"So am I fierce! He shall not get the better of me."

Penelope could only gaze at her, dumbfounded. "You were so desperate to avoid wedding him. You said you hated him."

"So I do. He is a loathsome barbarian. Naturally I don't want to wed him. Who would? But even though I am forced to have the cur to husband, you may be sure I shall never submit to his autocratic rule."

"Oh dear," Penelope said, quite appalled by the vision of domestic strife that filled her mind.

Looking rather wildly about her, she became aware that Fitzwarren was walking towards the carriage, in company with a handsome young man whose plump figure, encased in the tight-fitting breeches of present fashion, showed an incipient tendency to corpulence. His comely countenance, for all its youth, already bore the marks of dissipation.

These defects notwithstanding, Penelope gave a squeak of delight and clutched her sister's arm. "Oh, heavens! See whom Fitz has got with him? Look, he is bringing him over here!"

Persephone glanced round. "What is the matter, Pen?"

"It is the prince, Seph! For the Lord's sake, smile! What is more, if you dare to say one word out of place, I shall never speak to you again."

An introduction to the Prince of Wales could not compete with the iniquities of Chiddingly in Persephone's order of significances. But it was momentarily diverting. She knew the prince to be a keen tulip of the turf, but by all accounts a man of indifferent ability in picking a horse. But the prince was not interested in talking of horseflesh.

"At last I have the good fortune to meet you," young George said expansively. "I have heard so much of the nabob's *little peas* but I must tell you, Fitz, report does not in the least do them justice. By the lord Harry, you take my breath away."

"Not noticeably," Persephone murmured, and received a punitive dig in the ribs from her twin's elbow.

"We are flattered, sir," Penelope cut in. "And honoured by your grace's condescension."

"Pooh, nonsense!" said the prince, as if borrowing from the nabob's vocabulary. "I wish you will both come down from there and walk with me a little way. I can imagine no greater felicity than having one such delicious bloom upon each arm."

Since this was tantamount to a royal command, even Persephone could not commit the solecism of refusing. Accordingly, the twins found themselves strolling arm in arm with the genial prince, who declared himself baffled indeed to find the same face cropping up either side of him, adding merrily, "Upon my word, you have set my head in a whirl!" He contrived at the same time to slip his arms about their slim waists, indelicate fingers squeezing the soft flesh they encountered there.

This liberty brought the militant sparkle to Persephone's eyes and a blush to Penelope's cheek, but neither of them had any idea how to extricate themselves without discourtesy. Fitz, however, who knew his prince, was on the watch for just such an occurrence, and procured their release by reminding young Florizel his horse was about to run in the next race.

"By Jove, is it time already? I declare, I have been so agreeably entertained that had it been the passage of an hour I would not have noticed."

Bestowing with his pudgy hands one last squeeze on the neat waists, he released the twins and said his farewells.

"I am minded to snatch a kiss," he said, lowering his voice conspiratorially and winking, "but I see old Chid's jealous eye upon me. I should hate the fortunate dog to blow a hole through me. Ha, ha! No idea which of you is promised to the old fellow, you see."

The twins could only be thankful, though Penelope told Fitz she found the prince excessively droll. They were alone, for Persephone, unable to disdain any interest in the forthcoming race, had returned to the carriage to obtain a better view.

"Is he always so amorous?"

"If he can but get his hands on a pretty woman, I am bound to say, yes, he is," Fitz said. "I confess I was in dread your sister would send him to the rightabout."

"So was I. Especially as she had been in a furious temper just before you came up."

Fitz lifted an eyebrow. "She is taking it badly, then?"

"Badly? I think she is mad! Moreover, I am sorry to say this of a friend of yours, Fitz, but Chiddingly is a brute. I have a very lively fear he may beat her when they are married."

"I suspect your sister will give as good as she gets," Fitz said, a laugh in his voice.

"Yes, that is what she threatens. I dread to think of what sort of a life they will have together."

Fitz looked down at her with a good deal of amusement in his face. "It is as well he abandoned his pursuit of you, then."

Penelope shuddered. "Don't mention such a thing! Not that I would have married him, even when I had no idea of what a vile temper he has."

"Poor Chid. Hoist with his own petard. Yet I dare to hope they will both come about."

Penelope turned anxious eyes on him. "Do you think so indeed? Seph says she hates him. There is such venom in her when she speaks of him that I cannot but fear for her future."

Fitz reached for her fingers and lifted them to his lips. "Dear Pen, you are such an innocent. I beg you will not trouble your gentle heart unduly. I am certain there is no need, my love."

"If only I could be sure of —" She broke off, and her fingers quivered, her eyes flying to his. "What did you call me?"

He reddened. "Forgive me. A — er — familiarity between friends merely. It — it slipped out."

Bowing, he released her fingers and turned away, greeting with obvious relief the approach of Leopold to claim her attention.

Persephone was not the only one to view her approaching nuptials with concern. Mrs Cordelia Harraton, whose first intimation of events was received through the medium of the court notices in the newspaper, was shocked to discover her brother had offered for hoydenish Persephone rather than gentle Penelope. She descended upon his lodgings in a mood of righteous indignation.

"A fine sister-in-law you seek to saddle me with, I declare."

Chiddingly bristled. "Oh, indeed? I was under the impression it was you who proposed the match to me in the first place."

Mrs Harraton swept up and down the small parlour, her cherry-red petticoats rustling about her. "I know I did so. But I did not know then that twins were in question. When I realised how their fortune was divided, I could not think it large enough to tempt you."

"You realised it?" Chiddingly set down his tankard of ale and rose from his chair. "Then why in Hades could you not have told me?"

"Good heavens!" She came to a halt to stare at him. "Do you tell me, Christopher, that you have offered for this Persephone in the hope of gaining a fortune?"

His cheeks darkened and his jaw tightened. "So you have not yet visited with your friend Lady Alice."

Cordelia gazed at him in the liveliest astonishment. "No, I have not. What in the world are you talking of?"

"You will know soon enough."

"For the Lord's sake, Christopher, do you wish me to have the vapours? What has occurred?"

His blue eyes were sombre. "Well, I suppose you have some right to know."

But when he had related the story of the unseemly haste with which he had been obliged to contract an engagement, his sister's reaction made him regret disclosing the tale.

"And I am expected to greet this brass-faced hussy with cordiality?"

"She is no hussy."

"Is she not, indeed? Upon my word, Christopher, you are a great fool. Depend upon it, she will be dispensing her favours all over town within weeks of the wedding." She paused, frightened by the expression of fury on his face.

"If ever you repeat such remarks, Cordelia, you will bitterly regret it. You have it quite wrong. The whole episode was my fault from start to finish."

Mrs Harraton eyed him. "Are you trying to make me believe you sought to compromise the girl?"

Chiddingly looked at her, arrested all at once. Here was a loophole. Let Cordelia believe him villainous, rather than nourish such uncomplimentary — and indeed untrue — views of his Seph. He adopted a flippant tone. "Why not?"

"To what end, pray?"

"Don't be stupid, Cordelia. We may only see fifty thousand pounds at the start, but the nabob cannot last forever."

"So you have saddled yourself with a wife who, I am reliably informed, is a termagant of shrewish temper without the smallest pretension to conformable behaviour."

"That is my affair."

"If I am obliged to be conciliating to the wench, I suppose it is mine, too."

Chiddingly gave a short laugh. "Certainly, if you don't wish to have your eyes scratched out, you had better make it so."

So Mrs Harraton, perforce, went to pay her respects to her prospective sister-in-law.

"My dear, dear Miss Winsford," she said in patronising tones which at once set up Persephone's back as that young lady entered the saloon. "Or may I call you Persephone?"

Persephone shook her hand briefly. "I cannot think why you should wish to."

"Surely you know I am Christopher's sister?"

"You mean Chiddingly? Is that his name? Not very apt."

"He is not very saintly, I agree," Mrs Harraton said with a thin smile.

"Saintly? A hellion, more like."

"I beg your pardon? You are speaking of my brother, ma'am."

"Then you ought to know what he is. If you are indeed to become my sister-in-law, it will be as well for you to know the truth. There is no hypocrisy in *my* family, and I scorn to pretend with you, either."

Cordelia hesitated, undecided whether to march out in a dudgeon or stay and explore this odd girl's attitude. Curiosity won. She produced her grin. "Do not let us quarrel. I hope you will not take it amiss if I put you a little on your guard, however."

"In what respect?" Then, remembering her duty as hostess, Persephone invited the visitor to be seated.

"You would do well to take care how you expose yourself, my dear," Cordelia said, sinking into a chair. "You will certainly set people in a bustle if you mean to reveal the lack of sympathy and understanding between yourself and your husband."

"He is not yet my husband. I care nothing for what anyone may say or think."

Shocked, Cordelia stared at her. "I declare, you are so brazen, I could almost believe Christopher innocent, after all."

She came under instant fire from Persephone's grey eyes. "Innocent? Of what, may I ask?"

Mrs Harraton tittered. "Why, of seduction, my dear." There was a spark of malice in her glance. "He told me he engineered the whole thing. Just for the fortune, you know."

She had the satisfaction of seeing the grey eyes widen.

"He said that?" Persephone asked, her tone hushed.

Cordelia shrugged. "Unless I misunderstood him."

She took her leave soon after, but Persephone remained in the drawing-room for quite some time, staring bleakly into space. The despondency she had been unable to shake off since coming home seemed to weigh more heavily than ever. She might have taunted Chiddingly with being a fortune-hunter, but she had believed his offer sprang from chivalry. To learn that he had seized the chance to make sure of her cut her to the quick.

Until now she had believed that regrettable incident to be the outcome of an urgent and mutual attraction. To think now he had been merely using her made her burn with shame and humiliation. Worse, it pained her beyond anything she had thought possible. That Chid should prove a liar and a cheat was somehow unbearable. Much as she hated him, she had insensibly grown to respect him.

The overmastering hurt that consumed her found expression, naturally enough, in a deep rage that chased away her erstwhile gloom and smouldered steadily in her breast. It was fuelled by the intelligence, brought to her next day by Penelope, that the word had spread all over town. Everyone believed her to have been entrapped by Chiddingly's machinations, and there was apparently no doubt in anyone's mind that she had succumbed to his seduction. Persephone's fury knew no bounds and was, had she but known it, matched by Chiddingly's own.

"I cannot for the life of me guess how such a tale has got about," Fitz told him over the bottle of claret they were sharing in Padiham's cosy parlour.

"I should not be at all surprised to find Persephone herself had set it about."

"Gammon. To what purpose?"

"To give her an excuse for breaking the engagement."

"Hang you, Chid, you are not thinking. She cannot break the engagement. Her reputation would be smirched beyond recovery."

"And I suppose this morsel of gossip redounds to my credit?"

"Of course it does not redound to your credit. But neither does it lend any countenance to poor Seph."

"That would not weigh with her, I assure you. Depend upon it, she has done this to make me out a villain and curry sympathy as the injured party."

"My dear Chid, the female is always the injured party. If it will bring you to your senses, you had better call upon her and fight it out."

By some freak of fortune, both parties chose to ride in the park early the next morning, hoping to shake off their separate mental disturbances. On catching sight of one another, they rode together as if of one mind, and clashed instantly.

"You little cat, what in Hades do you mean by it?"

"Don't dare ring a peal over me, you unmitigated scoundrel! Have you not done enough?"

"I had not believed you capable of such a paltry revenge," he went on, riding over her response as if he had not heard it. "So I seduced you, did I? Damme, I don't mean to sound like a coxcomb, Persephone, but I rate my attractions a little higher than that."

Persephone looked at him, her own fury arrested. "What the devil are you talking of?"

"If I had wanted your damned fortune, woman, I would have wooed you in form, not played a cheap trick to force your consent. What in Hades possessed you to set such a tale about?"

The cheeks of his prospective bride flew colour and fire leapt from her eyes. "Do you dare to suggest I am responsible for these abominable rumours, you — you —?"

"Wait one moment," Chiddingly began, but he might have spared his breath.

Persephone launched into a hectic tirade. "Never in my life have I been so insulted! That I should be accused of stooping to so vulgar a level! You are the author of this outrage, not I. Did not your sister Harraton herself tell me you said you had deliberately compromised me?"

Shock washed over Chiddingly like a douche of cold water. "Oh sweet heaven! But that was because —"

He stopped, recalling how he had led his sister to believe that stupid piece of foolishness rather than let her hold a base opinion of Persephone. He had said it in defence of her, and now it had bounced back upon him. His harridan of a sister had no doubt confided in her friend Alice Chumleigh. From one female to another, and thence to the world, was an inevitable step.

"Seph, I owe you an apology. I can explain everything, but this is not the time nor the place."

"It never will be the time, nor the place. I want to hear no more of your lies," she cried on an angry sob. "I thought you a man of honour, at least, and now —"

"Will you be still a moment? Come, we will settle this now. Dismount and let us discuss it calmly."

"I don't want to dismount and there is nothing to discuss."

"Oh? Are you afraid?" he taunted, swinging himself out of the saddle.

"I am never afraid! Oh, very well, very well." She shifted her weight and loosened her foot from the stirrup, but as Chiddingly left his horse quietly standing and came to assist her, she waved him away. "I can manage perfectly, I thank you."

He ignored this, and, reaching up, caught her as she slid out of the saddle and set her down in the road. He then led both horses to the trees and tethered them.

Persephone stood in the road, beating her whip rhythmically against the skirt of her habit. Returning, Chiddingly reached out and relieved her of the whip.

"I will take that, I thank you. I have no mind to receive yet another of your vicious punishments."

"Well? I am waiting."

Chiddingly threw both whips aside and grasped her shoulders. "Seph, you cannot think I offered for you to get at your father's fortune."

"Oh, can I not? Am I expected to believe it was ardour that led you to offer for Pen?"

He let her go. "No — no, I did seek it on that occasion, I admit. But I was under a misapprehension. I thought the sum —" He broke off, realising how infelicitous were these words, and how little they must help him.

"Not enough for you? What changed your mind, I wonder? Indigo's indisposition, perhaps?"

"I did not change my mind. At least, I did, but not about your fortune. I never wanted to marry you."

"I am well aware of that. The feeling is mutual."

"Then I am scarce likely to have used that regrettable incident to tie myself to you on purpose, am I?"

"For all I know, you had been lying all along."

"Saints preserve me, you abominable little shrew!"

Balling her fist, Persephone dealt him a punch in the centre of his chest that deprived him of breath and made him stagger back. By the time he had recovered, she had retrieved her whip and, lifting her skirts, was vaulting unaided into her saddle. Once up, she paused to move her leg to the correct position to ride side-saddle, which gave Chiddingly an opportunity to run up and seize her bridle at the bit, holding her horse steady.

"Let go!"

"Not until I have said my say!"

"I don't want to hear it!"

"By thunder, woman, I am of a mind to tell the world the truth! It was your folly that began this intolerable situation. Had it not been for you chasing after me that day with your foolish suspicions of Bolsover, none of this would have happened. You have no one but yourself to blame, for you have fallen into a pit of your own digging." Then he released her rein and stalked away to fling himself into his own saddle. Next moment, he had ridden off, leaving Persephone to stare after him with tears gathering in her eyes.

Everything in her wanted to cry out to him, to call him back. But Chiddingly hated her, that much was plain. As much, if not more, than she hated him. She ought to be gratified but, oddly, the thought made hot tears course down her cheeks. She lifted a hand to dash them away, resolving never to sue for his forgiveness. But even as she decided so, her lips opened.

"*Chiddingly*!" she cried out brokenly.

But the baron was already too far away to hear.

Well, he was right, she thought, lashing herself mentally. The situation was intolerable. She might have dug her own grave, but had she asked him to leap into it with her? But he had, and the best thing she could do now was to ride to the devil and break her neck. Doubtless that would make the brutish fiend happy again. And she, tormented soul that she was, might rest in peace. Oh, heavens, but she wanted to die! Anything was preferable to marrying a man who held her in such contempt.

"Oh, Chid," she uttered involuntarily. Digging in her spurs, she urged her horse to follow him with all speed. But although she galloped like a demented runaway, the baron was long gone. There was nothing for her to do but return to Hanover Square.

CHAPTER TEN

When Persephone arrived home, for the first time she ignored the claims of her horse to her attention and instead tethered him to the railings by the area steps. Running inside, she instructed a footman to attend to him and have him returned to the Rossendale stables. Fearful of breaking down before the servant, she flew up the stairs, and, flinging into her chamber, she threw herself down on the newly made-up bed and wept bitterly into the mound of pillows.

Here Penelope found her some ten minutes later, the sound of her lamentations having roused her from sleep in her own bedchamber next door.

"Seph, Seph, what is it?" she cried, rushing to the bed to clasp her arms tenderly about the shaking shoulders. "Dearest, tell me, I pray you."

Persephone raised her tear-stained face from the pillows. "Ch-Chid h-hates me, and — and I am h-heartily glad of it," she announced in heartbroken accents.

"Hates you? Oh, Seph, he cannot."

"He *does*! He does not w-want to m-marry me in the very l-least. And I am glad of that, too," Persephone wailed.

"But — but, Seph, you don't want to marry him. You told me positively that you hated him, too."

"I know. I *do*. I mean, I *don't*."

Penelope's lips quivered uncontrollably. "Make up your mind, Seph."

Persephone sat up, sniffing dolefully. "My mind *is* made up and I wish I were dead!"

Her sister tried to keep her countenance, but her dancing eyes gave her away.

"It is not funny," Persephone protested as her twin went off into one of her fits of laughter.

"Oh, Seph, you are so droll. I do not mean to laugh at you, dearest, but you will contradict yourself so absurdly. What has occurred? I suppose you have quarrelled with him again?"

"Yes, I have, and the devil of it is the hateful wretch is right. It is all my fault." She dissolved into tears again. "N-no one in their right m-mind would want to marry me, let alone Ch-Chid, who has every reason in the world to despise me. Oh, *Pen*!"

Penelope received her in a comforting embrace, petting and crooning with automatic gentleness until her sister was quiet, her brain furiously buzzing meanwhile. Leaving Persephone resting drowsily on her bed, she went back to her own room to write a hasty note and then rang for the maid she shared with her twin.

"Send one of the footmen to deliver this immediately, if you please, and then come back quickly and help me to dress."

The recipient of her note was still abed when it was delivered in South Street, and the butler was disinclined to wake his master.

"Begging your pardon," said the footman, "but I was told as how I was to make sure it got into his lordship's hands before I departed."

"You'll have a long wait, then," the butler told him loftily.

Fortunately, the valet, passing through the hall on his way to his master's dressing-room, took it upon himself to enquire where the footman had come from. The answer caused him to override the butler and carry the note instantly upstairs.

"What the devil ails you, Weeke?" his master demanded wrathfully when he discovered the time of day to be barely nine.

"This note arrived, my lord, and I fancied your lordship would wish to see it without delay." He looked noncommittally the other way as he held out the silver salver. "The footman, my lord, is of the Winsford household."

"Eh? Give it to me at once," his lordship said, snatching the letter and instantly breaking the seal. He read the missive quickly:

Dear Fitz,

Forgive this unconventionality, which you must set at the door of my unusual manners, but I need you. Seph is in a dreadful way and your dratted Chiddingly is the cause, of course. We must Do Something at once. Please, please come.

In hope and haste,
Pen

Fitz flung off his covers. "Weeke, my shaving water! My clothes! Hurry, man! And find me a pen and some paper."

Hardly had Penelope received his scribbled response that he would wait upon her within the hour, when Fitz himself arrived, looking as elegant as if he had spent the usual lengthy time at his toilette. He was ushered at once into the large saloon. Penelope, who had been rustling agitatedly about the room in her chemise gown, came to him with her hands held out.

"Oh, thank you for coming so quickly."

Fitz bowed over her hands, kissing them each in turn. "Your word is my command, Pen."

She blushed a little and twinkled. "Truly?"

"I am entirely at your service, now and always," he said lightly, but his eyes held an expression that made her catch her breath. "Now, what have our ill-tempered couple been doing to alarm you so?"

"I found Seph in great distress," Penelope said, sitting on a sofa and invitingly patting the place beside her. "She had met Chiddingly out riding, I gather, and they quarrelled."

"What is so unusual in that?" Fitz asked as he took his seat.

"Nothing, only this time Seph was not raging at all, but weeping her heart out."

"Upon my soul, I wish she had done so in Chid's presence, then, for I am sure nothing could more easily bring them to an understanding."

"Yes, but she is so proud she would scorn to show her hurt. He seems to have been uncommonly cruel, for she says he hates her and has no wish to marry her."

"Did he say so?"

"Why — why, I do not know. He must have said something of the sort, I suppose."

"Well, for my part, I am convinced Chid is far more tender of your sister than he is yet aware of."

Penelope gaped at him. "How can you say so, when he is always so violent towards her? As is she to him, I must —" She broke off, her eyes popping as a thought occurred to her. "Great heavens! You do not think *she* is — it is not possible."

Fitz grinned at her. "Dear Pen, if you were in question, I must agree. But we are talking of Seph. Between her conduct and that of her affianced husband, I can descry not the difference of a hair. I have always thought them remarkably well suited, if they would but take the trouble to step back and look at each other instead of fighting all the time."

Under her very fetching mob-cap, Penelope's brow wrinkled. "It might be so, I suppose. But then what is to be done? I mean, how are they to find it out?"

Fitz smiled. "I fancy Chid is already in a way to doing so. Only he does not yet realise his sentiments are reciprocated."

"Well, I cannot blame him there," Penelope said unguardedly, but she was not thinking of Chiddingly and her sister. "How in the world is one to know if — I mean, that — that —?" Flushing, she stopped and fell to studying her fingers where they lay twisting around each other in her lap.

Fitz's hand reached out to cover and quiet them. "Some men, Pen, take an inordinately long time to know their own minds."

Her blushes increased as she looked up wonderingly and found his eyes upon her with so much meaning in them her heart leapt. But as he smiled, he removed his hand and reverted to the subject under discussion.

"There is only one thing for it. Chid must set about it like a sensible man and woo the woman."

"I doubt he is capable of it," Penelope said, disappointment lending her voice a sharpness she had not intended.

"At least he may have a chance with your sister if he begins with the one thing they have in common."

Directly as a result of this conference Persephone found herself, some two days later, aboard Chiddingly's phaeton and being driven down to Faversham to visit his stud and, incidentally, his home since the expanse of stables was situated on his estate.

The invitation had reached her by letter, couched in stiff and formal terms, to which she had sent her acceptance written in similar vein.

Miss Winsford thanks Lord Chiddingly for his kind invitation, which she will be pleased to accept, she had written, for nothing would have induced her to reveal the transports of delight with which she had read his words, not only at the treat in store which could not but appeal, but at the thought she would see him again before their betrothal party scheduled for the day following the excursion. She had toyed with the idea of sending for him, only to shy away from a meeting brought about for the sole purpose of offering the apology she had vowed not to make. This way, she might find a chance to introduce the subject without deliberately setting about it.

But so self-conscious was she, so embarrassed with the shame of her past actions, that the instant she set eyes on him she was stricken to tense silence. As a result, she affected a stiff manner, speaking in a cold voice that in no way expressed her true feelings.

Chiddingly, equally tongue-tied, behaved in much the same way, so that conversation on the journey was conducted in a desultory fashion that would have led anyone to believe the dislike they so often expressed for each other was in no way exaggerated.

Small chance, Chiddingly reflected, his friend Fitz's suggestion would be found to prove efficacious.

"Chid, you must make an effort to come to some kind of understanding. Preferably before the wedding," he'd said. "Else you will soon find yourselves so estranged you cannot begin to bridge the gap."

It was not a prospect Chiddingly could view with anything but dismay. Things were bad enough. The last thing he wanted was to drive a deeper wedge between himself and Persephone.

"I do not know how to approach her, Fitz. We cannot meet, it seems, without rubbing against one another."

"There is one thing on which you may readily agree. Why do you not begin there?"

"Horseflesh? Yes, but how?"

"Take her to see your stock, man. You could not more surely engage her interest."

Chiddingly's blue eyes had lit for an instant, and then dulled again. "She will deny herself, if she thinks she must spend a whole day by my side."

Fitz had laughed. "I should be very much surprised if she can resist."

He was found to be right, for the paralysis that seemed to afflict them both disappeared like magic as soon as they arrived at Chiddingly's estate and Persephone at once saw a line of nags exercising on the turf beside the carriage drive.

"Oh, they are splendid," she cried, stiffness melting away. "How many horses do you have?"

"If you count all the foals, between twenty-five and thirty. But that does not include my working horses, such as this team and those I hack in town," Chiddingly told her, his own manner lightening considerably. "And the farm cattle, of course."

"You farm, too?"

"Enough only to keep the stock well fed. I meant the horses I lease to the farm tenants. For they will never buy a second nag until they have worked the one they already own to death."

"Oh, abominable. You could not tolerate that."

"Do you care to go directly to the stables, or would you like to refresh yourself first? I sent word to my housekeeper."

"No, no, I cannot wait. Please let us go to the stables at once," she begged, with a warmer smile than she had yet shown him.

The stud stables were situated some way from the house, surrounded by several paddocks on land studded with hedges and trees, together with a training track. The land abutted acres of common, along which a worn path meandered down to the distant dunes and beaches of the Swale, an inlet from the sea.

Tidmarsh and Siegfried, who came forward to greet them as the phaeton clattered into the stable yard, managed, though indeed unintentionally, to fling both parties back into embarrassment.

"May I be permitted to offer my felicitations, ma'am," Tidmarsh said, "and to be the first to welcome you to your future home?"

"Thank you," Persephone said, her tone gruff.

"Aye, mistress," piped up the jockey. "An' I reckon as how his lordship will have his hands so full, he'll mebbe give me a bit o' peace."

"Hold your tongue, rascal!"

Tidmarsh, quite as annoyed but more direct than his employer, dealt Siegfried a buffet on the side of the head, and gave Persephone an apologetic smile. "Your pardon, ma'am. I'll take him away, my lord."

"Do so. And keep him out of my sight."

Whereupon Tidmarsh collected the jockey by means of attaching his fingers to his ear and led him off, his victim loudly complaining.

"You let go, you persecutin' Tidmarsh. I hopes you get nibbled to death by ducks, I do."

As their acrimonious voices died away, Chiddingly turned to hand Persephone down from the phaeton, trying to infuse naturalness into his tone. "I think perhaps it would be as well if we walked out to the paddocks, where we will find most of my best cattle."

Persephone merely murmured her agreement and stepped out beside him, her confusion increasing as she took in the covert glances being cast at her by the stable lads and grooms going about their business. She had dressed in an unusually frivolous way, in a blue cotton open robe over lighter-toned petticoats, with a chip hat perched at an angle on her golden locks, and this scrutiny made her feel shy and unlike herself.

It was a relief to leave the yard behind them and walk out by the field where several fenced-off areas could be seen ahead of them, in which pairs and groups of horses grazed in the peace of a sunny April morning.

Persephone halted, looking from one paddock to another. "Oh, how can you bear to spend your time in town when you could be here with all these beautiful creatures?"

She picked up her skirts and ran to the wooden palings that divided her from the animals inside the paddock. Holding out her hand, she leaned across to call out to the pair of horses within. They had been naturally curious, watching the approach of people from the stables, and now came trotting over to investigate.

Persephone greeted them with soft words and a soft hand to stroke their muzzles, and turned her glowing features to Chiddingly. "They are delightful. Such wonderful colours. I have never seen a bay so light. Why, he is almost gold. And this chestnut is like a flame."

The baron, following her, had remained standing a few feet away, watching with a smile. "I confess I love them too. In fact, they are my favourite pair."

"I am not surprised. Would I might try them at a light phaeton."

"You may certainly do so when once you are living here."

She blushed, consciousness returning, and made an excuse to move on. But the ice was broken and they found themselves deep in discussion on the idiosyncrasies of individual animals, and the difficulties of maintaining order and discipline in a large stable.

"And the worst menace, if you will believe me," Chiddingly said in tones of amused vexation, "is the clash of personalities among my people."

Persephone laughed. "People are always more troublesome than horses."

"Are they not? Well, you have seen what I am obliged to endure from Siegfried. But the little devil is so superb a racer I cannot let him go. He knows it, too, and takes atrocious liberties. Truth to tell, though, it is Tidmarsh — and he I would not lose for a fortune, believe me — who is like to create mayhem in my stables."

"Tidmarsh? Why, how is that? He seems to me to be an admirable person."

"So he is. Except that he must needs become amorously involved with my head groom's daughter. It only needs for Clatterbridge to get wind of the matter for me to find myself hovering on the brink of a domestic crisis."

Persephone could not help laughing. "Lord, if it is not just as it was in Bombay. Ufur — an autocrat, you know, but the greatest horseman in the world — was used to complain of the self-same problem. If you take his method, you will marry them off as quickly as possible."

"Like us." The colour flew into her cheeks. "That was maladroit. Forgive me."

Persephone shook her head, turning her eyes away to gaze unseeingly upon the two dark foals gambolling together in the paddock behind them. "It does not matter."

"Tidmarsh fondly believes me to be ignorant of his attachment," Chiddingly went on in a bid to cover the moment. "Though he ought to have realised with Siegfried on the loose, that were impossible. But I should not care to embarrass him by referring to it."

Persephone hardly heard him. At that precise moment, she had scant interest in Tidmarsh. Now, if ever, was her opportunity. She drew a resolute breath and turned to face the baron, leaning against the wooden palings for support and grasping them at either side. "Chiddingly, there is something I want to say to you. No, not that. Something I must say."

"Persephone, I —"

"No, let me speak, I pray you."

He stood silent, watching her face, pale but determined under the straw hat.

She met his eyes squarely. "Chiddingly, I — it was —" Then out it all came in a rush. "Oh, Chid, *forgive* me. It was indeed all my folly that compromised us both so dreadfully. I have been so wrapped up in my own stupid predicament that I had not even thought how it has affected you. I dare say there is nothing you desire less in the world than to be tied to such a harridan as I am."

Chiddingly stepped up to her and captured her hands which, having released their clutch on the palings, were now waving distractedly in the air. "Seph, don't, I beg you. I cannot bear to hear you talk so, when I have behaved towards you in a manner so unbefitting a gentleman."

"No, no. You would never have done so had I not created the situation in the first place," she cried, determined to shoulder the blame. "I am so sorry you find yourself obliged to marry me."

"Well, I am not," Chiddingly declared, imprisoning her hands more tightly within his own. "I assure you, I am growing every day more reconciled to the prospect."

"Oh, please, Chid, don't say what you do not mean."

"But I do mean it. My fear is that *you* —" He broke off, smiling. "The truth is, Seph, we have never had an opportunity to know each other."

"Believe me, you do not want to know me. What you have so far seen of me is all there is."

He laughed, and dropping her hands, caught her in his arms. His blue eyes, so close to hers, were alight with an expression she did not recognise. But her heart beat fast as his fingers came up to caress her cheek.

"Everything I have so far seen drives me wild in every possible way."

Then his lips were on hers. Not hard at all, but gently persuasive, drawing from deep within her soul a rush of tenderness that made her dizzy, and she sagged a little in his arms. Chiddingly cradled her closer, his mouth passing from her lips to her cheeks, and up to kiss her closed eyes, which fluttered open to gaze in wonder into his own.

"Persephone, you are the most beguiling, the most miraculous creature — and the most infuriating." He kissed her again, and then drew back to smile into her eyes. "We will probably end by slaughtering each other, but I confess I find the prospect infinitely enticing."

Persephone's low gurgle of laughter escaped her, and her eyes warmed to a luminous glow. "You are undoubtedly unhinged, Chid. Now, do not say that is to be set to my account."

"Totally." He hugged her with rough tenderness, and then let her go. "Come, I have something to show you which I think — no, I am sure — you will like."

Taking her by the hand, he led her to where a group of young horses played and cantered together about a large paddock. Chiddingly pointed out his Barbary mare, whose dainty white legs were twinkling across the green as she raced, easily outstripping her companions.

Persephone looked, and a gasp of dismay left her lips. "*Shiveen!*" she cried out in sudden anguish, and tore her hand from Chiddingly's grasp, covering her eyes against so painful a sight.

"Why, what is amiss? Seph, my heart, what is amiss?"

She was shaking, and as he drew the hands from her face, the deep sadness in her eyes rent him in pieces.

"I b-beg your pardon. It — it is only that the horse reminded me — she is so like —"

"You had a mare the same. And you had to leave her. Lord, you poor girl."

She drew a shuddering breath, her fingers clinging tightly to his. "It was the greatest wrench of all. Yet I did it to myself." Haltingly, she explained how Shiveen had been too old to start afresh and that she had given her to Ufur. For the first time, she spoke to him of all she had left behind and what it had cost her to do so. "All, Chid! All my horses."

"That is indeed a tragic thing to happen to a girl like you."

"I have not yet been able to bring myself to purchase any over here. I told Papa I had not made up my mind, but the truth is I could not bear to replace my loved ones. So foolish of me."

"Foolish indeed, but I would feel exactly as you. But it is time to lay all these ghosts aside. We will begin with this one."

So saying, he left her side and vaulted easily over the paddock fence. He went into the knot of horses, fetched the Barbary mare and guided her back to the fence with a hand to her sleek neck. She came willingly enough, followed a little way by her fellows, who stopped to stare when they saw Persephone waiting.

A pang shot through her as she stepped up to lift a hand to the filly's muzzle and the picture of her lost Shiveen flashed momentarily through her mind. But she was not proof against the gentleness and beauty of this new animal, and could not close her heart against it. Within a very few moments, she had made friends. The filly nuzzled her neck as she turned once more to Chiddingly, her eyes in a fresh glow of exhilaration.

"What is she called?"

Chiddingly smiled, and his eyes held tenderness. "That is for you to say, Seph. She is yours."

"Oh no," she cried involuntarily, feeling she could not blot the memory of Shiveen with another such grey mare. Then she recalled Ufur's words. *You will be knowing many horses, Miss Sephy.* Yes, Ufur would have told her to stop being a fool. Still she hesitated. "I — I could not. Such a lovely horse. Also — as I can clearly see — your especial pride."

"Take her, Seph. A betrothal gift."

"Oh, Chid. You could not have found anything I would treasure more."

Chiddingly seized her hand and jerked her into his arms, making her straw hat slip off. His kiss was fierce, his arms about her crushing the breath from her body. Persephone melted against him, drowning in the demanding pressure of his lips. He released her as suddenly and held her away from him, his voice harsh with passion.

"She is pure Barb. I had her brought all the way over from Constantinople. Until this moment, I did not think I valued anything above her. Not even Indigo. Then you —"

A shout from behind cut him off.

"My lord! My lord!"

He let go of Persephone and turned to see Tidmarsh running headlong towards them. "What in Hades —?"

Persephone moved past him. "Something is amiss!"

"My lord!" Tidmarsh called, as he neared. "It is Indigo. He has disappeared!"

"I knew we had something still to fear!"

"Nonsense, he cannot have gone," Chiddingly rapped out. "You have looked everywhere?"

"The grooms are searching the grounds now, my lord," Tidmarsh said. "Siegfried, too. But I fear they will not find him."

"Do you tell me he has vanished? With I don't know how many persons about my estates, we are to think a horse — and a distinctive one at that — may so easily slip away unseen?"

"It is more sinister than that, my lord. The stable boy assigned to make Indigo his particular concern is nowhere to be found."

"*Ooloo!*" Horror crept into Persephone's breast.

Chiddingly paled. "Sweet heaven!"

Then he was running, Tidmarsh hard on his heels, back towards the stables. Persephone picked up both her hat and her skirts and chased them, but she was soon left behind, and by the time she came panting into the yard Chiddingly was striding about, barking instructions at his assembled minions.

"Search every stall. I care not if you have already done so, do it again. At once. Some of you to the common — look for tracks. You and you, to the training ground. Check every tree. And find me Clatterbridge."

"He is out with the grooms, my lord," Tidmarsh said.

But at that moment the head groom came running into the yard, out of breath. "My lord! Ned has been to the western gates. He reports a vehicle has stood in the lane. There are tracks, and the marks of several horses."

Chiddingly grasped his arm. "Did he note which way they led? Answer, fool!"

"Y-yes, my lord. Away to the north, past the forest."

"They have not entered the forest, then? They kept to the lane?"

Clatterbridge gaped. "I — I dunno, my lord. I think he did not look."

"Then we had better do so. Have them fig out Thunder. Quick!"

The head groom flew to obey as Persephone appeared at Chiddingly's elbow. "I want to go with you."

He glanced at her with impatience. "No, wait here. I shall not be long."

Her eyes held his. In an under-voice, she grated, "I am coming!"

"Oh, very well, I have no time to argue. Clatterbridge! Forget Thunder. Let me have the gig."

But Thunder was already being made ready, and as he was led out, Chiddingly took the bridle and swung himself into the saddle. "Bring the gig yourself, Persephone. Clatterbridge will show you the way."

He rode out of the stable yard, followed by Tidmarsh on a horse he had already ordered to be saddled before running to warn his lordship of this fresh disaster.

Awaiting the gig with one impatient foot tapping away, Persephone seethed at being left behind, though she cared nothing for the cavalier treatment she had received from her betrothed. In her view, he was right to put his attention where it was most needed.

With Clatterbridge up beside her, she drove the gig as speedily as the horse could go in the direction he indicated, plying him all the while with questions.

"How was it discovered Indigo was missing? Who saw him last? And, heaven help us, at what hour?"

"We dunno who saw him last, miss. Could be any one o' we, for the stable boy took him for his exercise as usual, and could've gone anywhere. I seen him myself this morning, but it were only when the lad took in his feed that he seen the horse were missing. Should've been back from exercise nigh an hour afore that."

"Did it not strike anyone as odd they had not seen him return?"

"Miss, we got ever so many horses here. You don't look for no horse particular. You see them all every day, like."

Persephone could appreciate this, but it still seemed careless. "But the stallion is special, Clatterbridge. After his sickness at Newmarket —"

"Aye, miss, I know. But you gets used to them quick here. Even the real good 'uns."

When they reached the western gate, a little-used exit from the estate mostly given over to tenants taking a shortcut across to the shores of the Swale, they found Tidmarsh and Chiddingly minutely inspecting the marks in the lane.

Persephone was careful to stop before she could eradicate the evidence with the hoofs of the horse pulling the gig.

"What have you found?" she called out, climbing down from the gig once Clatterbridge had gone to the horse's head.

"It seems certain they kept to the lane," Chiddingly said, coming towards her. "I must follow as soon as may be."

"But are you certain these marks mean what you imagine? They could be any horse — a cart, perhaps."

"No, not only does one set of prints join up here from my gates, but Tidmarsh recognises Indigo's pattern."

"He was reshod at my lord Buckfastleigh's place," Tidmarsh put in, seeing her cast him a questioning glance. "Preparatory to the race, as we expected him to run. His lordship's smithy uses a particular shoe. It is quite distinctive."

Persephone bit her lip, her eyes clouding. "Then he has been kidnapped!"

"Yes, ma'am. One must suppose the stable boy to have been party to the plot."

"A fine thing when my own boys are not to be trusted," Chiddingly said, with an ill look at Clatterbridge.

"Aye, but young Sawleigh was new, my lord," the man said in a self-exculpatory tone. "Seemed to know his work, like. A good lad. Joined us at Newmarket."

Persephone was on him like a flash. "You hired a boy at Newmarket? After what occurred there?"

"It weren't my blame, miss. I weren't even there," protested Clatterbridge, aggrieved.

"Nevertheless, it is a foolhardy thing to have done," Chiddingly said. "I suppose my own groom took him on. I shall have something to say to Fenwick."

"My lord, Fenwick was not to know," Tidmarsh intervened. "He took the lad on well before Indigo took ill."

"But surely to goodness," Persephone burst out, "after such an occurrence, anyone new to your retinue must have fallen under suspicion. Did not anyone enquire into the boy's history?"

"O' course we did," Clatterbridge said, affronted. "Leastways another groom, a friend of Fenwick's, offered him the lad, saying as how he had no need of a boy and had undertaken to find him a post."

"What groom was this?" Persephone demanded, quick suspicion kindling in her breast.

"Sir John Lade's, miss."

"Oh," she said, dashed. The scarred man was definitely not from Letty's stables, or Letty would have recognised him. But she was far from satisfied. "But Sir John Lade was not his former master. So who was?"

Clatterbridge's leathery countenance writhed in embarrassment. "Can't rightly say, miss. But he come with as good a character as you're like to see, my lord," he offered, turning to his master as if he feared an attack from that quarter.

But Chiddingly brushed it aside. "Come, Persephone, one does not enquire into all the previous employers of a mere stable boy."

"Well, with a valuable stud, you ought to."

Tidmarsh spoke up. "I believe Siegfried can help us there. He told me the boy had mentioned Lord Goole."

"Goole?"

"Yes, my lord. It seems that since his lordship has been putting down most of his stable, on account of not being permitted to race, the boy had to go."

"Then that is our answer!" So saying, Chiddingly took Persephone by the arm and pulled her towards the gig, throwing an order at his head groom. "Take Thunder, Clatterbridge. I will drive Miss Winsford back. Go directly to the stables and have both my phaeton and my travelling coach made ready."

He handed Persephone up into the gig and took the reins in his hand.

"Aye, sir," Clatterbridge said, leaving the horse's head and taking Thunder's reins from Tidmarsh's hand.

Then the two were off, leaving their master to follow in the gig.

"What will you do, Chid?"

"I will follow the tracks as far as I can. If I find nothing, I shall go to London to seek out Goole."

Persephone sat frowning in silence for a moment. At length she said, "You hold by your belief it is he, then?"

"What in Hades else am I to think? You are not going to try and tell me you believe Billy to be responsible?"

She did not reply to this, but her frown deepened and she struck her gloved hands together. "We are both palpably to blame. Had we not wasted precious time in petty arguments —"

"It is of no use to repine over that now."

"But I have not given the matter a moment's thought. Neither, I am very sure, have you."

A tinge of red crept into his cheek. "I have had other things to think of."

"Yes, our idiotic betrothal."

"Oh, Seph, be quiet. What is that to the purpose now?"

"You are very right. Regret will not mend matters. If we hurry, do you think we may catch them?"

"We?" he said, turning his head. "You, my girl, are going back to Hanover Square."

"I most certainly am not."

"Persephone, don't start to argue with me, for I have no patience to deal with you at present."

"Do you think I don't care as greatly as you about what has occurred?"

"Doubtless. But I am not carrying you with me on this fetch. It is of no use to dispute with me, for my mind is made up."

Persephone's breast rose and fell in speechless indignation.

Glancing at her flushed cheeks, Chiddingly felt a stir of remorse. He reached out his whip hand and briefly touched the clenched fists in her lap. "Seph, have a little sense," he said more gently. "We have this infernal betrothal party tomorrow, for one thing. For another, we truly cannot afford any further scandal."

They were coming within sight of the stables. Persephone did not look at him and her voice was gruff. "Will you send me word?"

"To be sure."

She turned, her hostility waning. "Do you promise?"

Chiddingly sighed, smiling a little. "Very well, I promise you shall hear from me as soon as I have anything to report."

Persephone softened. "Thank you. For I shall not know a moment's peace until I know Indigo is safe."

She made the relatively short journey to London in Chiddingly's coach, accompanied very correctly by an abigail, together with a footman who rode with the coachman on the box, and a groom on the perch up behind.

As she thought over all that had occurred, she found she could not believe Goole responsible. Who, after all, had so far shown himself to be the ruthless author of every other vile scheme? Yet how to proceed with an investigation into the matter she did not know. Chid would have her wait for the outcome of his own hunt for Goole. But what if he was wrong? What might happen to Indigo in the meantime? He could be carried so far away he might never be found.

CHAPTER ELEVEN

The journey home was slower by coach than by Chiddingly's phaeton, and Persephone chafed at the delay. It was late afternoon when she was at length set down in Hanover Square, and she ran straight into her mother who, finding her unaccompanied, demanded at once to know what Baron Chiddingly was about sending her back alone.

"I am like to give that man a piece of my mind," said Clarissa, marching into the small parlour and rousing her husband from his perusal of a document that seemed to be taking up a good deal of his attention.

"What the deuce is it now?" he asked testily, looking up.

But when he learned the cause of Persephone's return without her prospective spouse, he nipped his wife's intentions in the bud.

"Deuce take it, Clarissa, what do you expect from the man, eh? Eh? Damme, he had a deal more important affairs on his mind. And so too have I, I might add. Women! Ha!"

"What in the world ails Papa?" Penelope asked as her father removed himself from the parlour, shutting the door behind him with unnecessary force.

"Oh, it is something to do with this matter of Warren Hastings. Do not ask me. They are expecting Edmund Burke to demand in the House tomorrow for some sort of redress, I gather."

"An impeachment," Persephone supplied, for she had heard of the matter at length from the nabob. Warren Hastings, the former Governor of Bengal, was to face trial for alleged crimes committed while in power. Edmund Burke would be one of the Members of Parliament managing the prosecution. "I had better go and talk to him."

"You will do no such thing, Seph. You must dress at once. We are due at Lady Buckfastleigh's rout."

"Oh, Mama, must I go? I have no heart for it, with Indigo in this trouble."

"Do come, Seph," Penelope said, jumping up and drawing her towards the door. "It will divert your mind."

"What is more to the point," their mother put in, "you cannot possibly offer such an affront to Lady Buckfastleigh after all her trouble at Newmarket."

Persephone groaned, but she knew there was no way of avoiding attendance at the gathering. In the event, she was glad she went, for Fitz met them with a message from Chiddingly.

"He asked me to tell you he has gone off to Norfolk."

"Norfolk?" Penelope repeated.

"Is that where Lord Goole's seat is situated?" Persephone asked.

"Exactly. Goole is but recently gone out of town, so Chid has gone haring after him. For my part, I cannot think he will find his horse there."

"No more can I, I assure you. It is not Goole who has kidnapped Indigo."

Fitz looked her over with interest. "Oh? You have reason to suspect some other?"

"Every reason. But of course *he* will not credit me."

Penelope and Fitz exchanged glances. There was mute question in his eyes, but Penelope very slightly shook her head. There had been no time to discover how her sister had fared on the mission of peace. Besides, it seemed as if this appalling kidnap had prevented them from spending as much time together as had been hoped.

Fitz turned to Persephone again, but found her attention had been caught elsewhere. Murmuring an excuse, she moved away, heading purposefully to where she had seen a podgy little man with merrily smiling baby-blue eyes.

"Good evening, Mr Bolsover," Persephone said, in as pleasant a tone as she could manage.

"Why, Miss Winsford." Billy's jovial laugh rang out. "Or should I learn to call you *Lady Chid*, perhaps?"

"That would be a trifle premature." Although to Persephone's surprise, she found the name pleasurable to her ears. "Speaking of Chid —"

"Ah, yes, a bad business indeed," broke in Billy. "As if that poor animal had not suffered enough."

"How do you come to know of it, may I ask?"

"Oh, all the world is talking of the stallion's disappearance, dear lady."

"Yes? It is strange, then, that yours is the first tongue I have heard to touch upon the subject."

"Stuff and nonsense, ma'am!" Billy blew out his cheeks. "Ask anyone. Had it from Bunbury myself."

Persephone looked about her. "Indeed? I do not see Sir Charles here."

"Met him at Tattersall's."

"Oh, I see." Persephone regarded him steadily. "Naturally, you have not passed on this tidbit yourself."

The little man's chubby cheeks took on a purple hue and his lips pouted for an instant. Then he laughed again. "Miss Winsford, you have found me out. To be sure, I am a little guilty. Come, come, ma'am. You must know we horse-mad fellows are all too eager to gossip about each other's nags. Can't blame us, now can you? Kidnapping, I mean to say. Upon my word, it affects us all, so it does."

"How did you know it was a kidnapping, Mr Bolsover?"

He stared at her, little round eyes popping. "Well — what else is one to think? Horse vanishes into thin air. No trace to be found. I ask you, what is one to think?"

"Very true," she said, keeping her tone bland. He must not divine her suspicion.

"All I can say is, I hope Chid catches up with the villains. Damme, I've a mind to set a guard over my Magnet, so I have."

Persephone could not resist a snide smile. "Don't trouble, Mr Bolsover. I am quite certain any of your horses must be safe from attack."

She inclined her head and walked away from him, her jaw tight shut to prevent hot words issuing from her lips. The audacity of the man! If he was innocent, she was no judge of the matter. Just as she had suspected, Chid was gone on a wild-goose chase. But how was she to find convincing proof to show him?

One thing she could check on, however. Looking about, she saw Fitzwarren still engaged with her sister. They were locked in what looked like intimate conversation. Persephone halted, staring at them as an abrupt realisation shot into her mind. In the press of her own affairs, she had entirely forgotten about Pen.

Pen, who had been so oddly behaved at Newmarket, clearly troubled in spirit. Persephone now thought she knew what that trouble had been. The most casual observer must see for themselves what was apparent to Penelope's twin.

A mischievous smile on her lips, Persephone descended upon the couple, and linked her arm in Pen's. An arch look at her sister accompanied her first words.

"I am devastated to be obliged to interrupt you," she said, aping Penelope's musical tone, "but I am afraid I must borrow Fitz — just for an instant."

Penelope, blushing, cast her sister an unloving glare from under her fashionable hat with its fringe of lace trimming about the enormous brim. But Fitz grinned appreciatively, and turned his eyes upon her.

"As long as it is not going to cause Chid to call me out."

"Don't be absurd. He is more like to call me to account."

Again Fitz exchanged a glance with Penelope, but one of veiled triumph. This was better, his look seemed to say.

"Tell me, Fitz," Persephone went on, "is the town truly buzzing with the story of Indigo's disappearance?"

"Buzzing? No, indeed. Though some of Chid's racing cronies have somehow got hold of the tale."

"I knew it!"

"Why, what have you found out?"

Persephone shook her head. "I cannot tell you. When will Chid return?"

"He cannot reach back here before tomorrow afternoon at the earliest. But he must be back for your party in the evening."

"The party! Oh, the devil, I had forgot it."

"Seph," said Penelope in direful tones, "what are you about? I know that look. You are planning something dreadful."

"No, no. At least —" Persephone snapped her fingers. "I have it."

Fitz looked from her to Penelope in startled question.

"It is no use turning to me," Pen said. "I have no more notion than you what she will be at."

"Seph," Fitz said with urgency, "I do beg of you to consider well before you embark on one of your crazy ventures. Whatever you have in your head, wait at least for Chid."

But Persephone had no notion of waiting for her intended spouse. For one thing, he would heartily disapprove of what she meant to do. For another, he would — even if he could be induced to listen to her — inevitably put a stop to her participation.

Accordingly, the next morning she slipped out before breakfast and had herself driven in a hackney to Bloomsbury.

Laetitia Smith was delighted to see her. "I've been in such high gig over you and Chid," she said. "Not but what I thought it typical of you, Seph, if you'll pardon the liberty. Didn't surprise me to hear you rushed upon your fate, as the saying goes."

"Oh, Letty, don't. If you knew the agonies of mortification I have suffered!"

"Plague take it, Seph, do you take me for a noddy? Of course I know. But I'm bound to state I'm glad of it. For, married to Chid, you'll always be sure of having the finest horses to hand."

It was some time before Persephone could induce her to talk of anything else, but at last she managed to break in. "Letty, forgive me, but I am here on a very urgent matter. It is about Indigo."

Miss Smith had heard all about the drugging, of course, and was exclamatory over it. But her eyes fairly popped when Persephone told her of the kidnapping.

"You can help me if you will, Letty."

"Anything in my power, Seph. But I don't see how it'll do much good for us to set off if Chid has already gone after Goole."

"Yes, but it is not Goole. Do you remember at Epsom, Letty, those three men we saw? There was Goole and Billy Bolsover, and another."

"Couldn't see, though, Seph. I must say I didn't notice him particular."

"Well, he is very important. But first, can you tell me this? Sir John's groom recommended a stable boy to Chid's household while we were in Newmarket. I know it is asking a lot of you —"

"No, it ain't. Easiest thing in the world. Johnny is mighty particular, you see. He knows all his lads. Every one, from top to bottom."

"That is admirable," Persephone said, curbing her impatience with difficulty, "but this boy was not one of his. He came apparently from Goole, who is putting down his stable and had no use for him. Sir John's man had —"

"Said he would find him a post," Letty finished. "I recall the case. But you have it wrong, Seph. The boy went from Goole to Billy and Billy sent him to us."

Persephone pounced. "Bolsover! Devil take him!"

Letty gazed at her with popping eyes. "Billy? You're saying *Billy* did this?"

"I have no time to explain it all now, Letty. There is one more thing I must know. Billy Bolsover's groom — do you know him?"

Letty shivered. "I should say I do. Nasty, evil-looking brute. Not his fault, of course, poor man. He had a terrible accident with an unbroke horse, I believe."

"Go on."

"Well, that's it. Walks with a limp. His face is almost broke in two by a devilish ugly scar."

Staying only to extract from Letty the information that Billy Bolsover had a place at Flambards out by Wembley Green, Persephone thanked her profusely, promising to let her know the outcome of events.

"And though I know we can't ever be true friends, Seph," Letty said in parting, "I vow I'll make it a mite easier when I get Johnny's ring on my finger, which I mean to do before the year is out. As Lady Lade, at least you may acknowledge me with impunity."

"You *are* my true friend, Letty," Persephone said, warmly clasping her hands. "Moreover, if Lady Chid chooses to make a friend of Lady Lade, the world may go hang."

"Lord, you'll set 'em all by the ears — and Chid will murder us both."

This was extremely likely, Persephone could not but acknowledge to herself as she was driven back to Hanover Square. But she in fact met with opposition from an unexpected quarter. Penelope, when she found out what her sister meant to do, was aghast, and expressed much the same views as Letty Smith.

"But Chiddingly will slay you!"

"He will not find me, Pen, you fool. He will only find you."

"Then he will slay *me* instead. I won't do it, Seph. You cannot expect it of me."

"Pen, dearest, you must help me, I pray you. It is a matter of life and death."

"Yes, mine," retorted her twin. "Oh dear, you are dreadful, Seph. Why in the world cannot you wait for Chiddingly's return?"

"Because there is no time. Only consider, Pen. He cannot be here before this afternoon. He will not believe me, and we will waste precious moments in fruitless argument. Then he will insist we remain to attend this abominable betrothal party to ensure we do not create any scandal. He will finally set off tomorrow — if at all — by which time that evil man could have carried Indigo anywhere. Across the seas to France, perhaps. Or Ireland. How are we ever to find him again?"

"Yes, but —"

"But if I go now," Persephone pressed on, "I may catch them before they have a chance to move him. Recall that Bolsover was in town last night. With luck, he is at present still abed, knowing Chid has gone off and cannot be here for hours."

"Yes, but you are asking me to pretend to be you," Penelope said in an agitated way. "To make a public exhibition of myself —"

"It is only what you have been playing at forever. You do me just as well as I do you, Pen."

"Oh, in fun, yes. But this is real. It is an imposture."

"Yes, and you will contrive it splendidly," Persephone said, apparently having no appreciation of the reprehensible nature of such an undertaking.

"Moreover, if you do find Bolsover and the horse — not that I believe for one moment he will be there, for I think you are quite off your head — what can you do to retrieve him?"

"I do not know, but I dare say a dozen things. At least I can delay Bolsover." Persephone suddenly smote her own forehead. "Papa's pistol! I must not forget to take it — though how I am to refrain from blowing the head off that hateful man's shoulders I do not know."

Penelope was gazing at her. "Seph! You will not — oh no, this is dreadful. I know you do not like him, but you cannot murder Chiddingly."

"Dolt! I am talking of Bolsover. Of course I will not shoot Chiddingly." A sudden mischievous smile lit her eyes. "Except if I do so in a fit of temper."

Penelope threw up her hands, declaring she would have nothing whatsoever to do with her sister's vile schemes. Persephone at once became serious again, seizing her hands and squeezing them.

"Oh, please, Pen. You will do it for me. I know you will."

"I wish to heaven we had not been twins. Moreover, if you suppose Papa will not instantly see through this charade, you are even more addlebrained than I thought — and that is not possible."

"Dearest Pen, I knew you would not fail me," Persephone cried, releasing her sister's hands only that she might throw her arms about her.

"I ask only one thing," Penelope begged, subjected to a ruthless hug. "Write to Chiddingly what you mean to do, then he may chase after you at once. For if I am obliged to pretend to be engaged to him, I shall very likely fall into a swoon."

"Fudge. Ten to one I shall be back before the party in any event, and so you may be comfortable."

But Penelope was not in the least comfortable. Not only was she in a state of dread at the task her sister had set her, but no sooner had Persephone left the house than all the dangers she might be running into struck her forcibly. She had been so appalled at the part in her twin's scheme assigned to her she had not until now given a thought to the risk Persephone was taking.

"Oh, heavens! She will run straight into the lion's den and be swallowed up whole. And I shall be called to account for it."

She toyed with the idea of sending for Fitz, but she was pledged to secrecy and she could not betray her twin's trust.

She derived what comfort she could from the fact Persephone was not quite alone. She had been obliged to take a groom, for the simple reason she did not know the way to Wembley Green. From the thought of the pistol Persephone carried she derived no comfort whatsoever, visions of her sister's lifeless corpse being brought home on a hurdle chasing through her unquiet brain.

But even this fear paled beside the enormity of the task she had been given and Penelope set about her preparations in trepidation, her heart jumping and her nerves in shreds.

She must first arrange to dispose of herself for the evening, to which end she attended at breakfast in the parlour complaining to her parents of the headache, a fabrication to which her unnatural pallor lent credibility. Clarissa was all concern in an instant.

"My love, I do trust you are not sickening for something," she fluttered, coming over to place a hand on her daughter's brow. "You are certainly a trifle hot. I hope you don't have a fever."

"Oh no, Mama. It is merely the — the exigencies of the season, I dare say," Penelope said, improvising desperately. "I am not used to so much gaiety and — and dissipation."

"Very true. We have scarce been a night at home. What with all the worry your dreadful sister has plunged us into, I vow I am astonished we are not all of us prostrate."

"Pooh, nonsense," barked the nabob, raising his eyes from the letter in his hand and entering the conversation. "You are beginning to sound exactly like your sister Harriet, my dear. I wish you will strive for a little sense."

"Well, really, Archie! I am sure it is no matter for wonder if I am like Harriet. We are sisters, after all."

"Ha! That is nothing to the purpose. Look at Pen and Seph." He glanced round the table. "Where is Seph?"

"She — she has gone to visit a — a friend, Papa," Penelope said, a faint flush rising to her cheeks. "She will return presently."

"Well, I hope she does not mean to be late," worried Clarissa. "There is so much to do for this party. I must say I am thankful Harriet insisted on holding it in Grosvenor Square, for this house is barely adequate for the purpose."

"If that is a hint, my dear," Archie said with an amused look, "you are wasting your breath. You won't find me frittering away my blunt on one of these draughty great mansions. Particularly with Seph leaving us so soon. I dare say it won't be long before Pen is off our hands, too. Eh, Pen?" He winked broadly at his daughter, who flushed hotly.

"Papa, please."

"Couldn't expect me to be blind, my love, now could you?" demanded the nabob, laughing. He then rose, bestowed a kiss on Penelope's brow and went off, saying he was going to East India House.

His wife turned an avidly enquiring gaze on her daughter. "Pen, what in the world —?"

"Mama, don't, I beg you," Penelope pressed her fingers to her temples, which had begun to throb in earnest. "I — I have such a pain."

"Oh dear, if I had not forgotten," her mother said, contrite. She rose from her chair again and came around the table. "Come, my love. You had better lie down upon your bed. I will send for the doctor, and —"

"No, please. If I could just be left alone to sleep, I am sure I will be better directly."

"Oh dear, oh dear," Mrs Winsford fussed, going along the corridor with her to her chamber. "If it is not one thing, it is another. I hate to leave you like this, but I promised Harriet I would come over to help."

"You go, Mama. The maid can do all I want, truly."

But Mrs Winsford had first to procure some drops of laudanum in water, which Penelope promised to drink if her headache should get any worse. She also left a box of *sal volatile* by the bed and a plethora of instructions with the maid before she could be induced to leave her daughter alone.

Having got rid of the maid, Penelope waited a good hour, screwing up her courage, before rising from the bed and sneaking to the passage outside to make sure none of the servants was about. She then used her pillows to create a mound under her bedclothes, drew the curtains around the bed and pulled the drapes at the windows. Going to the bed, she swept aside the drawn curtain and decided the mound would pass muster as long as no one took it into their heads to probe deeper.

Then she crept into her sister's room, and, selecting one of Persephone's numerous riding habits, she put it on and practised her sister's mannerisms before the mirror.

"Oh dear, I shall never manage it," she said in despairing tones, but, in spite of her fears, she began to be infected with excitement at the game she must play.

After further practice, it struck her she had perhaps overestimated the difficulties. After all, to others she and Persephone were exactly alike, and if they were given to believe she was one twin, why should they suppose anything different?

It was therefore with renewed confidence that she confronted her mother when that lady later returned to the house.

"Seph, where have you been?" Clarissa demanded. "You were to help us at Harriet's, you know."

"I had something to do at the stables, Mama," Penelope said offhandedly, hoping her mother would not ask for further details.

"You and your dratted stables. This is supposed to be your party."

Penelope shrugged. "You know well it means nothing to me."

"Do I not! I declare, I shall not be sorry, Seph, when I have got you off. It will then be up to that dratted Chiddingly to put up with the trouble you cause."

Penelope said nothing for a moment, merely flicking away and hunching an impatient shoulder. She had never realised, she reflected, how different was Mama's manner to her twin than to herself. She was smitten with an unexpected pang of compassion for poor Seph. But there was no time to indulge such thoughts, for Clarissa was declaring her intention of going to Penelope's room to see how she did.

"Oh, Pen is sleeping," Penelope said hurriedly. "I went in to her and she begged to be left alone. I cannot think she will be well enough to come tonight."

"Oh, how vexatious. It will look very odd if she is not present."

"She may have my place for the asking," Penelope dared to say. "Let her go in my stead."

Predictably, Mrs Winsford began scolding at once, forbidding Persephone — as she thought — to disturb her sister, and instead harrying her to go and begin her own preparations for the party.

"Meanwhile, I will go and see about something for your sister to eat," added Mrs Winsford, throwing Penelope into instant alarm. "I am sure some broth will do her good. I shall take it up to her myself."

She left the room on the words and for a moment Penelope stood transfixed. Then she flew to Persephone's room and threw off her riding-habit. Snatching a dressing-robe, which she flung about her shoulders, she dashed back to her own chamber and hastily got between the sheets. By the time Clarissa came softy into the bedchamber a few moments later, Penelope, though still clad in her stay-laces and chemise, had managed to disarrange her hair as if she had been sleeping without a nightcap, and began artistically groaning as soon as she heard the door open.

"Pen, my dearest, my poor darling," said her mama in distressed accents, coming to the bed and drawing aside the curtains. "How do you do now, my love?"

"Oh, Mama, I am so sorry," said Penelope in a faint voice. "I do not think I can possibly attend this party — and poor Seph — oh dear."

"Never mind, my love," soothed Clarissa, taking her hand and caressing it. "You will stay quietly in bed. Dear me, your pulse is tumultuous."

As Penelope's heart was thumping like a drum, this was hardly surprising. However, it lent colour to her imposture. Too much, it appeared for one dangerous moment.

"I wonder if I should send for the doctor, after all," worried her mother.

"Oh no, Mama. I am certain it is just the — the excitement we have all undergone. My headache is a little better, but I don't feel quite ready to rise."

"Certainly not. But see you eat this broth, my love. You must keep up your strength."

"Oh yes," Penelope agreed, adding, "and then I think I will take the laudanum."

"Have you not yet done so?"

Mrs Winsford tutted and fussed, but was at length persuaded to go off and attend to her own toilette, leaving her daughter to sleep. She gave her a bad moment when she promised to pop in before leaving for the Rossendale mansion, but Penelope managed to avert this adroitly.

"Oh, I beg you won't, Mama. I have been awakened so often by the opening of that door. The hinges creak so."

Having proved the truth of this assertion by trying the door, Clarissa was at length persuaded her daughter was best left to herself. Penelope waited a few moments before leaping out of the bed and creeping next door to resume her toilette in the character of Persephone.

While she dressed, all in her twin's clothing, she half hoped Persephone herself might return to save her from having to go through with it. But her nervousness had been replaced by fear for Persephone's safety as the day wore on. If this Billy Bolsover was indeed a villain, what might he not do in revenge, when he discovered himself to have been unmasked? His accuser a young girl, virtually alone, to boot.

In fact the early part of Persephone's day had been attended by the most unprecedented good fortune. Arrived at Rossendale's stables, and watching the groom saddling one of his lordship's great brutish chestnuts, she was struck by sudden inspiration. Might she not make better time on one of Chiddingly's blood steeds?

"Do you know where Lord Chiddingly keeps his horses in London?" she asked the groom.

"Aye, miss." The man paused in his work to look at her. "Hard by his lodgings, miss. Sizeable set o' stables and all."

"Excellent. We will go there at once," Persephone said, urging him to complete his task.

The groom set to with a will and was soon leading the way to the mews near Ryder Street. The journey did not occupy very many minutes, and Persephone spent them fighting down a slight qualm of conscience. She knew what she would think of anyone who took out any of her horses without permission. But this was a little different, she persuaded herself. She was, after all, engaged to be married to Chiddingly, and who had more right to make use of his stock than his wife? Granted she had not yet that distinction — if one could call it so, indeed — but she was going to rescue his horse, and she was surely entitled to take one of Chid's own animals for the purpose. Besides, if he had not wanted her to do so, he should have paid better heed to her warnings. On his own head be it.

Having convinced herself her intention was justified, she determined to take a high hand with Chiddingly's servants, supposing she should meet with any opposition. But arriving in fighting mood at the stable yard, the first person she saw was Tidmarsh, his head bent over the raised hoof of a horse, examining the frog.

"Tidmarsh," she called out, all the pugnacity she had built up melting. "The very man!"

Startled, Tidmarsh looked up, dropping the hoof he held and coming forward. "Miss Winsford! What do you here?"

"Tidmarsh, you must help me," she cried, releasing her foot from the stirrup and sliding from the saddle.

"Anything in my power, ma'am."

Grasping his arm, she pulled him aside, saying quietly, "Tidmarsh, I am going after Indigo and you must come with me."

"But I thought his lordship —"

"His lordship has mistaken his man. I could probably convince him, but I am not waiting for that. He has gone to Norfolk."

"I know, but —"

"On a wild-goose chase, Tidmarsh. It is not Goole who has kidnapped Indigo, and so he will find."

"Why, then, he is likely on his way back, ma'am, and we should await his coming."

"We cannot wait. Already we are a day behind. His lordship may not be back for hours, and by that time Billy Bolsover may have done his worst."

"Billy Bolsover?" Tidmarsh exclaimed, almost as astonished as his own master had been.

"He ain't never," chimed in a new voice. "What, that roly-poly lump o' lard?"

Persephone turned to find Siegfried ducked down between herself and the trainer, his monkey-like little face flitting back and forth between them.

"He has, I tell you. You are both as bad as your master. Why will you not believe me?"

"I believe you, missie, and I'm game," declared the little jockey, fists flailing as he began to shadow box. "I'll hammer the stuffing out o' that pork belly of his."

"Bravo! Well, Tidmarsh? Are you with us?"

"An' don't you pull no long face, neither, you glumpish Tidmarsh," chided Siegfried, "when you knows as how the master'll skin us alive. Leastways, if'n we lets the missie go off alone, he will, no mistake."

Tidmarsh noted with approval that his prospective mistress had sensibly worn a plain blue habit and a hat adorned only with a couple of nodding plumes. But, for all this inconspicuous costume, she could not be permitted to go alone. He grinned suddenly. "Siegfried is in the right of it, ma'am."

"Ah, ain't I just. Nor I doubt the master hisself could stop her neither. Got the bit between 'er teeth proper, she has."

Correctly interpreting this to refer to herself, Persephone lost no time in reinforcing the notion. "Yes, I have, and you are perfectly right. No one is going to stop me."

"In that case, ma'am, you leave me no choice."

"Good. I need another horse, Tidmarsh. In fact, that is what I came for. Do you think I may borrow one of his lordship's?"

"Certainly, ma'am." The trainer turned to the grooms to issue several fast instructions.

"Lucky for him, the master'll know as how it were you, mistress, what wants one of his nags," remarked the jockey, grinning. "Don't reckon he can take agin that."

Persephone was by no means as confident of Chiddingly's acquiescence, but there was no time to worry over that now. Besides, Chid was going to be as mad as fire in any event merely because she had not waited for him. Borrowing his horse was a small matter in comparison, though she dared to suppose the presence of her two companions would go some way towards assuaging his wrath.

Leaving the Rossendale groom to take the chestnut back to his lordship's stables, the rescue party set off. Persephone, mounted on another of Chiddingly's light-mouthed Arabians, a dapple grey of singular beauty, beguiled the journey by relating all the circumstances that had led her to suspect Billy Bolsover of making away with Indigo. Tidmarsh's brow grew blacker as the tale unfolded, and Siegfried, already convinced, gave vent to a series of cant exclamations which were fortunately incomprehensible to his prospective mistress.

By the time they reached their objective, the afternoon was well advanced and Tidmarsh wanted to call a halt outside Bolsover's gates to decide what was best to do. But Persephone was in no doubt.

"We will ride straight to the stables. Come on, man. Already it may be too late."

She spurred her horse and the trainer had perforce to do likewise in order to keep up.

It was not a very large estate and keeping to the turf by the side of the short driveway, the rescuers skirted the house and made their way around to the back of it. There was no need to search out the stable block, which was visible ahead of them, a short distance from the house. Furthermore, all Persephone's instincts were at once seen to be vindicated, as a tableau opened before them and they brought their mounts to a startled halt.

They were only just in time. Any later, and all might have been lost.

A huge covered carrier's wagon stood in the yard. Before it, held by a long rope leash in the hands of a stable boy — instantly recognised by Tidmarsh as the boy Sawleigh — was the great inky black stallion. By dint of sidling and tossing, and whinnying in protest, he was resisting all efforts to make him mount into the wagon.

Two planks had been placed against the open back by means of which he was presumably expected to enter the vehicle. Moving around the horse, and attempting to encourage his co-operation by nudging him with long-handled whips, were a couple of grooms. To one side stood several other men, among them the squat figure of Billy Bolsover, fairly dancing with impatience.

The assembled company were far too intent on their task to notice the newcomers at first, and, before they could do so, a man moved out from the side armed with the long-lashed whip of a coachman.

"Leave him to me. I'll handle him," he was heard to call out. As the other two men moved aside, he lifted his arm, and the wicked length of his whip flew through the air. With a cracking sound, it coiled about Indigo's inky flank.

The horse bellowed in pain. Turning to challenge this new attacker, he reared up on his hind legs and came down with a resounding crash. As he reared again, there was a concerted backward movement from the group of watchers and a fusillade of warning shouts.

"Take care!"

"Mind his hoofs!"

"You fool, watch what you are about!"

The man with the whip ran around to the horse's other side. As the lash flailed out once more, his scarred face could be seen, contorted with savage enjoyment. When the heavy thong cracked into his side a second time, Indigo's bellow of anguish brought the party of rescuers alive again.

A howl of fury tore itself from Persephone's lips, and her knee dug into the flank of her mount. The tableau broke up as startled faces whipped about, and Scarface jerked round in time to see the Arabian grey thundering down upon him, its rider screaming like one demented, her own whip raised to strike.

"Brute! Fiend! Devil!" yelled Persephone, her lash wreaking merciless vengeance as she flayed the man about the face and shoulders, controlling her own mount with automatic ease as she rode in circles about her quarry.

Dropping his own weapon, the man raised his arms above his head, crouching away to escape the punishing blows.

"Take that, you evil ruffian! And that for my father!" As she beat him, Persephone drove him towards the now scattering crowd.

Roaring in pain, the groom plunged among his fellows as Persephone at last ceased her attack, panting with effort. The men about her stared in a mixture of fear and curiosity.

Tidmarsh and Siegfried, who had ridden forward with her, but had perforce held back in open-mouthed astonishment during the late attack, now rode to flank her on either side, ready for action.

"I knew it was you, you vile cheat!" Persephone cried, catching sight of Billy Bolsover where he stood gazing up at her, as shocked as the rest. "Oh, but you will regret this day!"

"My dear lady —" Billy began, recovering himself.

"Don't you *dear lady* me!" Persephone transferred her whip to her left hand and dug into the voluminous pocket of her skirts. "No tricks, sir. I am armed!"

In proof of which, she produced her pistol, cocked it, and levelled it at Bolsover's person.

"Now, don't be foolish, Miss Winsford. You cannot mean to shoot that thing."

"You know very well I am quite capable of it. I have killed one of your henchmen already, have I not? Stand back!"

Not only Bolsover, but all his retinue, thought it prudent to obey. Then, with no warning, Persephone wheeled her horse and rode up to the stable boy. He still held the tether against which Indigo was straining, having backed away from the whirlpool of whips. Sawleigh's mouth, already agape, now sagged wider and horror entered his starting eyes.

"D-don't shoot, miss!"

"Let go that rope!" Persephone jerked her pistol hand forward for emphasis.

The boy dropped the end of the rope with alacrity and raised his hands above his head. Indigo, finding himself suddenly loose, wasted no time but galloped away, heading first in the wrong direction towards the rear of the house. Finding his way blocked, however, he turned and sped off down the side of the building, and was soon around the corner, heading for freedom, the long rope dangling behind.

"Siegfried, go after him," Persephone cried. "But take him home. Don't dare come back here."

"Aye, mistress," the jockey returned and was off.

Tidmarsh followed a little way and then turned back, only to find himself confronted by a phalanx of men separating him from Persephone. He looked up and caught her eye. Seeing something move to her left, he uttered a hoarse alarm. "Behind you!"

It was too late. Persephone felt a sharp blow on her wrist. With a cry of pain, she dropped the pistol, which exploded at once, deafening her momentarily. In the ensuing chaos, Tidmarsh was torn from his horse by many hands and overpowered in seconds.

Next instant, a stinging pain slashed about Persephone's abdomen. Looking down, she was shocked to see the end of a leather lash coiled about her waist. She seized it in both hands, looking down its length at the same time to arrive at the baby-blue eyes of Billy Bolsover, malevolently smiling.

"Now who will regret this day?" The little man tugged viciously at the handle of the whip that had lately lashed Indigo, and which he had retrieved from the ground unobserved.

The violent jerk unseated Persephone and she came tumbling to the ground, rolling as she fell. Her head, unprepared and unprotected without the hat that had fallen off, struck the cobbles sharply. There was a bursting of stars in her vision, and then infinite blackness.

CHAPTER TWELVE

Penelope's acting powers had not been much called upon in the short carriage journey from Hanover Square to Grosvenor Square, what with her father's preoccupation with the news of Warren Hastings' impeachment, and her mother's animadversions upon *Penelope's* unlucky indisposition. She found herself looking forward to the evening with the same flush of mischievous enjoyment she had felt on being first mistaken for Persephone when she had entered society all those weeks ago.

The first person she encountered after running the gauntlet of Lady Rossendale and her cousins was Fitzwarren. Her heart missed a beat and it was with a flutter in her stomach that she greeted him in Persephone's husky voice.

"Good evening, Fitz. I suppose you have had no word from my future husband? I certainly have not."

"None, I am sorry to say," he admitted, smiling. "Though I am glad to see you have thought better of whatever crazy idea you had in mind last night."

Penelope shrugged in Seph's manner, thinking, *If only you knew!* "What could I do, after all? But I am vexed to find Chid has not yet returned."

"Doubtless he will be here directly. But where is Pen?"

"She is indisposed," Penelope answered, and her heart leapt when she saw his features crease into an expression of deep concern.

"Indisposed? Why, how is this? Nothing serious, I hope?"

"Oh no. A headache, merely."

"A headache to keep her from a party? *Pen*? No, no, Seph, don't trifle with me, I beg of you. If she is indeed seriously ill, you must not keep it from me."

Penelope could not but be gratified by his words, and it was hard indeed to sustain her role when everything in her wanted to cry out her reassurance.

"Oh no, truly, Fitz, she is not ill. Mama thinks she is worn down by the season, and I dare say it is true, such a gadabout as she is."

Fitz's smile was perfunctory. "Yes, perhaps. I pray you will give her my deepest regrets and wish her well again with all speed."

"Certainly," Penelope said, refraining from permitting her eyes to light up in the fashion she knew would reveal her identity. Fortunately, perhaps, they were interrupted by Count Leopold, also seeking Penelope. She repeated her excuses, in the character of her twin, and watched the two of them retreat. She again wished she had confided in Fitz, but, at the same time, he had revealed to her far more than he would have done had he known she was in fact Penelope.

But in a moment her mind was distracted, for she was approached by two gentlemen whose names escaped her, but who had been in her sister's company at the Newmarket races.

"Miss Winsford, any news?"

"Yes, we have been so anxious. Has Chid returned?"

Penelope shook her head. "Alas, not yet. I can tell you nothing."

"To happen at such a time," the first man said, "when I dare say there is nothing you would less wish to be troubled with."

Assuming he referred to the betrothal, Penelope shrugged. "Nothing is of more importance than the safety of the horse."

"To be sure, yes," the second man said, twitting her slyly, "if only it does not make poor Chid miss his own betrothal party."

"He will care nothing for that," Penelope said, seizing her chance to escape. "No more will I."

Turning her shoulder, she walked away, assuming Persephone would certainly not relish such comments and might be counted upon to dismiss them without ceremony. Within a very short time, however, she began to be annoyed in earnest, for it seemed as though each person who came up to offer their felicitations found it necessary to comment upon Chiddingly's absence.

Though she would herself have formed excuses, she knew well what Persephone's response to such impertinent curiosity would be.

"Oh, is he not here?" she said daringly to one enquirer, glancing about her. "I had not noticed."

But, in spite of this, she began to feel concerned herself. Suppose Chiddingly had found Indigo with Goole, after all? Then why would Seph not have returned from her own abortive rescue attempt? Perhaps she was even now in Hanover Square, readying herself to come to the party. Would she come as herself or as Penelope?

Before she could make herself quite distracted, she caught sight of the baron himself in the doorway of the ballroom. All her fortitude deserted her. Her heart knocking against her ribs, she moved forward to greet him, wondering what in the world she was to say. In the event, he spoke first, solving the problem.

"It was not Goole," he said, "so you may delight in your triumph."

"Oh, I do," Penelope said, quite at a loss.

He looked at her oddly and she hurried on.

"Everyone has been at pains to discuss your non-appearance, so you are arrived just in time to rescue me from embarrassment."

"Since when do you care for that?"

"Oh, I don't," Penelope agreed, smiling, though her heart was raising a tempestuous tattoo in her breast. "But I knew you would mind — I m-mean, the proprieties and — and such things as you care for so greatly…"

Her voice died as she realised what a shambles she was making of it. His eye was on her in so stern a fashion the colour rose to her cheeks.

"I think," he said in a menacing tone, "that we will go apart a little, ma'am."

"Oh no," Penelope quavered. "I mean, we cannot. We are — we are the principal guests."

"Oh, I think we may safely disappear for a moment or two," he said, taking a firm grip on her elbow and steering her inexorably towards the door of one of the little antechambers that gave on to the ballroom. "After all, I have been separated from my affianced bride for more than a day. I am sure no one will wonder at it if my ardour suffers impatience."

Penelope could not utter a word. Her heart beat madly and she had to dismiss a wild idea of calling out for help. Heavens, what could she do? Her impersonation had not been supposed to include making love to Chiddingly in a private room. More than ever she wished she had confided in Fitz, and she cast a desperate eye about, hoping to catch a glimpse of him just before the baron unceremoniously pushed her into the little room and shut the door.

He released her and watched with an unmoved countenance as she retreated as far from him as the small space of the antechamber afforded.

"And now, *Penelope*," he said, "perhaps you will be good enough to tell me where is your sister."

Penelope gasped, gazing at him with horror-filled eyes. "H-how did you know?"

"Don't be ridiculous, girl. Do you imagine I merit such smiles as you have given me from my affianced wife? Furthermore, her first words to me will undoubtedly be those of reproach for not having listened to her in the first place."

Penelope sighed and sank into the one small sofa provided in the little room. "Oh dear. I had fooled everyone else so successfully."

"No doubt. You aped Seph's manner very well, but not her manner with me. Besides, there are intimacies between a man and his promised wife which —" He broke off, unwilling to point out to her that Persephone's very presence affected him with so much fire that Penelope could not long have maintained the imposture in his company.

But he had said enough. Penelope gazed at him with a new understanding. "I had not thought of that. But then, Fitz did not know me. I mean —" Flushing, she turned away, afraid of revealing how much it meant to her that his friend should apparently not have sensed her own presence under her disguise.

"Never mind that now," Chiddingly said, bringing her back to his present urgency. "You have not answered my question. Not that it needs for you to do so. I suppose I may guess. If she has inveigled you into taking her place, then I need not doubt where Seph is at this very moment."

Penelope shook her head, turning to look at him again. "I tried to stop her, I swear it. But nothing would do for her but to go after this Bolsover with nothing but a groom at her side and Papa's pistol to protect her."

"Oh sweet heaven! What in Hades did I ever do to be cursed with such a bedlamite? What time did she set out?"

"This morning. Nor is she yet returned."

"This morning? Fiend seize it! Why she could not have waited passes my comprehension. I only hope to heaven I may be in time." He turned and wrenched open the door.

Penelope leaped up, stepping forward to grasp his arm. "Are you going to save her?"

"Believe me, ma'am, when I catch up with her, it is I she will need saving from!"

Then he was striding across the ballroom floor, leaving Penelope alone. Becoming aware that people were staring first at her, then at Lord Chiddingly's tall figure heading straight out of the ballroom he had entered just a few moments before, Penelope flushed hotly. Heavens, they would think she and Chiddingly had quarrelled. Now what was she to do? Then a voice at her shoulder made her whirl about in startled gratification.

"Pen! Just what is happening here?" demanded Fitz in the severest tones she had heard from him.

"You *do* know me!" Light flooded her features.

"Hush, not so loud," he warned. Slipping his hand to her elbow, he began to guide her across the room, murmuring in her ear, "We will pretend to follow Chid, so people will imagine me to be the peacemaker and leave us alone."

He was right. Though eyes followed them and whispers began behind fans, no one approached them, and they traversed the room unmolested. Once through the main ballroom door, Fitz led Penelope across the hall and bundled her into one of the supper saloons which for the moment stood empty.

"Now," he said, releasing her, but abating not one jot of the stern reproach in his voice, "you will please to tell me, Miss Penelope Winsford, the meaning of this outrageous prank."

Penelope quailed. "It is not my fault, Fitz. Truly it is not. I will tell you the whole, only I beg that you won't look at me so. You have no notion how it distresses me."

His face softened at once, and he quickly put out a hand. "Dear Pen, forgive me. That is the last thing in the world I wish for. It was only the needless worry to which I have been put this last hour and more over your health. If you knew —" He broke off, smiling. "Well, never mind. You are plainly in as high bloom as ever, and that must content me."

Having no idea how her fingers clung to his, Penelope gazed up into his face with her heart in her eyes. When he raised her hands to his lips to kiss the fingers with unwonted fervour, she blushed prettily.

"Oh, Fitz."

He seemed to catch hold of himself. Though he retained his clasp on her fingers, he stood back a little and the quizzing gleam came into his eyes. "Dare I suppose your enterprising twin to be the author of this game? I confess when I realised it was you I thought so."

"How did you realise it?" Penelope asked, a little shy.

"Oh, when I saw Chid march off from you. The expression in your eyes, my gentle Pen, had nothing to do with your fierce sister." He released her hand at last. "I take it she has dashed off to rescue Indigo?"

"Yes, she has. Chiddingly has gone after her. He was not fooled by me for a moment, you know." She went on to give him a rapid review of the day's events, and was relieved to find him rather enjoying the recital.

"She is outrageous," Fitz said at the end, a laugh in his voice. "I must say I am happy to think it is not I who must control her quirks."

"Oh, no one can do that. At least, Ufur could do so. But no one else."

"I fancy Chid may prove equal to the task."

"Yes, that is all very well, Fitz, but what are we to do now? He has gone off, leaving me to bear the brunt of it when everyone must suppose a terrible quarrel has taken place between us — I mean, between him and Seph, for I am she at this present."

"No longer. Upon my soul, I am glad of it. For I do not think I could have borne much more delay."

Penelope felt a pulse beat in her throat. "What — what do you mean, Fitz?"

He took her hands once again in his. "I mean, dear Pen, that since the guests of honour have deserted their party, there is nothing for it but for us to step into the breach."

"But — but you cannot impersonate Chiddingly."

"I have no intention of so doing. Nor, my sweet Pen, are you going to continue with your masquerade. You are again, from this moment, your own dear self."

Penelope's lip trembled. "I cannot think what is in your head, Fitz."

"Can you not?" His eyes gazed into hers with so much tenderness in them that her heart turned over. But his raised eyebrow teased nevertheless. "How am I to explain? Pen, you know my pose. I have been designated an arbiter of beauty, and an arbiter of beauty I must remain. And you are — did I ever tell you so? — very beautiful. May I … may I add you, sweet Pen, to my collection?"

She hesitated, only half understanding what he meant, hardly daring to believe he was — at last — speaking of what lay between them. Yet at the same time, this whimsical notion was not the declaration she had longed for. Where was the romantic attachment she had imagined in her dreams?

"I — I do not know what to reply. Are you asking me — you must be asking me to —"

"To marry me. Yes, Pen. Will you?"

She drew a breath, biting her lip to stop the trembling. His eyes were on hers, in a burning look that seemed to belie the lightness of his words. Dared she hope he might yet say what she yearned to hear?

"Oh, Fitz, is it truly what you want? Because if not —" She broke off, took a breath, and the words tumbled from her lips. "Fitz, I will marry you, in — in any event. But you must not imagine I do so for such a f-foolish reason. Add me to your collection, forsooth! As if you could keep me thus forever. For I will grow old, you know, and perhaps you would be sorry to have done so at the last. Only you see, I do love you so, and I will marry you whatever your reason. But I will not have you think of me as some sort of — of object."

"Pen, Pen, stop!" Fitz tightened his hold on her hands and she winced. "Oh, my idiotic little love! My *darling*! Don't you know I adore you?"

She gazed at him, dumbly shaking her head. Tears sprang to her eyes, and with a catch in her voice, she whispered, "I th-thought you would never say so."

A shaky laugh escaped him, and, dropping her hands, he swept her into his arms. Penelope felt her knees weaken as she returned an embrace filled with as much passion as she could have desired.

"Oh!" she uttered, emerging breathless from his kiss. "Oh, then you *do* love me."

He held her close and murmured, "With a passion great enough to withstand both the onset of years and your unusual manners, my sweetest life."

Her delicious trill of laughter pleasurably assailed his ears and he kissed her again. When she could at length speak once more, Penelope, her eyes shining, leaned back in the circle of his arms to look up at him.

"Oh dear. And I have been in such an agony of apprehension, for fear you did not return my regard. All this time! Why, why has it taken you so long? I believe even now you would have said nothing if —"

"You are perfectly right. I have been overscrupulous, my darling, for I had thought to wait until all the hue and cry over Chid and Seph had died down."

"*And* you had not made up your mind. Confess it now."

Fitz clasped her more strongly. "Though I blush to confess it, you are right, Pen. I have been so long in the habit of thinking myself immune to the tender passions that I could not believe myself caught at last."

"Caught? I vow you would have come by your deserts had I accepted Leopold or my cousin Rossendale."

His eyebrow flew up. "Ah, you would have me pretend I did not guess you were not — shall we say? — indifferent to me."

Penelope tried to pout at this conceit, but the smile would not be suppressed. "You are shameless, Fitz. Did I give myself away so obviously, then?"

He smiled. "You gave your heart away in a hundred delicious little ways that were — and are — a constant delight to me."

"Wretch! I did not mean that."

"Have I not your heart, then, Pen?" His lips hovered tantalisingly over hers. "Have I not your heart?"

"You know you have," she gasped. The blood rushed through her veins in a pleasurable wash of heat when her lips met his again, and there was silence in the empty saloon for some considerable time.

At length she raised her head from his shoulder where it had been so peacefully resting, and was startled into awareness by the sight of a face peeping round the door with blank amazement. Seeing her take note of it, the face disappeared.

"Fitz, what are we about? Someone has just seen us. For heaven's sake, what are we to do? Only think of the scandal, if everyone should suppose Seph to be kissing Chid's best friend."

Fitz laughed, but he let her go. "Have no fear, my love. They will know the truth soon enough."

"But how?"

"Very simply, dear Pen." He took her hand and led her to the door. "Come. Your parents must by now be thoroughly concerned by the whispers doing the rounds. Let us beard your father at once. For this, my darling, is now becoming our betrothal party."

"Oh, famous," twinkled Penelope. "Then no one tonight will have the least interest in what has become of your abominable friend and my equally abominable twin."

Persephone felt abominable as she came sighing back to consciousness. Her head throbbed, as did her ribs, when she drew an incautious breath. There was an ache in her stomach, and her arms and wrists were agonised. Striving to move first these most painful items, she discovered her wrists were bound together behind her back, and she was lying on her side on a bedding of hay.

Opening her eyes, she found a grey gloom about her and wrenched upright. Hissing against the pain, she held her breath, gasping at the sharp stab in her ribs.

When she was able once more to pay attention to her surroundings, she realised she had been left in a stall, for the low whickering and muffled stamping about her revealed the presence of horses, if their aroma had not already told its own tale.

She tried to rise, but felt too weak to be able to do so without assistance, and with her hands tied she could not help herself. Cursing softly, she was just wondering how long she had been there, when a light flickered at the edge of her vision.

Persephone held her breath and sat perfectly still, but the light came close, resolving into a lantern behind which, as he entered the doorway of the stall, she could make out the puffy features of Billy Bolsover.

"So you are awake. I am glad. I have no wish to be had up for murder, and you looked devilish sickly earlier."

"You will be had up for kidnapping, you evil little man," Persephone said through her teeth, her discomforts at once forgotten.

"Oh, I hardly think so, ma'am."

"And that is not the least of your crimes."

He nodded, coming further into the stall and holding the lantern higher. He peered into her face, as if what he found there was of profound interest. "So you guessed it all." He sighed, adding without heat, "Damn you. Left alone, Chid would never have put two and two together."

"Why should he? How should he guess his so-called friend would display a villainy that is beyond belief?"

Billy laughed with something of his old joviality. "Oh, not villainy, Miss Winsford. Merely desperation."

"Money! I knew it."

"Yes, as you so sapiently remark, money." He frowned, his little mouth falling into the petulant pout he had hitherto kept so well hidden. "Yet is that quite fair? For money, yes, I might have tried for the hand of one of the richly endowed nabob's *little peas*. For money, I might enlist certain aid to obtain a strongbox full of gold. But the matter of Indigo is — different."

His voice took on an edge, and Persephone thought she understood. With a Hindi oath, she made a supreme effort and rose shakily to her feet.

"You need not tell me. You have no love of horses. It is all pretence. Only one thing motivates you, Bolsover, and it is a petty, dishonourable thing." Persephone came close to him, her white features taut with disgust, her eyes glittering in the lantern's light. "You cannot bear to lose, and that is all."

"You she-devil!" he got out, chubby features purpling with choked fury, and Persephone knew she had struck home.

The sound of running feet interrupted them, and Billy turned to hold the lantern up as one of his men came in.

"We cannot hold the stallion, sir. He is kicking and bucking like one demented."

"Then he is still here!" Persephone cried.

Bolsover turned on her with a snarl. "Yes, you thought you had trounced me finely, did you not? Well, you were mistaken, ma'am. My men scoured the countryside all afternoon and finally managed to catch the devil."

"Siegfried too?"

"Ha! Did you think that scrawny little runt a match for me? He was taken in a trice."

"Oh no!"

"Oh yes. Chid thought he had a winner there, a super champion. Mayhap he did. But no longer, ma'am. No longer."

Sounds of increased commotion reached them from outside, together with hoarse shouts and a great deal of stamping and hammering of hoofs. The servant glanced apprehensively towards the stable doors.

"Sir, he is like to trample us all. What can we do?"

"Do? I will tell you what to do. You will shoot the beast. That is what you will do."

"*No!*" Persephone screamed, and even the servant looked dubious.

But Billy began to waddle purposefully towards the stable door. Persephone, notwithstanding her tied hands, ran after him, trying to put herself in his way.

"Billy, no, you must not! You cannot shoot Indigo! I forbid it! I beg you!"

He pushed her aside and strode on.

Persephone, frantic now, ran past him and flung herself into the doorway before him. "Billy, if you kill Indigo it will be the lowest, vilest, meanest trick you could play. Billy, in the name of the Almighty, I had rather you shot me!"

"Don't tempt him," said a new voice from behind her.

Bolsover froze and Persephone whirled about, her face radiant in the light of several flambeaux in the yard outside.

"Chiddingly!"

"You abominable little wretch, Persephone! Thank the Lord you are all right!" With one hand the baron caught her to him, while in the other he held a large and eminently serviceable pistol. Releasing her after a brief hug, he became aware that she was tied. "Good grief!" He swung the pistol to cover the servant who cowered behind Bolsover's short bulk. "You! Untie her at once."

"Oh, thank you, Chid! You have come in excellent time." Persephone questioned him as the servant struggled with the stubborn knots at her wrists. "Have you Indigo safe? What of poor Tidmarsh and Siegfried? Are they —?"

"They are both freed, never fear. When I learned at the stables that they had accompanied you, I thought it prudent to bring reinforcements. We had little trouble, as you see, for the fools were all struggling with Indigo."

"Is he safe again? I set him free, but the villains recaptured him."

"I know. Tidmarsh told me. Never fear. Siegfried is taking care of him."

Persephone's hands came loose at last and she rubbed her wrists and arms almost unconsciously, glaring at Billy Bolsover. "What are you going to do with this miserable coward, Chid?"

"Ah yes. Come out, Billy."

He took Persephone's hand and backed away from the door, pulling her with him. His pistol was still pointing straight at Bolsover's waistcoat. The little man slowly inched forward, his eyes on the pistol.

As he came out into the yard, he saw all his men overpowered and under guard, at pistol point like himself. His scarred groom, welts and weals on his face and hands from his recent encounter with Persephone's whip, stood separately, under Tidmarsh's personal guardianship.

"Well, Billy? Have you nothing to say?"

Bolsover shrugged, his sangfroid apparently recovered. "That depends on your intentions."

"What would you do in my place? Not only am I confronted with a kidnapper and a cheating liar who will stoop to drugging a horse, but I am also forced to believe you are hand-in-glove with thieves and highwaymen. And as if this were not enough," he added, a flame of anger throbbing in his voice, "you have offered harm to my woman. That will not go unpunished."

Persephone looked at him, a thrill of delight shooting through her veins. "Will you fight him, Chid?"

"It is scarcely worth the pain, but I appear to have no choice. You will find swords in my phaeton, Seph. Fetch them."

Nothing loath, Persephone ran to the phaeton, while Bolsover, turning a ghastly colour, began to protest.

"Stuff and nonsense, Chid. Why should we fight? Surely you are not so Gothic as to imagine your honour can be so satisfied? Besides, you should take care how you provoke me. I can ruin you, you know."

"You may try," Chiddingly said, unperturbed, as he handed his pistol to one of the men and began to divest himself of the greatcoat he had thrown on over the formal attire he had donned for the party. "Though I fear you will find it is you who are ruined, Billy. I shall certainly spread the tale of your doings all over town."

Bolsover licked his dry lips. "If I too spread a tale, what then? Has not your affianced wife had enough scandal?"

"No one knows Persephone is here."

"Oh, indeed? What of the servants? Can you keep their mouths shut?"

"Your servants, sir, will be rotting in Newgate. I hardly think anyone will pay their words undue attention."

Billy blenched as Persephone returned with the swords. Having handed one to Chiddingly, she came over to give one to Bolsover. He took it in a clammy hand, panic lending him a waspish tongue.

"They will attend, never fear," he said, his voice hoarse. "They will certainly attend, Chid, when they hear that where you have been — and had to marry for it — I also have taken my toll."

There was a sudden tense silence. Persephone broke it. "It is not true, Chid. I swear it is not true!"

"Oh, but you cannot know that, dear lady," Bolsover said unctuously. "You have been unconscious for some hours. How can you know I did not taste you as you slept?"

Persephone gave a distressed cry, and Chiddingly strode forward.

"May you rot in hell, you vicious, lying little cur," he growled, and flung his sword up in a careless salute. "On guard!"

But Billy Bolsover, fear coursing through him, did not even bother to salute. Raising his foil, he threw himself into ferocious attack, with scant regard for the established rules of fencing. Wielding the sword like the cutlass of some pirate of the Spanish Main, he slashed it back and forth at terrifying speed, both stubby hands grasping the hilt.

Chiddingly could do little but meet his blade in a parry or two, backing from the vicious snick-snack that came up at him from Bolsover's inferior height.

Transfixed, Persephone watched in horror as the man kept on, bouncing back and forth like a crazed butterball, the foil snapping to and fro before Chiddingly's face.

The baron tried to hold his ground, expecting the man would soon tire, when he might find an opening to bring his skill into play. As it was, this was no fight, merely a bungling fiasco. The flailing blade whistled more fiercely still as Bolsover's fear increased.

Driven back, Chiddingly suddenly tripped on the cobbled surface and fell heavily.

Bolsover's mad attack ceased all of a sudden, and he stood with a heaving chest, clearly unable to think, let alone deliver the *coup de grâce*.

Recovering, Chiddingly scrambled up, lifted his sword arm and aimed, getting a purchase on the uneven cobbles with his heel that would enable him to lunge. But, as he made ready to plunge the point of his foil into Billy's tubby body, there was a dull thud, and that individual wobbled uncertainly. Then his eyes rolled and his short bulk crashed to the ground like the trunk of some stunted tree, revealing to Chiddingly's cleared view the sight of his promised bride, standing over the fallen man with an iron horseshoe in her hand, raised ready to strike again.

"Blast you, Seph! Now I can't kill the villain."

Persephone looked across at him as he got to his feet. "Maybe he is already dead?"

Chiddingly bent over Billy and felt his pulse. "No, more's the pity. You should have struck him harder."

Indeed, Billy was already groaning as he came to. Chiddingly rose to his full height and towered over him where he lay, gazing up with terror in his baby-blue eyes.

"You are done for, Billy. Never show your face in town again. If there was any honour in you at all, you would take a pistol to your own fat head and blow your brains out."

Then he moved away. Retrieving his greatcoat, he placed it about Persephone's shoulders and led her towards his trainer, who looked rather dazed at the outcome of events.

"Tidmarsh, my dear fellow, I leave you to clear up this mess. Deliver these rascals to Bow Street and see Siegfried takes Indigo back to London."

"You may rely on me, my lord," Tidmarsh said, and glanced down to where Billy Bolsover was struggling to sit up. "And him, my lord?"

"That?" said Chiddingly in a voice of scorn. "You may toss it in a midden."

"With pleasure, my lord."

Then without further ado, Chiddingly dragged his affianced bride to the phaeton, lifted her unceremoniously into the vehicle and climbed in himself. "And now, Persephone," he said, setting his horses in motion, "I have only to deal with you."

"I wish you had killed him, Chid. I am sure he will do you another mischief."

"Seph, I am no longer interested in Billy. Perhaps you will be good enough to explain to me why, for one thing, you had to needlessly expose yourself to danger?"

"Needlessly? Why, you should be glad I did so. Another hour and we would have missed them altogether."

"And for another thing," Chiddingly continued, as if she had not spoken, "why, you heedless, brainless little fool, did you interfere in a sword fight?"

"Fight? It was nothing of the sort and you know it."

"The man was crazed. What if he had turned on you?"

"What if he had slaughtered you?"

"Heaven preserve me! Can't you understand, you featherbrained fury, that I cannot bear to see you risk your life so recklessly?"

"*Salla*! Do you expect me to change my ways merely to satisfy your male pride?"

"Is that what you think? I don't know what you deserve."

"Don't dare start to threaten me, for I won't bear it, Chid. I may be ten times your wife, but I will never submit to be browbeaten and bullied."

With an oath Chiddingly pulled up his horses, throwing his reins into the spring clip to hold them steady.

"What in the world —?" Persephone began.

But he turned and seized her by the shoulders. "You know very well you are quite as passionately attached to me as I am to you!"

"Yes, for I passionately *hate* you."

Chiddingly shook her, albeit gently, the motion emphasising his words. "Don't — lie — to — me! You love me. Admit it at once!"

Persephone brought her fists up and pummelled his chest. "I loathe you!"

"No!"

"*Ooloo*! Very well, then, if you must have it," she yelled, "*I love you*!"

They both went still and silent, staring at each other. Then Persephone added, in a small, defiant voice, "But much against my will. Are you satisfied?"

Chiddingly began to laugh. "The more so for that last. Oh, Seph, you adorable witch, you will drive me to Bedlam and I do not care."

Dragging her into his arms, he kissed her hungrily. Instant flame lit Persephone's loins and she clung to him, heedless for a time of her bruises, the warmth of her blood quite banishing their pain.

"Oh dear Lord," Chiddingly groaned, "I am minded to cheat the marriage bed and take you here and now."

Persephone gurgled. "In a phaeton?"

"Anywhere!"

But her amusement sobered him and, though he kissed her again, he gave his horses the office to start.

"You terrify me," Persephone laughed. Then she winced in discomfort. "Especially since you have already broken me to pieces. I am bruised enough today, I thank you, you brute."

"Then you have come by your deserts," he said, but he took her hand and brought it up to his lips to be kissed. "I can be tender, you see."

Persephone snorted. "You are nothing but a savage and a barbarian, and you know nothing whatever of tenderness."

"Do you care to try me? Only wait until I have you down at Faversham!"

"*Salla!*" Persephone cursed, reminded of what day it was. "Chid, our betrothal party! Poor Pen must be in a sad way."

"On the contrary, she is doing very well. Nevertheless, we must hurry. We may just get back in time to put in an appearance."

"Not if you drive. You had better let me take the ribbons."

"If you imagine I am going to let you loose on my team, you were never more mistaken. At night, too. Moreover, I have no wish to be jolted in your reckless neck-or-nothing fashion."

"Don't be absurd. I am never reckless with my horses."

"I don't know how you dare make such a claim. With my own eyes I have seen you —"

"Chid, if you say one word against my driving —"

"Now, listen to me, my girl —"

They argued thus most of the way to their betrothal party, each certain that they had met their match.

A NOTE TO THE READER

Dear Reader,

Before I wrote this book, many moons ago, I had to research the whole field of horse racing and horse breeding, with particular reference to the 18th century. I quickly found out that I didn't know enough about horses either, so I had to read up on the basics: the horse body and how it functions, plus how to discuss horses and their qualities. I discovered that horse talk is a whole language in itself!

In those days, there was no internet and all research had to be done via books, so I hunted down relevant volumes in the library. By good fortune I happened to be temping at the time and my fellow worker had a son who knew all about horses. I borrowed several books from him and, in gratitude, named Chiddingly's trainer after him — hence Tidmarsh. I will say he was chuffed to bits.

All the expressions I have used to describe horses and their "points" I culled from this research. I found out how the English racing thoroughbred grew out of matings between English mares and Oriental stallions: Arabian, Barb and Turkoman breeds. My setting of 1786 was very much the era when the thoroughbred was coming into its own.

Several of the "racing men" in the story are real, although I have fictionalised them to suit my purposes. Sir Charles Bunbury was indeed the President of the Jockey Club. He and Lord Derby did have that discussion at the Oaks about whether the Derby or the Bunbury would be the name of the race they were establishing at Epsom. The Derby it became and is still run to this day.

The lords Clermont and Egremont are real too. I have visited Petworth where Egremont had his stud, and it's a beautiful house. Aimwell did win the Derby for Clermont in 1785. The three unfortunate horses — Miss Nightingale, Tosspot and Rosebud — were actually nobbled in the ways described. Tattersalls is still the main auctioneer of race horses and I was luckily able to include the founder, Richard Tattersall, after finding out about his life and work. Last but no means least, we have George, Prince of Wales, as a young man, already notorious for his amours and his extravagances.

My other area of research was of India in that period, Bombay in particular. Although it does not feature very much in the story, I had to know enough about it to be as authentic as possible. The background of the impeachment of Warren Hastings became a feature for my nabob Archie.

I recall the whole episode of researching for the story as one of fascination. I could have written a treatise on horses and racing by the end! I've forgotten most of it by now, sadly, but luckily almost everything is readily available via Google and Wikipedia nowadays.

I hope you have enjoyed this romp through the somewhat crazy adventures of the Winsford twins and their respective heroes. If you would consider leaving a review, it would be much appreciated and very helpful. Do feel free to contact me on **elizabeth@elizabethbailey.co.uk** or find me on **Facebook**, **Twitter**, **Goodreads** or my website **www.elizabethbailey.co.uk**.

Elizabeth Bailey

Sapere Books is an exciting new publisher of brilliant fiction and popular history.

To find out more about our latest releases and our monthly bargain books visit our website: **saperebooks.com**

Printed in Great Britain
by Amazon